The Last American Hero

The Last American Hero

G. B. Mooney

Writers Club Press

San Jose New York Lincoln Shanghai

The Last American Hero

Writers Club Press
an imprint of iUniverse.com, Inc.

For information address:
iUniverse.com, Inc.
5220 S 16th, Ste. 200
Lincoln, NE 68512
www.iuniverse.com

ISBN: 0-595-16847-7

Printed in the United States of America

This book is dedicated to all military personnel who have been declared Missing In Action, and to their families and loved ones who my never have closure

PROLOGUE

It had taken ten years for the political system to approve and fund the construction of an east-west US Route 30 by-pass around Greenwood, Pennsylvania, thankfully removing the thundering eighteen-wheeler traffic from the downtown streets of the county seat. The by-pass had finally been completed in the late sixties and was already showing signs of needing major repair. What had been the western end of Pittsburgh Street, that became US Route 30, was now the last westbound entrance ramp that climbed out of a valley and merged with the bypass.

A compact car stopped at the outlet road at the bottom of the valley. The driver cautiously made a right turn and started up the ramp. At the top of the hill, just before the ramp merged with the bypass, the car pulled over to the berm and stopped. A tall, slim man, wearing knife-creased gray gabardine slacks and a brilliant white oxford cloth shirt, got out and walked around to the front of the car. He smoothed his salt and pepper hair with suntanned hands and looked out over the valley. What he was looking at had once been a weed patch hill. Now it was part of the state highway system.

The man stood rigidly. His gaze gradually shifting to the old homes that remained in the valley. His head and shoulders sagged and emotion overcame him, destroying his attempt to control his composure. Tears welled up in his eyes and soon dampened his craggy, lined face. He put one foot up on the guardrail, placed an elbow on the raised knee and buried his face in a large hand and succumbed to uncontrollable sobbing. It took a few minutes for the man to regain control. Eventually he stopped sobbing and removed a handkerchief from his pocket and dried his eyes and face.

He carefully walked around to the driver's side of the car, opened the door and slid into the seat and started the engine. After checking for traffic on the ramp he accelerated to highway speed and merged with westbound Route 30 traffic, settling in for the fifty-mile drive to the Pittsburgh airport.

He was looking forward to what was sure to be a much happier part of his homecoming.

CHAPTER *1*

Western Pennsylvania, USA, Spring, 1934

"Okay, Ollie, start running and let out more string when you get it up in the air."

Ollie looked over his shoulder to make sure his brother Tommy was ready. Tommy was standing down-wind, holding a homemade kite high in the air with his right hand and the cloth tail in his left. Ollie turned and started running into the wind as fast as his short six year old legs could carry him, lifting his feet high to avoid tripping in the weeds. He felt the kite string tension starting to increase and then heard a whoop of excitement from his brother and his cousin. Ollie looked over his shoulder just in time to see his first kite dart into the blue Spring sky. Tommy and his cousin Billy were jumping up and down, their ragged clothes flapping in the breeze, shouting with unrestrained glee. It was a moment Ollie would remember the rest of his life.

The whole family had participated in the kite project. Ollie's cousin Billy, the only boy in the neighborhood who had a penknife, had cut the thin wood strips for the frame from a fence paling. His brother Tommy had helped him tie the short horizontal wood strip to the longer vertical strip to make the cross-shaped frame. They had then attached string to notches in the outer tips of the wood strips to provide a place to anchor the tissue paper covering.

Aunt Cil had mixed the water and flour paste to just the right consistency to allow a light but strong attachment of the tissue papers to the string. After the paste dried Ollie had tied a string to the tips of the short wood strip and tightened the string to pull the stick into a bow, tightening the tissue paper to a taut smoothness.

They punched a small hole in the tissue paper at the intersection of the frame members and made a string bridle for attachment of the flying string A cloth tail had been made by tearing an old shirt into strips and then tying the strips together. There had been considerable discussion about the length of the tail. If the tail was too short the kite would loop uncontrollably and crash; too long and the kite would be too heavy to fly.

Now, as Ollie slowly let out string from the ball he had been collecting all winter, his kite was soaring with the birds and the clouds. He could barely contain his excitement. The electrical waves going up and down his back made his small body shiver uncontrollably.

Tommy and Billy were almost as excited as Ollie. Ollie offered them the opportunity to fly the kite but they both refused.

"You fly it Ollie; it's your kite," Tommy said as he helped tie the end of the ball of string to a short piece of fence paling. "Don't forget to wrap the string on the stick like I showed you."

When they started down the hill toward the houses Ollie said, "Thanks guys, this is a great kite."

Ollie stayed all afternoon on the top of the hill overlooking the grimy Greenwood Coal Company owned houses in the valley, happily engrossed in flying his kite. When he noticed smoke coming out of the chimney of his house he began pulling in the kite, carefully wrapping the string in a figure eight on the string stick. He knew his mother would soon be calling him to get cleaned up for supper.

Just as he got the kite to the ground he heard a strange faint buzzing from the east. He listened intently as the buzzing steadily increased. Then, in an instant he saw the source of the noise that was now a roar. Two blue, bi-wing airplanes were streaking toward him, almost at ground level, just skimming the tops of the hills, following the railroad tracks. When they went past Ollie thought they were close enough to touch. In the brief instant of their passing he saw the red, white and blue stars painted on the wings and fuselage. Ollie also clearly saw the pilot in the cockpit of the nearest plane. He started to wave both arms, unable to control his excitement. As the planes too quickly vanished Ollie shook his small head in wonderment. What must it feel like to fly faster than the birds? In that instant, when the planes flew by, he knew that someday he would have to fly an airplane.

"First the kite and now this. What a day!" He exclaimed, gathering up his kite and rushing down the hill to share his experience with his family. When he reached the road halfway down the hill he noticed that most of the neighborhood was out talking about the planes.

After that first wonderful day, every time Ollie heard what he thought was an airplane he would run to an open space and start looking skyward, hoping to see one. If Ollie's mother couldn't find him she would send someone to the top of the hill. He would be there, lying on his back, waiting for the next beautiful airplane.

There were three dirt roads running north and south in the valley; one at the base of the valley and two higher up the hill.

The northern end of the valley was blocked by a man made earth fill that supported the main line of the east-west section of the Pennsylvania Railroad. A tunnel through the earth fill provided a path for the miners to walk to the coal company tipple on the north side of the tracks.

The residents of the coal company houses, for some unknown reason called "The Patch", were Italian, Polish and Irish immigrants who had been sponsored into the country by the coal company. The immigrants had been tagged after being cleared for entry at Ellis Island in New York, and then placed on a Pennsylvania Railroad train. After a day of traveling on the crowded train they disembarked at Greenwood, in the heart of the western Pennsylvania soft coal fields. The coal company officials checked in the new workers and their families and directed them to their new duplex homes.

In return for the men doing strenuous and dangerous backbreaking work in the timber supported dark tunnels of the mine, the families received free housing and chits for the purchase of food and clothing at the company store. If there was anything left at the end of the month the chits could be reclaimed for cash.

When the big depression, that started in 1929, caused Ollie's father to lose his job as a mechanical draftsman, his family moved into the coal company provided house of his uncle George and aunt Cil. George was the only member of the Miller family who hadn't left the Coal Company and was still working. Soon after Ollie's family moved in, Ollie's Uncle Mike and his family moved in. All told there were six adults and seven children living in the five-room house.

Ollie's father Louis and uncle Mike spent most of every day chasing job leads, frustrated by the many NINA, *No Irish Need Apply* signs, or doing odd jobs for the wealthy coal mine owners. His mother Hilda, aunt Cil and Aunt Mary cleaned house for the same people.

The parents did not discuss the daily struggle to survive with the children. Ollie, as young as he was, realized that many times he went to bed hungry and during the past winter had been cold most of the time. During the winter nights Ollie would lie on the floor of his makeshift bedroom, fully dressed except for his shoes, bundled up in his blanket, watching his breath condense into vapor in the near freezing room.

He liked the sounds the heavily loaded train locomotives made in the night, trying to move their attached coal cars up the grade out of the coalmine loading area. They would chug very slowly, trying to gain traction, and then chug very quickly when the driving wheels slipped on the slick tracks. Sometime it would take a dozen attempts before the train got going.

He didn't believe his Uncle George when he said he liked working in the coal mine. Every night when George came home, his face blackened except for his eyes, aunt Cil would make him stay outside until she brushed the black grime from his clothes. He then would go into the cellar for a cold sponge bath, in the wash tub, to remove the black dust from his face and body. After putting on clean clothes he would finally be allowed upstairs. He withstood this nightly routine with good humor, making funny faces, laughing and telling jokes to the children who often would sit on the cellar steps watching the ritual.

Near the end of summer Ollie became ill. He was recovering from measles when he came down with chickenpox. Ollie missed the first three weeks of school and when he was well enough his mother took him to the small, four room Catholic school to start first grade. Ollie tightly gripped his mother's hand, his small heart beating furiously in his chest, unwilling to face the Nuns dressed in their frightening black robes or the strangers in the classroom. Finally, after his mother explained that his brother would be there to help him and to walk home from school with him, he let go of her hand and sat down at the small desk.

Starting late put Ollie behind the rest of the class. The whole first year was a frustrating experience. No matter how hard he tried he could not catch up. The learning experience became a source of apprehension and stress. The nuns at Sacred Heart school wanted him to repeat first grade but reluctantly agreed to allow him into second grade when his mother pointed out that second grade was in the same room as the first grade. That would allow Ollie to participate in both grades at the same time. His mother also promised to work with Ollie so that he could catch up with his classmates. That summer Ollie's mother and the rest of the family spent at least an hour each day reviewing the first grade books that the nuns had allowed them to take home. Second grade went smoothly and Ollie no longer felt sick in the stomach when he walked up the steps to the school. The new teacher was a young nun who actually seemed to like the kids and teaching.

By fourth grade he had not only caught up with, he had passed the rest of the class. In fifth grade he was following the work of the sixth graders on the other side of the room.

By the time Ollie was twelve, in 1940, the country was starting to come out of the depression. The factories in the area were starting to get busy because of the war in Europe. All the men in the family went back to good paying jobs. The entire family that had lived in the patch house moved into a huge red brick row house, one block from the main street of Greenwood.

The house had a living room, dinning room and huge kitchen on the first floor, four bedrooms and a bath on the second floor and three bedrooms and a bath on the third floor.

When they moved in the kids walked around in disbelief. They were moving into a mansion! Having a bath with running cold and hot water for their weekly bath was a huge improvement from taking a bath in a wash tub filled with luke-warm water that had been heated on a stove.

Ollie shared a third floor bedroom with his older brother Tommy and younger brother Tim. He had his own bed and a huge desk that the previous tenants had left behind. Their bedroom window overlooked a backyard, a hill leading up to a paved alley behind the commercial buildings on Main Street. The desk was continuously cluttered with parts of model airplanes that were under construction. After investing in a few store bought model airplane kits, Ollie began to design and build his own planes. His father taught him how to measure pictures of airplanes he found in books and draw plans of his models to scale.

Researching for plane designs led Ollie to another magnificent discovery; the public library. He read every book available that had anything to do with aviation. When he had devoured all these he started reading adventure and sports novels.

ACKNOWLEDGEMENTS

You may not recognize the names of the people who I have listed in this Acknowledgement. Please indulge me in this recognition of their efforts on my behalf. My patient reader group struggled with me through early drafts and provided guidance, constructive critiques, and encouragement. The group includes John and Karon Mallon, Eddie Perri, Jennifer Lewers, Don and Dolly TeBeau, Joan Peterson, Sharon Majerzak and Norb Cudnowski. Norb, a former F94 pilot during the Korean War, and retired United Air Lines captain, was also my aviation consultant.

Oliver was even starting to like some of the snobs in his new school. In fact he had started to notice the girls in his class. One in particular had started to smile at him when she caught him looking at her, causing a strange feeling in his stomach.

Like most of his friends, who had just graduated from the Catholic grade school, Ollie eagerly awaited for the middle of August and the start of high school freshman football practice. His parochial school team had been playing sandlot ball against the public schools for two years and kicking the tar out of, as Ollie called them, the sissies. When the local newspaper ran a story in the paper announcing the date for the start of football practice, Ollie and all his friends showed up and waited outside the dressing room at the high school football field. When the doors opened the parochial school boys filed in and were directed through the dressing room and out the door to the practice field. Ollie noticed that the boys from the public schools had stayed in the dressing room. Soon the public school boys started wandering out on to the practice field, dressed in practice uniforms. The catholic schoolboys waited patiently for the coaches to come out. When they did, they gathered the public school kids at one end of the field and started talking to them. An assistant coach walked over to the catholic school kids and said, "You boys can leave, we have given out all the uniforms."

Bewildered, Ollie said, "Do you mean we aren't even going to be given a chance to play?"

"I'm afraid that's right," the coach said without emotion. "The boys who got the uniforms have been using our plays for years and know the system. They reported for uniforms last week. You people didn't report so you aren't on the team."

As the coach started to leave Ollie, his face flushed with anger, yelled, "That's not fair. How could we report if we didn't know? Anyhow, we beat those sissies every time we played them in grade school. Get them together right now and we'll play them."

The coach continued to walk away without acknowledging Ollie's outburst.

Ollie continued to shout at the coaches until his friends convinced him to leave. He was heartbroken.

Ollie was waiting at the bus stop when his father came home from work. When Ollie explained what had happened he could see the pain in his father's eyes. His father called the Athletic Director and the high school principal and got the same story. There were only a given number of uniforms and positions on the team and the coaches had filled them.

That night Ollie's father sat with him and tried to explain. "I know you don't understand," he told a dejected Ollie. "But some things in life are not fair. The people with money and power control who does what. It has always been that way. You were too young to remember this but during the depression all the help wanted signs had NINA printed on them. It meant No Irish Need Apply. I don't know why the rich people don't like us. For some reason they think we are bad. Maybe it's because most of them have English ancestors and really hate the Irish because we have been fighting them for hundreds of years. Or it might be because we are so stubborn. My grandfather used to tell people not to pick a fight with an Irishman unless you brought a lunch. We have a reputation for never giving up when we think we are right. Someday it may change, but for now you will just have to be strong and live with it. Just never give up. Always do your best no matter how you are treated. I don't know if we will ever be able to make something of ourselves but I don't want you to quit trying."

When school did start after Labor Day, the Catholic School kids soon found that there was discrimination in the public school; not by the teachers, but by the students. The public school students stayed together in cliques that kept out the parochial school children. The catholic school kids didn't mind at all. Like Ollie, they were enjoying being out from under the thumbs of the nuns. Instead of spending the whole day in one classroom with the same people, they rotated class-rooms and teachers and had study halls; gym and every Friday after-noon had an assembly.

When football practice started the next fall, Ollie's catholic friends were there on the right day at the right time. They were issued uniforms but soon found that most of the public school kids were on the varsity while the parochial school kids and the public school rejects were on the junior varsity.

Three weeks into practice, before the start of the regular season, Ollie approached a varsity assistant coach and challenged the varsity to a scrimmage game. The head coach thought it was a good idea. His var-sity had been practicing against each other for three weeks and were getting bored. He made a major mistake.

The junior varsity was put on defense. On the first two plays the var-sity didn't get the ball out of their own backfield. On third down Ollie knew that the varsity was going to pass. As soon as the ball was centered Ollie bolted between the linemen from his linebacker position. As the quarterback started to drop back he saw Ollie bearing down on him so he turned and started to run. Ollie delivered a crunching tackle that knocked the wind out of the quarterback.

The catholic school kids had been laughing about the selection process for the quarterback, a position acquired because he was the team doctor's son. While the flattened quarterback was trying to get his breath his face started to swell and blood dripped from his mouth. The coach rushed to the players and physically lifted Ollie off the ground and tossed him aside.

"Get off the field," he shouted angrily at Ollie, "and stay off. You are no longer a member of the team."

"I am sorry," Ollie said with obvious disgust, "I didn't mean to hurt the big baby."

When Ollie started off the field the rest of his friends followed. One of his friends turned to the varsity and said, "So long sissies, I hope you win a game this year."

"I guess he hates Micks, Wops and Polacks," Ollie said as he left the field.

For weeks Ollie was very bitter about football. His love for the game was snuffed by the attitude of a coach who was nothing like his hero, Knute Rockne. His father again tried to explain that the people he would meet in life would not always be nice or honest. Ollie's disappointment ran unabated for the entire football season. He did not attend any games and eventually gave up the dream of playing for Notre Dame.

By the end of the second year, the students who came into high school from the public schools started to mix with the kids from the parochial school and the clique line began to blur. There were still some children who were in an unofficial "400" club. They were the children of the wealthier parents who did place themselves above the riffraff. By the end of three years that line had almost disappeared and the absorption of cultures was nearly complete.

On reflection, later in his life, Ollie would consider high school as one of the most pleasant periods of his life. They had dances and hayrides and once in awhile somebody would be allowed to use a parent's car. They drained gasoline out of the hoses at gas stations and occasionally siphoned gas from another car. Mostly they traveled around the small town on foot, visiting their girlfriend of the moment and having house parties. Unfortunately, the drama unfolding in Europe would soon change the lives of Ollie and his classmates.

CHAPTER *2*

Life changed for Ollie and most of the world one clear winter day in 1941. He had been to an afternoon movie with one of his friends. When they came out of the movie they heard the news about the Japanese attack on Pearl Harbor. Ollie ran home and joined the rest of the family that had gathered around the radio, listening to news reports. At first Ollie thought the idea of his country being in a war was romantic. The older people knew better. All the parents knew that their older, male children would soon be in the military. Tommy and Billy where both nineteen and would probably be drafted immediately. His other cousin Bobby had just graduated the past summer and would probably be the next to go. Ollie's father was in his forties and had poor eyesight and probably would not be called. The family discussed the possibilities of his Uncle George and Uncle Mike being drafted. His uncles both wanted to enlist but after a tearful discussion with their wives decided to wait to see what developed.

By January of 1942 Ollie's brother and two cousins where in the military and Ollie felt lost. Each morning on waking he had to face the fact that his best friends were gone. He missed them and wanted to be with them.

In the fall of 1942 Tommy returned home on furlough. He had just finished Air Force gunnery school. His leave went by so swiftly that the family barely had time to catch up on the news. Before Tommy left he dug into his duffel bag and pulled out a small blue box and handed it to Ollie.

He smiled when Ollie opened the box and gazed speechlessly at the silver pilot's wings in the box. "I know that someday you will earn them, I wanted to be the one who gave them to you. Put them in a safe place till you need them."

Like most of their neighbors and relatives, the Miller family struggled through the war years, knowing that the small inconvenience of food and gasoline rationing were not comparable to the daily sacrifices being made by the men and women fighting the war.

Ollie joined the Civilian Air Patrol and on weekends flew as an observer, patrolling the railroad tracks and highways looking for potential saboteurs. Just being in the sky was reason enough to walk the three miles to the small airport east of town. He became a fixture at the airport, helping and pestering the handful of plane owners. Eventually they realized that he would not go away and started to take him on short flights in their old Curtis BI-wing "Jennies" and under powered Piper Cubs.

One of the pilots he flew with was a local doctor. Both the doctors sons where in the military. The doctor offered to teach Ollie to fly in return for helping the doctor take care of his yard and house. For Ollie it was a dream come true. He worked for the doctor three nights a week after school and flew with the doctor on weekends. Since he had read every book available on aviation he was a quick student and was soon doing all the flying on CAP patrols. One of his math teachers volunteered to help him study navigation and the science teacher helped him understand the physics of flight.

Ollie's busy schedule was a blessing; it helped him to have less time to worry about his brother and cousins who were in the middle of the war.

The war was very personal for Ollie. He read and reread the letters from Tommy, who was flying missions from England over Germany with the Eight Air Force. The letters were censored, but Ollie could read between the lines and felt the fear and apprehension that was behind the bravado of the letters.

Ollie knew that the Eight Air Force was carrying out dangerous daylight raids on Germany with high casualty rates. He was overjoyed when Tommy wrote to tell them that he had completed his combat missions but would be staying in England as an instructor and ground crewman.

His cousin Billy had enlisted in the Navy and was in the south Pacific on an aircraft carrier.

Uncle George had been drafted and was in Europe in an armored division.

Bobby was in the Marines and was somewhere in the South Pacific. They hadn't heard from him in months. It was a time of constant worry.

Their house was just around the corner from the Western Union telegraph office. The family could observe the daily coming and going of the delivery boy on his bicycle. The families with service men would hold their breaths in fear when they saw the messenger on their street, not relaxing until they were sure that he was not stopping at their house with a message from the War Department.

One gray morning in late October of 1944 Ollie woke up shivering. He didn't know what was wrong. He wasn't sick, he just had the feeling that he had swallowed an ice ball. His mother noticed that he was a little pale at breakfast and felt his forehead.

"What's wrong Ollie?" She asked, concerned about the cold, clammy feeling that she discovered when she touched his forehead.

"I don't know," Ollie said, shaking his head in bewilderment. "It's like I am scared and I don't know why."

Ollie could not shake the feeling and his mother and father started talking about taking him to a doctor. One afternoon a few days later Ollie was returning from a pick up ball game in the park when he saw the Western Union telegraph delivery boy turn into his street. When the messenger stopped in front of his house he felt a jolt of immobilizing fear surge through his body. He tried to run but he felt like time had switched to slow motion. It took forever to get to his front door. The delivery boy was just leaving when he ran up the steps to the front porch. His mother was standing just inside the front door, in shock, holding a telegram. She kept repeating in a strained voice "This couldn't be true, this must be a mistake."

Aunt Cil came into the foyer and took the telegram out of his mother's hand and read it and began to cry and tried to comfort his mother.

"What does it say?" Ollie asked in a near whisper, not really wanting to know. He was not able to withstand the unbearable fear that had gripped him since he saw the delivery boy stop in front of the house.

"I am sorry sweetheart," his aunt sobbed. "It says Tommy was killed in action"

"That can't be right, they must have made a mistake. Tommy was not flying anymore. It has to be somebody else." Ollie said with a mixture of fear, and hope. "We better call dad. He will straighten this out."

Ollie's father was home from his work in half an hour. While Cil tried to comfort Ollie's mother, his father called the local congressman in Washington and the Air Force recruiting station to try to get more information. Within an hour both had called back to express their sorrow that the telegram was correct. Ollie retreated to his room, unable to accept the heartbreaking fact that his brother would never come home. He knew the exact time his brother had died; it was the morning he woke up shaking with unaccountable fear. He sat staring out the back window, holding the pilots wings his brother had given him, unable to remove the vision of his brother releasing his kite on it's first flight.

Three weeks later they received a letter from Tommy's commanding officer. Tommy had volunteered to fill out a crew that was short a gunner. The plane had taken a direct hit in the bomb bay during the bomb run and had totally disintegrated in midair with no survivors. The CO was recommending Tommy for a Distinguished Flying Cross.

The following week they received a package from the Air Force with Tommy's personal belongings. Ollie's father put the package away unopened; unable to cope with the pain he knew he would feel if he opened the package. His mother was still wandering around in a daze, unable to talk to anybody. What was once a noisy house, full of laughter and talk, was now always eerily quiet.

Ollie bravely tried to accept the tragedy and over the course of several months began to resume normal activities. He made an extra effort to spend more time with his pesky little brother. He was now the big brother. Ollie took his little brother with him as often as he could and soon realized what a drag he must have been for his older brother and his cousins.

Just after his sixteenth birthday, with the help of a flight instructor friend of the doctor, Ollie flew solo and then later took a check ride with an examiner and successfully passed the test for his private pilot license. Like everything else in his life, the joy of the moment was somewhat dimmed by his personal grief.

He tried to fill his time from morning to night with activities.

His two older cousins, Rose and Mary Jo began to spend more time with Ollie, gradually indoctrinating him into the intricacies of the feminine world.

Rose, a slim beauty with chestnut colored hair and developing sensuality had initiated the education.

Ollie was aware that the young friends of his brother and his male cousins had spent hours at Ollie's house. It was also painfully clear that the same young men apparently became stupid when Rose was in the house. When the young men asked one of the Miller boys to intercede with Rose on their behalf, Rose would start to laugh and say, "Tell them they are wasting their time. I am going to be a nun."

Mary Jo was not as tall or as beautiful as Rose but was darkly attractive and possessed a ripping wit.

Both of the young ladies had become Ollie's unknowing protector after his brother and cousins left for the military. The girl's current project was teaching Ollie to dance.

Ollie, unlike the typical stocky, muscular Miller men, had developed into a tall, slender teenager with a narrow handsome face topped with coal black hair. He didn't have a real girlfriend but several girls had shyly told his two girl cousins that they would be happy to have Ollie escort them to an upcoming dance. After a week of prompting and cajoling by his cousins, he called one of the girls and was surprised when Marcia Allen accepted his invitation. Both his cousins agreed that she was the cutest and helped Ollie get ready for his first real date.

Just as he was about to leave for the dance, Rose, noticing his obvious apprehension, said, "Remember Ollie, you're not going to marry Marcia, so just have a good time and talk to her like you talk to us. Ask her questions to get her to talk. She will be as nervous as you are so make sure she has fun."

The evening went smoothly, all things considered. There were a few minutes of awkward silence in the beginning but they were both soon having fun. Ollie was surprised when Marcia started holding his hand between dances.

When the dance ended Ollie walked Marcia home. Marcia's mother put out a snack for them and then went upstairs, leaving the door to her bedroom open. Ollie and Marcia looked at each other and began to laugh.

"She must think I am a maniac." Ollie said, unable to control his laughter.

"Maybe she thinks I am the depraved one," Marcia said, taking his hand while smiling mischievously and then sitting on his lap.

"Have you ever had a girl sit on your lap like this?" She asked while boldly kissing his cheek, "It's lots of fun."

"Aren't you worried about your mother?" Ollie asked nervously, glancing up the stairs toward the bedroom door.

"She was young once," Marcia said breathlessly as she kissed Ollie on the lips.

Ollie was enjoying the contact and the fresh mint taste of the kiss. When Marcia became more aggressive Ollie began to get nervous. He really didn't know what was happening nor did he know how to respond when Marcia tried to lead him. She gave up when Ollie stood up and announced that he had to leave.

Both his girl cousins were waiting for him in the living room when he got home. They started to ask questions about the evening.

Ollie took their kidding gracefully, telling them about the evening, and said, "I will say this for sure, dancing with Marcia is sure more fun than dancing with you two."

"You ingrate," Rose said with mock hostility. "Wait till you want to learn how to kiss. I won't teach you."

"What makes you think I need your help with that?" Ollie smiled as he headed up the stairs.

Rose and Mary Jo looked at each other for a few seconds and Mary Jo said, "Ollie seemed a little nervous to me. What do you think?"

"Maybe Marcia was a little to advanced for Ollie." Rose said. "Maybe we better start teaching him more about worldly stuff."

"Yeah, like we know." Mary Jo answered, rapping Rose with a rolled up magazine.

Just when Ollie was about over thinking daily about Tommy, disaster struck again, twice. Within a two week period the Western Union messenger made two more visits to the Miller house. The first message from the War Department advised that Bobby had been wounded in action and was being transported back to the states. The second was more devastating; Billy had been killed in action. Once again the war plunged the family into grief. Visions of Billy and Tommy helping build and fly his first kite kept popping into Ollie's mind.

In time, after spending months in a military hospital, Bobby came home on crutches. He had lost his left leg below the knee. When his mother first saw him she began to sob uncontrollably.

"Mom," he said, while hugging his mother. "Believe me. I am just happy to be alive."

VE and VJ day brought little joy to the Millers. They were happy that the war was over and that the rides of the Western Union death messenger had stopped. The two gold star flags in their window reminded the neighbors that their family had paid dearly for protecting their country.

The family was overjoyed when Uncle George finally came home. The kids immediately noticed a change in their favorite uncle. He was quiet and seemed to be somewhere in the distance when they tried to talk to him.

His first night home he awakened everybody in the house screaming hysterically. "Get out! Get out! My God let them get out!"

Everybody in the house rushed in panic to Cil and George's bedroom door.

A visibly shaken Cil opened the door and said, "It's OK, he just had a nightmare."

It was a nightmare that would return nearly every night.

Months later they learned that George's tank had been hit by artillery. He was in the turret and escaped just as the tank erupted in flames. George could hear his crew screaming inside the burning tank but could not help them. He began to drink occasionally and then more frequently, just trying to forget or to go to sleep in a drunken stupor to escape the night horrors.

Once when he was partially drunk he told his brother, "I wish I had died with them, everybody would have been better off."

The entire family and their parish priest tried unsuccessfully to bring him back. Finally he reached some inner peace but never was the same happy, outgoing person that Ollie remembered from his days in the old coal company house.

Ollie's high school graduating class of 1946 found themselves in a dilemma. Most of the young men had assumed they would be going into the military after high school. With the war over they found themselves competing with returning veterans for jobs and placement in colleges. The veterans were getting preferential consideration. During his senior year Ollie, who had maintained an A average in his college prep courses, had been applying to colleges for a scholarship. After a year of relentless submittal of applications he sadly realized that he would not be going to college and might be spending the rest of his life working in a menial job

Ollie applied to every commercial airline, seeking any kind of entry position. None answered his letters or returned his phone calls. The local tire manufacturer, where he had worked summers while in school, eventually did hire him. The job did pay well and provided Ollie with free time to pursue his instrument and commercial pilot's license.

Ollie also wrote letters to and visited all the military recruiting offices in Greenwood and Pittsburgh, trying to get into flight school. They all had the same discouraging advice; they were over staffed with pilots and had discontinued flight training. They told him he could sign up as an enlisted man and would have preference if and when they started flight training again.

In February of 1947 Ollie made a decision; he was going to enlist in the Army Air Force. His mother burst into tears when he got up the courage to tell her.

"I won't sign the papers," she said with conviction, between her tears. "This family has given enough. I hold my breath now every time you go flying. I have been on the verge of asking you to quit many times, and now this. You can't do this to me."

Ollie tried to convince her of the advantages of his decision explaining that he would still be eligible for the GI bill of rights and could go to college after his enlistment if he didn't like the military. His mother remained adamantly opposed. His father also objected at first but gradually, albeit reluctantly, agreed and helped convince his wife.

"You know Hilda, all Ollie has ever wanted to do is fly. If we say no we will be responsible for ruining his dream."

His mother finally agreed to his enlisting telling her husband, "If anything happens to Ollie I will never forgive you."

This statement almost caused Ollie to change his mind. He didn't want to ruin his father's life because of something he wanted to do.

His father told him not to worry. "I would feel terrible the rest of my life if I stopped you. Just be careful and don't volunteer for anything."

Ollie enlisted the following day. His parents had a going away party for the family and Ollie's friends the day before he left. Ollie said goodbye to his friends and his childhood.

Fortunately, the difficult years of his childhood had molded his character and had prepared him for what would be a difficult journey into manhood.

CHAPTER 3

San Antonio, Texas, USA, February, 1947

Oliver slowly awoke out of a troubled dream. In the dream he had been wandering naked on an open, freezing cold, wind swept hill. His body was trembling uncontrollably and he realized that the cold was real. It was about three am and he was in an unheated tent in Texas.

The trip by railroad to San Antonio, Texas had been long, tedious and demoralizing. He had traveled by train to Pittsburgh, reported to the Air Force recruiting station, had a physical examination while nude in a freezing cold room, had taken a written exam and then, along with a dozen other men, had been sworn in and became the property of the Air Force. The group was then walked to the Pennsylvania Railroad station and along with an Air Force escort, boarded a train heading for San Antonio, Texas. At each major city more recruits boarded the train. By the time they reached Saint Louis, Missouri the car was filled. On the first night a fight broke out among four of the recruits who were playing Black Jack. During the fight a window was broken and the car immediately filled with February cold, sooty air.

The rest of the trip was miserable. Box lunches with dry bread and baloney sandwiches, sickening sweet artificial orange drink, cookies and an apple were provided periodically to the shivering young men. After two days of agony they arrived in San Antonio and loaded onto an Air Force bus and were transported to Lackland Air Force Base. The recruits were directed into a mess hall where they were served tomato soup, bread and liquid acid that was supposed to be coffee. There wasn't much complaining. At least the food was hot and the mess hall was heated.

After finishing the meal the recruits were formed up in straggly lines outside the mess hall and marched to a large warehouse. As they rounded the mess hall they noticed that the card players who had broken the train window where outside the rear of the mess hall, scrubbing huge, greasy pots. The message was clear; screw up and you would be punished quickly.

Inside the warehouse the recruits formed single lines and as they approached a counter were greeted by an enlisted man that sized up the line and shouted "small, medium or large," to a clerk behind the counter. The men behind the counter selected a duffel bag and threw it across the counter to the recruit. The recruits were then led through a side door and assembled into groups of eight and then, toting the heavy bag, were marched, what seemed like miles, to a tent area.

"Okay, this is your tent." A young, warmly dressed Airman advised them. "You will be in the tents until we have enough people to start a basic training group and then you will be moved to your regular barracks."

With those few instructions, he left to pick up another group of recruits.

Ollie dragged his duffel bag into the tent and dumped it onto a steel frame cot. The end of the cot was covered by a thin, rolled up mattress, sheets, a pillow and one thin blanket.

The tent, just big enough for eight cots and a pot bellied stove, was the same temperature as the cold Texas wind blowing down from the hill country.

Ollie and another recruit started looking around the inside and then the outside of the tent, but found no fuel for the stove.

The recruits began to unpack the duffel bags. They discovered that all of them had been issued large size clothes. One by one they pulled the issued clothes over their civilian clothes and got into their bunks and tried to sleep.

Before the sun came up the recruits in the tent were jolted out of sleep by somebody walking up and down the rows of tents, shrilly blowing a whistle and shouting, "Everybody up and fall out and line up outside your tents in five minutes."

The recruits stumbled clumsily out on to the dirt street and formed two lines.

"Looks like something out of a Three Stooge's movie doesn't it." Ollie said to the recruit next to him as they viewed the others in their miss-fitting clothes.

When the non-commissioned officer in charge arrived he started to bellow, "Is this your idea of a joke? Who is responsible for this? Somebody speak up or you will all spend your entire enlistment pulling KP."

Ollie raised his hand and said, "Sir, I don't know about the rest of these people, but most of us arrived last night and they gave us all a bag with these clothes in the bag."

"Okay, Okay," the non-com replied, the flush starting to leave his face. "I'll find the simpletons who did this. I want you all to keep in formation and follow me to the mess hall."

Breakfast was fried corn mush, fried Spam, cold dry toast and strong coffee. The mess hall was warm and the warm food helped lift the spirits of the recruits. While they where eating Ollie noticed the non-com talking to an officer who had entered the mess hall. The non-com pointed to Ollie and then left. By the time they finished breakfast the non-com had returned and after speaking to the officer blew his whistle and announced, "I want you men to go back to your tents and put all the clothes you have been issued back in the duffel bags. We will be around to take you back to supply to get proper uniforms. You are dismissed, I trust you can find your tents."

As the recruits were filing out of the mess hall the non-com tapped Ollie on the shoulder and said, "The lieutenant wants to talk to you."

Only in the Air Force one day and already I am in trouble, Ollie thought as he approached the officer with noticeable apprehension.

"What's your name?" The officer asked

Ollie responded, "Oliver Miller, sir."

"Be at ease," the lieutenant said. "I just want you to answer a few questions."

He proceeded to ask questions about the activities since the recruits had arrived. When he was done he said, "You are dismissed."

Ollie hesitated and started to leave.

"Was there something else you wanted to say?" The officer asked.

"I was wondering if the lack of fuel to burn in the tent stoves and only cold water in the latrines was intentional. Is it part of a plan to toughen us up, sir?"

"I will look into that too," the officer said as he turned and walked away.

It took the rest of the day for the new recruits to get measured and issued proper uniforms. By nightfall no fuel had been delivered to the tents so half of the recruits in Ollie's tent went out to scavenge anything that would burn. They found a large group of unoccupied tents and borrowed a few wooden tent pegs from each tent. They then located a dump area and retrieved some cardboard and old wood that had been discarded. They set the fire in the stove and decided not to light it till it really got cold. Between wearing the long johns, adding clothes to the top of the blanket for additional warmth and the meager heat given off by the stove, they managed an uncomfortable sleep.

The next day they where marched off to lectures on Air Force History and when they returned to their tent they found cardboard boxes filled with coal and kindling wood.

A non-commissioned officer assigned the personnel from different tents to build and maintain a fire in the latrine boiler. The next day they rotated into the latrine for a hot shower and shave. Ollie began to feel like a human again.

They lived in the tents for nearly two weeks and then moved into permanent, two story wooden barracks, and began basic training.

Basic training was just what Ollie expected it to be; physical conditioning, close order drill, lectures on military chain of command, inspections and military discipline. With the exception of KP, an ordeal that consisted of eighteen hours of continuous work in the mess hall kitchen, Ollie actually enjoyed basic..

On Saturday, the final day of basic training, the training officer addressed the graduates and told them to check the bulletin board at Company headquarters for their next assignment and traveling instructions.

Ollie patiently waited and when he finally worked his way up to the postings found that he was to report to Biloxi, Mississippi for radioman school. He noticed that most of his company had been assigned to general duty at various Air Force posts. He was one of the few scheduled for a school. The next day the new Airmen spent the day packing their gear in duffel bags and saying good-bye to friends.

Monday morning Ollie boarded an Air Force bus to the Greyhound bus depot in San Antonio and was soon on his way to Biloxi, Mississippi and then to Keesler Air Force Base. He hitched a ride to the Radio school headquarters, signed in and was directed to his barracks.

One of his new classmates directed him to an available bunk and he unpacked his gear into a footlocker and clothes locker.

The young airman that had helped Ollie introduced himself, "Bill Thomas," he said, extending his hand. "I got here three days ago. I was just going to the mess hall. Want to go with me?"

Ollie finished storing his gear and the two young men stepped out into the humid air and started toward the mess hall.

"The last word I got was that the next class would start next Monday so it looks like we will have a few days to scout the area." Bill said as they entered the mess hall.

After eating Ollie patted his stomach and said, "Well, at least the food is better here and the living quarters are like a four star hotel compared to Lackland." Ollie said, obviously having enjoyed his dinner.

During the next several days their barracks gradually began to fill. On Monday morning the class was assembled outside the barracks and marched to the Radio Training center where they were issued books and supplies. They were directed to a small amphitheater classroom and after being seated a stocky Master Sergeant entered the room and walked to the lectern.

He held up a typewritten sheet of paper and said, "Look for this document, titled 'Schedule', in the kit you were just issued. This is the schedule that you will be following for the next eight weeks. You will note that each day will start with a lecture in this room starting at Oh-eight hundred. The subject of the lecture is listed on the schedule. Read your text before the lecture and be ready to ask questions if you don't understand something.

We will wake you up every morning for roll call, physical training and chow. After that it will be up you to get to the right place at the right time. Screw up and you are gone. Now follow me and I will take you on a tour of the facilities."

The eight weeks passed quickly, the hours filled with studying, practicing code, broadcasting, tearing down and rebuilding equipment and taking endless written and oral tests. The class had a small graduation party and celebrated being awarded their first promotion. It was only one stripe but it was a step up.

Most of the class where issued orders to report to various Air Force Installations for duty. Ollie received orders to report to Omaha, Nebraska for Flight Engineering school.

The school at Moffit Field in Omaha was run just like the radio school except it covered the mechanics and electronics of aircraft. After graduation Ollie was assigned to Military Air Transportation, stationed at Moffit field.

After reporting for duty and being assigned quarters, he was granted a seven day furlough. He was pleased with his assignment. He would receive enlisted man preferential status for off duty MATS flights and flew into Pittsburgh on an Air Force DC4.

Ollie called all his old friends and found that most of them had enlisted in the military. The furlough was over in what seemed like an instant and his parents drove him to the military installation in the Pittsburgh airport.

Ollie reported into MATs for duty the next day and was fitted for tailored flight clothes and the new blue dress uniforms and was assigned to a crew consisting of a pilot and co-pilot-navigator and Ollie. He met the two flight officers an hour before his first flight and participated in the walk around inspection of a striped down, humped backed, four engine Constellation, loaded with cargo bound for Japan via Hawaii and Wake Island. The pilot, Captain William Snelling, was a young, slim ex B17 pilot who had flown twenty missions with the Eight Air Force during World War II. Ollie had instant rapport with the Captain as soon as the Captain learned that Ollie's brother had flown with the Eight. The co-pilot, Bobby Clemens, a muscular, ruddy faced, self proclaimed Georgia Cracker was a Second Lieutenant who had arrived in England for duty as a fighter pilot two weeks before VE day. He had returned to the States for transfer to the Pacific Theater and had crashed landed after being shot down by ground fire on his first mission. By the time he recovered from his injuries the War was over. Both men had re-enlisted to obtain training that would help them obtain airline jobs at the end of their enlistment. Ollie immediately both liked and admired both of the unpretentious officers. They reciprocated by treating him as an equal, without cognizance of the difference in rank. They insisted that Ollie call them by their first names.

The crew flew on a regular schedule to all parts of the world, sometimes in a plane filled with cargo and one or two human hitchhikers and sometimes in a plane setup for passengers only. For most crews the long flights could be excruciatingly boring. Ollie and his crewmates never complained, they were just happy to be flying.

During a long trip to Japan they stopped for fuel in Hawaii and picked up a lone passenger, a Women's Army Auxiliary Corp second lieutenant returning to General MacArthur's staff in Tokyo, from a furlough. She was the lone passenger in the noisy, cold cargo section. When the woman climbed on board Ollie introduced himself. Even in her rumpled olive drab uniform, with cotton hose and flat shoes, it was obvious that this was an extremely attractive young woman. She was almost as tall as Ollie and had long brunette hair, worn in a page boy bob popular in the WAAC, a very attractive, perfectly proportioned face and expressive dark brown eyes.

When Ollie introduced himself she held out her hand and smiled. "I'm Mary Callahan. I'm pleased to meet you."

Ollie noticed two things immediately. She had not introduced herself as a lieutenant and when she smiled her nose wrinkled and her face lit up in a genuine smile.

He invited her to stay in the cockpit during the long flight and set up an area where she could sleep. Mary had not carried any food on board so Ollie shared his thermos coffee and food with her. During the flight, when she was awake, she put on earphones and a mike so she could talk to Ollie without shouting over the drone of the engines. The other two crew members looked at each other frequently during the flight, raising their eyebrows. It was obvious that Ollie and Mary were really striking up a nice friendship.

When they landed in Tokyo, Mary insisted that she wanted to repay Ollie for his kindness and cook him dinner in her apartment. They visited the airbase commissary and picked up supplies and drove to Mary's apartment in her Jeep. The first night in Tokyo, after dinner and an hour of conversation, Ollie started to leave. Mary smiled and put her arms around him and said, "I really think you should stay here tonight. I haven't finished repaying you for your kindness."

Mary led him into the bedroom and started helping him remove his uniform. When Ollie tried to explain that he was totally inexperienced, Mary said softly, "Just relax and I'll teach you every thing you need to know."

Mary led him to the bed and lay down besides him, caressing and gently kissing his lips and body, telling Ollie where to touch and kiss her.

Hours later a smiling, contented Mary lay beside Ollie, stroking his chest. "You are an excellent student. I think after a few more nights you can move on to graduate school."

From that time on, Ollie was ecstatic when he was flying to Japan. Mary Callahan became the first diversion that interested Ollie in something other than flying. Ollie ignored the good-natured kidding by the rest of his flight crew. When they were in Japan, Ollie spent every possible moment with Mary.

During long flights the crew talked incessantly about the future of the Air Force and military politics. From the discussions Ollie became aware that an internal struggle was going on inside the Air Force leadership and in Washington. The make up and deployment of the Air Force was a continuing debate. For the moment it appeared that the Strategic Bombing proponents were winning the battle for their projects. Money had been allocated for the development of a new bomber to replace the B29 and any money left for fighters was being spent on interceptors and not attack fighters. Ollie was somewhat interested in the maneuvering but only to the extent to which it might provide new flight training opportunities. Both the officers in his crew thought by the time Ollie was near the end of his enlistment that the majority of the World War II pilots would be leaving for civilian flying jobs and that the Air Force would have to start training new replacement pilots.

In 1948, after a routine cargo flight to England, Captain Snelling informed the rest of the crew that they would be temporarily stationed in England for an unknown amount of time.

The Russians who controlled all the land accesses to Berlin, Germany had set up a blockade of rail and road transportation into the Allied controlled western sector. Within days the residents were running out of food, medicine and fuel. MATS was assigned the task of air lifting supplies into Berlin.

For the next six months Ollie and his crew worked without a day off. They would fly a full load into the Templehoff airport in Berlin, using precision navigation. The Russians had warned that even the slightest deviation from the landing approach to the airport would be cause for the ground anti-aircraft guns to shoot down the American planes. The planes landed continuously with just a few minutes between plane landings. Sometimes Ollie could feel the turbulence from the prop wash of the plane landing in front of them. At night it looked like a continuous stream of skylights tracking into the airport. The crew ate and slept while the planes were being loaded and unloaded and occasionally had a few hours off while in England.

When it became apparent that the Americans were not going to give up and that the blockade was not entirely effective, the Russians removed the blockade. The MATS flying and ground crews received special commendations from the Air Force and thirty-day furloughs.

Ollie spent the first week of his furlough at home, catching up on sleep and visiting old friends. After a week Ollie hopped a MATs flights to Japan. The next three weeks he had a marvelous time with Mary in Tokyo. Dressed in civilian clothes, he would pick her up after work and they would drive out of the crowded city and tour the beautiful flower garden parks that had been maintained even during the war.

When Ollie returned to Moffit Field he got the bad news that he was no longer assigned to Captain Snelling's crew. He was advised that he would be receiving a new assignment in a few days. When he called Captain Snelling to tell him how disappointed he was that he was not going to be on his crew any longer. The Captain told Ollie that he had been re-assigned to the Strategic Air Command's 55th Reconnaissance Wing at Topeka Kansas. He was starting flight training in B29's. Bobby had been reassigned to jet fighter school.

"I'm not sure," the captain said, "but you may be soon getting your wish. I have heard rumors that flight training is going to be opening up again. When I heard the rumor I immediately contacted the CO and made sure he had your name on the list for flight training. Keep your fingers crossed and good luck."

Two days later Ollie was summoned to the CO's office.

"I have your new orders," the colonel advised, gesturing toward the paper work on his desk. "Thank God this has come in. Now you and your ex-crew can stop pestering me. You are to report to Air Cadet school at Columbus Air Force Base in Mississippi no later than noon next Sunday. I have already booked you on MATS. Think you will be ready?"

"Sir, I have been ready for this since I was six years old."

The feeling of elation and excitement flowed through Ollie's body. He felt warmth in his chest and body that he had never experienced before. He barely remembered shaking the colonel's hand or leaving his office. He kept pinching himself to make sure he wasn't dreaming.

Ollie called Captain Snelling as soon as he got back to his quarters. The captain was almost as excited as Ollie.

"One thing I wanted to tell you," the captain said. "Don't tell the instructors that you have had flight lessons. They will try to prove to you that you don't know anything and will do their best not to cut you any slack. Flying the trainers will be much more difficult than flying light planes. It will even be more difficult than the big planes we let you fly. Pay attention, even if you think you already know what they are trying to teach you. You will learn something new. If you have trouble with anything give me a call. I'll get my phone number to you as soon as I get to Topeka."

CHAPTER 4

Columbus Air Force Base, Columbus, Mississippi

Ollie arrived at Columbus Mississippi on a cold, dismal day in January 1949. The cold did not dampen Ollie's euphoria. Nothing could have restrained the warm feeling that had taken over his life since learning that he was to become an Air Cadet.

Ollie reported into Cadet headquarters and received instructions and rooming assignment. He was issued Cadet uniforms, flight equipment and training books and supplies, soon stored in the prescribed manner.

The training schedule was posted outside the Cadet Headquarters. Most of the first few weeks would be a repeat of Ollie's Basic Training since some of the new cadets had entered as civilians. The next month would be devoted to ground school.

After what seemed an eternity, the first day of flight instruction arrived. Ollie and three other cadets reported to the cadet flight-training center and met Captain James Perry, a career Air Force officer.

Perry had been a flight instructor since enlisting in the Air Force in 1942.

He greeted the cadets without histrionics or for that matter emotion. It was immediately apparent to the cadets that Perry was a no nonsense, competent instructor that expected their complete attention. After talking to each cadet for a few minutes he started for the door that led out to the hangar apron and over his shoulder said, "Follow me and let's go get really acquainted with the T6."

Ollie's heart was pounding in his chest as they approached the North American T6 single engine trainer. The huge radial 600 horsepower Pratt and Whitney piston engine was many times more powerful than those in the light planes Ollie had flown. Ollie knew every feature, control and instrument of the trainer and could not wait to take the controls.

After a detailed walk around and cockpit inspection Captain Perry asked, "Who wants to be first?"

The other three cadets hesitated, looking at each other, and Ollie said, "I would, sir."

"Okay, Miller," the captain said, looking at his nametag, "let's go."

Ollie climbed up on the wing of the trainer and carefully slid into the front seat and fastened the seatbelt, put on his flight helmet and plugged in the radio and intercom leads. The captain leaned into the front cockpit and checked him out, gave him a thumbs up and then climbed into the rear seat.

A few seconds later the captain's voice asked if Ollie could hear him. When Ollie answered in the affirmative the captain said, "All right, lesson one is about to commence. Pay attention and do what you are told and don't touch anything unless I tell you too. If I do let you touch anything, let go as soon as I say 'I have got it' or 'I have it'. Are we clear?"

Ollie answered, "Yes sir."

Captain Perry talked through the start up procedure, covering each step in detail and asking if there were any questions.

They received clearance to taxi to a runway and then to take off.

Ollie felt the thrust of the huge engine pressing him back in his seat. They quickly gained air speed and Ollie experienced the thrill that he always felt when he became airborne. This time it was more intense, sending a shiver up and down his spine. As soon as they reached cruising altitude the instructor made some gentle banked turns and then leveled out.

"Okay, Miller, take the controls. Keep a firm grip on the stick and pressure on the rudder pedals. Let me know when you are ready."

Ollie grasped the stick lightly with his right hand and firmly pressed the right rudder pedal with his foot, anticipating the movement of the plane caused by the torque of the engine.

"I am ready, sir." Ollie said. It had taken several seconds to wet his dry lips before he could reply.

He felt the controls come under his direction and immediately reacted to the torque of the large radial engine and smoothly corrected the plane flight to the correct heading. The feeling of elation was immediate. He couldn't stop himself from muttering, "Hot damn!"

"What did you say?" The flight instructor asked, mild surprise reflected in his voice. This was the first student that had ever corrected for the torque without being surprised or being told how to correct.

"Sorry for that sir. I was momentarily overcome by the experience of being in control for the first time."

They maintained level flight for a few more minutes with Ollie keeping the attitude of the plane exactly level with the horizon. The instructor talked him into several gentle banking turns and then into descending and climbing turns.

"Do you think you could find your way back to the field?" The instructor asked.

Almost every student he had up for their first flight by now was usually totally dis-oriented and could not even be sure of up and down. Many of the cadets threw up on their first flight.

When Ollie said he thought he could find his way back the instructor said "It's all yours, line us up for a landing from east of the runway."

Ollie put the plane into a tight right turn, straightened out, and after a few minutes made another right turn and was lined up perfectly with the runway a few miles in the distance. He was just reaching for the throttle to reduce power when Captain Perry said, "I have the controls Miller."

With reluctance, Ollie relinquished his grip on the stick and pressure on the rudder pedals. He would have flown till it was dark.

The instructor landed smoothly and taxied to the apron where the three other students were waiting. He killed the engine and they unbuckled their seat belts and climbed out of the cockpit. As they were walking away from the plane the instructor asked Ollie if he had ever flown a plane before.

Ollie replied that he had flown with MATs as a flight engineer and that the flight crew had let him fly the big planes on occasions.

The instructor looked at him skeptically for a few seconds and then looked at the other three cadets and said, "Which one of you wants to be the next to threaten my life?"

For the next five months the Cadets lived and breathed flying. Each week the number of cadets declined as they were washed out due to poor scores in classroom or poor instructor ratings. Ollie was the first in his class to solo and the first to fly cross-country.

The training staff held a small graduation exercise for the cadets, followed by a party in the Officers Club. During the party Captain Perry drew Ollie aside and said, "You can tell me the truth now. You had flight instruction before you arrived here, hadn't you?"

"I knew you suspected that but the pilots on my flight crew told me to not say anything about my previous flight training. They thought I would get flack from the instructors if they knew that I have been flying since I was sixteen. I realized after a few weeks that it wouldn't have made any difference to you but I didn't want to take any chances. This is too important to me."

Captain Perry smiled and patted Ollie on the shoulder, "I knew the first second that you took the controls that you were going to be the best student I had ever had. I also could tell that you and I are the same. We really are only alive when we are flying. Not that I don't enjoy teaching, but I only do this because the Air Force lets me fly nearly every day and pays me for having fun. I won't tell any of my buddies in advanced school that you had previous instruction but I will make it a point to tell them to give you their full attention. Most of them are like us. They fly because they love it. Wait until you fly your first jet. The experience is unbelievable."

The next morning orders were posted. The class was moving to Perrin Air Force Base in Denton, Texas for advanced training in the T28 Trainer.

The T28, a single engine two-seat trainer with an 800 horsepower radial piston engine, was much faster than the T6 and was much more difficult to fly. After a few hours Ollie felt very comfortable and soon was learning aerobatics, formation flying and tactics. After three months at Perrin the class was split. Some were assigned to multi-engine school. Ollie was surprised to find that he had been assigned to Webb Air Force Base in Big Springs, Texas were he would be flying a T33 jet trainer.

When the orders were posted he called Captain Perry at Columbus Air Force Base.

"Does this mean I will be going into fighter training next? That really surprises me. I thought that because of my training in MATs I would be going to multi-engines."

"Yes it means jet fighter training is next," the captain said. "Would you have preferred multi-engines? They usually take the top of the class for fighters."

"No, I am very happy," Ollie replied. "I guess I was just surprised that fighter training had opened up."

The captain smiled and said, "You are going to have to read a newspaper once in awhile. Occasionally read something other than a flight-training manual. Before you started flight training the US guaranteed Japan that we would provide fighter interceptor defense for them until our government figures out what they are going to allow Japan to do for self defense. I thought you knew that. That's why flight training was re-started."

Ollie really didn't care about the politics; he just considered it fortunate that he was in the right place at the right time.

Jet training exceeded Ollie's wildest dreams. The first time he took the controls of the sleek T33 two-seat trainer he wore the plane like it was a part of his body.

His instructor just said, "It's all yours Miller. Jim Perry said you have the potential to be a hotshot pilot so show me what you've got. Turn it loose but don't go too crazy on me."

Ollie gently moved the controls to get the feel of the jet trainer. The jet propulsion system provided no torque to the plane and the plane seemed to fly in a straight line by itself. After a few minutes of checking the controls, Ollie advanced the throttle to max, gently brought the stick back to his stomach, stood the jet on it's tail and felt the "G" force of the acceleration press him back into the seat. They burst through hazy gray clouds into crystal clear air beneath a bright cobalt blue sky. Ollie regained level flight and started a series of aileron rolls and then leveled off to let his adrenaline return to normal.

"Now that you have that out of your system," his instructor said after he stopped laughing, "let's get down to some serious training."

After three months at Webb Air Force Base Ollie moved to Moody Air Force Base in Georgia for a month of training in a T33 equipped for instrument and night flying.

The last phase of his training at Moody Air Force Base included training in gunnery, strafing, formation flying and tactics.

On January fifth, 1950, Ollie and the rest of his class were commissioned as second lieutenants in the Air Force. The Base Commander pinned the gold lieutenant bars on the graduating class and then the coveted silver pilots wings.

When the Base Commander was in front of Ollie and had pinned on the bars and was preparing to pin on his wings Ollie said, "Sir, would you please use these wings," retrieving a small, worn blue box from his pocket. "My older brother was killed in action flying with the Eighth. He gave them to me when I was a kid."

The Base Commander took the extended box, withdrew the wings and as he pinned them to Ollie's jacket said, "I am sure your brother would be proud of you today."

Immediately after the ceremony Ollie visited the communication center and had them put through a long distance call to Mary in Japan.

After the first joyously wild moments of their conversation, Ollie said, "I have really good news. I have been assigned to an advanced training program and will probably be stationed in Japan as soon as the training is complete."

Mary was ecstatic; the long separation had been unbearable.

Two days later the new pilots where flown to Tyndall Air Force Base in the Florida panhandle. When Ollie opened the door to his shared Bachelor Officer Quarters he was greeted by Bill Thomas, his friend from radio school.

Bill, sporting obviously new second lieutenant bars smiled broadly as he shook Ollie's hand and simultaneously pounded him on the shoulder. "I'm your assigned Radar Observer. I'll be riding in the back seat of our F94 Interceptor and you better be smooth. I don't want to barf on you."

They spent the next several hours catching up on the news and their activities during the year and a half since they had parted after radio school. Bill had gone on to Radar school and had been stationed at various radar installations around the world until being selected for training as an in-flight radar observer.

The pilot of the interceptor flew the plane and controlled the onboard munitions. The radar observer directed the pilot to potential enemy targets while scanning for possible approaching enemies. The pilot and "RO" worked as a team and needed a total rapport to maximize efficient operation and to stay alive in combat situations.

After ground school that covered every aspect of the F94, both by book and by lectures from experienced pilots, Ollie and Bill were assigned an F94. Before their first flight Bill jokingly asked, "How about you taking this machine around the block a few times by yourself before I get on board."

"We live or die together," Ollie said with mock seriousness. "So get on board and I will try to get you back on the ground in one piece. Besides, you have airtime in this beast and I don't. You are probably going to have to talk me through everything."

Their first of many familiarization flights was smooth as silk. Ollie put the plane through routine maneuvers while Bill scanned his radar screen. After the first few flights they began mock interceptor runs on any aircraft that Bill picked up on the screen.

In May 1950, Ollie and the rest of the F94 trainees finished their advanced training. Just as Ollie had expected, they were assigned to the Fifth Air Force in Japan.

CHAPTER *5*

Johnson Air Force Base near Tokyo, Japan

Ollie and the rest of the crews assembled their belongings and took the long MATS flight from Florida to Johnson Air Force Base, thirty miles northwest of Tokyo, Japan. As soon as Ollie was settled in his Bachelor Officer Quarters he found a phone and called Mary's office phone. The woman who answered the phone surprised Ollie by telling him that Mary was no longer at the number he had called. When Ollie asked for her new number there was a slight hesitation and then the woman gave Ollie a number that he recognized as Mary's home number.

Mary answered her home phone on the second ring. "I knew you would be in today, I have been pestering my friends in the Air Force and they told me to stay at home today so I knew this was the day. I am so happy that I am almost ready to cry. How soon can we get together? I have so much to tell you."

"What has happened? Why aren't you at work? The woman at your office wouldn't tell me anything, just that you weren't at your work number."

"Well, it's a long story and I will give you all the details when we get together. The short version is that I'm no longer in the WAAC. I'm now a civilian and have started a new career as a liaison between American and Japanese businesses. I had the opportunity to take an early dis-charge and when you called and said you might be coming to Japan I decided to stay here and wait for you. It is going to be wonderful. I can't wait to see you."

"This sounds too good to true." Ollie was delighted with the prospect of not having to deal with Mary being in the military. "I will call you as soon as I know when I have time off. "

"Can't I just hop in the car and come up there right now?" Mary asked wistfully.

"That would be okay by me but I don't think my new CO would approve. As much as I want to see you I don't want to ask him for any favors the first day and get on his shit list. I have to go now, we are having a briefing in ten minutes and I don't know what is planned after that." Ollie replied. "I will call you as soon as I have a free minute. I promise."

One hour later he called back, "I have terrific news. We have nothing scheduled until Monday so I will have three days off. I am hitching a ride into Tokyo and with any luck will be at your apartment in an hour. The guy I am riding in with has an apartment just a couple of blocks from you. See you soon."

Ollie could barely focus on the conversations that took place between the other two passengers and the driver. He was thinking only of once again holding Mary in his arms. He was remembering her soft fragrance and the warmth of her body when the captain driving the car pulled up in front of Mary's apartment.

"I'll pick you up here at twenty-one-hundred on Sunday," the captain shouted as Ollie retrieved his bag from the trunk and headed for the stairs leading up to Mary's apartment.

Her apartment, built by the American government for American civilians working with the Army of Occupation and American Officers, had replaced the rubble of a bombed out section near the southwest corner of Tokyo. It was called "The Enclave" by the residents and was patrolled by American Military Police.

Mary's apartment was on the second floor. The front of the apartment faced the street and the back had a view of a park, completely encircled by the "cookie cutter" design apartment buildings.

Ollie bounded up the steps and found the door to Mary's apartment open. She had been looking out the front room window and had opened the front door just as Ollie arrived. Ollie lifted her off her feet and then lowered her and buried his face in her hair.

"You don't know how much I missed this," he said, gently stroking her back with both hands.

"I think I do," Mary responded with a tremor in her voice and her body emphasizing her response.

"Come with me," Mary said softly, taking him by the hand and starting to walk down the hall toward the bedrooms. "I want to show you something."

Ollie was about to speak when he realized that she was turning into the door to the spare bedroom. He stopped to take in the contents of the room when Mary turned on the light. Total confusion registered on his face. Before he could say anything Mary said, "Ollie, this is your son, Kevin Oliver Callahan," gesturing toward a baby sleeping peacefully in a crib.

It took several minutes for Ollie to fully grasp the meaning of what had just transpired.

Mary led him back out to the living room and poured two glasses of wine from a chilled bottle that was open and sitting in a bowl of ice.

"Here, drink this," she smiled. "As soon as you rejoin me mentally I'll fill in the details of the long story I told you about over the phone."

Several hours later Ollie was still shaking his head in wonder. Mary had filled him in with the details of the events since they were last together.

A month after Ollie had left Japan after his three week furlough, Mary suspected she was pregnant. With the help of a civilian friend she made an appointment with a civilian doctor who confirmed her suspicions. She worked until it was obvious that she was pregnant and then received a medical discharge. She delivered the baby boy without difficulty and received overwhelming support from the wives and mothers who lived in the Enclave.

When Ollie asked her why she hadn't told him she answered that he had started into Cadet Training and she knew how important that was to Ollie and that she did not want him to worry about her and the baby. The wives of the officers and American civilians had set up a child care center and one month after Kevin's birth she had started her new job.

"We are going to have to do something about the baby's last name," Ollie said as he took Mary into his arms.

Mary's voice, muffled from being buried in Ollie's chest, was barely audible. "Is that a marriage proposal?" She asked softly.

"Lets make it official," Ollie said tenderly. "Mary Callahan, will you please marry me as soon as possible?"

"I'll take that under serious consideration," she replied, pressing her lips to Ollie's. "You are going to be a great husband and father."

They were married three weeks later by a Chaplain and had a small reception for their friends, at the Air Base Officer's Club. They didn't have time for a honeymoon but did decide to keep Mary's apartment in Tokyo and Ollie's quarters in the base BOQ.

The first several weeks of Ollie's duty were uneventful. They flew on routine patrols bordering the West Coast of Japan and the Tsushima straits of the Sea of Japan. He and Bill studied every ground feature in their patrol area and flew a few overnight patrols to Misawa Air Force base on the tip of a northern island in the Japanese Island chain.

On June 25, 1950, the North Koreans invaded South Korea. The South Koreans were overwhelmed and within days the North Koreans had captured Seoul, the capital of South Korea. The American troops stationed in South Korea were poorly trained and armed. They retreated south to Pusan and set up a defensive perimeter, waiting to be evacuated.

For Ollie and the Fifth Air Force the war in Korea meant increased patrols along the West Coast of Japan and limited Air Force activity in the combat zone. The Fifth was prepared for interception but not for aerial combat or ground support. The fighters available for duty were nearly obsolete F80 Shooting Star jets, manned by inexperienced combat pilots, flying from dirt strip runways and living in mud surrounded tent cities. Spare parts and armament was barely existent.

Ollie and his RO rotated in three-week stints between flying patrols out of Johnson Air Force base near Tokyo and the Air Force base in Misawa in Northern Japan.

The United Nations forces began an offensive and started to push the invaders north. Shortly after Seoul was recaptured, Ollie and Bill included time flying in Korea in their flight rotation. They would fly out of Misawa for three weeks, return to Johnson for three weeks and then be stationed near Seoul, at an air base designated K13, for three weeks, and then start the rotation again.

The war was very strange for Ollie. During other wars the US warriors were away from home for years at a time. For Ollie, he went home to a family life every six weeks. When he rotated back to Johnson Air Force Base he spent nearly every night with Mary and the baby in their Tokyo apartment.

Mary worried when Ollie rotated to Korea but was enjoying her new job and had the baby for companionship when not working.

Living alone in a foreign country was not a problem for Mary. Her father had been a life long US State Department diplomatic career officer. Mary, an only child, had spent all of her youth in foreign countries, with only her mother and an occasional friend for companionship. To keep her from being lonely, her parents had tutors teach her the local language and customs. By the time she was ready for college she was proficient in five languages and could converse in five more.

She had been in Japan with her mother and father when the Japanese attacked Pearl Harbor. They returned to the US as part of a diplomatic exchange. Her father had entered the military and her mother had joined her father in England when Mary went off to college. She was orphaned in 1944 when her parent's apartment in London was destroyed by a German buzz bomb. It had taken awhile to overcome the trauma of losing her parents. During the first year after her parent's death she had started drinking and partying to dull the pain. She had a succession of lovers that did not diminish her sorrow. After a year of deep depression she forced herself to reapply her activities to school. Enlisting in the WAAC after college, meeting and falling in love with Ollie, and now her new, interesting job, new baby and husband had restored happiness to her life.

Life in the Korean combat zone changed dramatically when the Chinese crossed the Yalu River and swept south, catching the United Nation and US forces by surprise. Once again the US was on the defensive.

The Air Force was finally getting the new F86 Sabre jets operational. They were being flown across the Pacific using in flight, tanker refueling. The UN Korean air bases were withdrawn to the south for safety and the fighter pilots started to have daily contact with Chinese fighters on raids into North Korea. The Chinese would eventually break contact and head north across the Yalu and the US pilots would have to break off pursuit. They were not allowed to fly across the river.

Little changed for Ollie and the rest of the interceptor crews. The Chinese did not venture far enough south for the interceptors to be scrambled. Ollie flew routine patrols just to the north of the UN battle lines.

Bill Snelling, the pilot on Ollie's MATS crew was flying a B29 and was stationed at Yokota on Hoshu Island in Japan. When Bill was in Tokyo he frequently would accept Ollie's invitation for dinner. Bill didn't talk about the missions he was flying and ducked the issue when Ollie asked questions. Ollie thought that the B29s were going to be used to bomb North Korean military targets. During dinners, Ollie passed along the comments and observations about the MIG maneuverability and pilot proficiency that he had picked up from the fighter pilots in Korea. They had been reporting for months that they knew that Russian pilots were flying in Chinese MIGs. When they tangled with Russian pilots they knew immediately that they weren't Chinese because of the increased skill. There had even been one report of a MIG pilot parachuting from a damaged plane taking off his helmet, exposing red hair, and waving at the American pilot as he flew by.

The UN forces had the North Korean and Chinese armies pushed back above the original north south border and the rumor were circulating that an armistice would soon be signed. It couldn't be too soon for the US Air Force. Although the kill ratio for fighters favored the US, nearly three hundred American jets had been shot down by MIGS or ground fire. Pilots were in short supply and National Guard and Reserve pilots had been placed on active duty and were flying combat missions. The B29 raids where being challenged by massed Chinese fighters and losses on both sides were becoming intolerable. Photo recon of areas just north of the Yalu indicated that there were over four hundred MIG fighters available for action. The UN Air Force units were desperately trying to replace lost fighters and pilots.

In the midst of this activity Ollie was summoned to a special meeting at Johnson Air Force base. When he entered the room he looked around at the small group of officers and realized that he did not recognize anyone. The highest ranked officer, a paunchy, round faced colonel, introduced Ollie to the other two Air Force officers, neither of whom was wearing pilot's wings.

"Lieutenant Miller," the colonel said without emotion, "because of your special training you have been selected for a top-secret mission."

Ollie could not imagine what special training he had that the other pilots did not have.

The colonel, noticing Ollie's perplexed look, said, "I'm going to explain this to you in detail in due time. For now I want to tell you that this is top secret. There are only a few people, other than those of us here in this room, that knows what the complete mission is. We are not even going to tell you what the complete mission is. We are just going to tell you what you have to do. You will be leaving for a base in northern Japan where you will be trained. You will be escorted from this room to a plane. Your equipment has already been loaded. No contact is to be made by you to anyone until the mission is complete and after the mission you will not be allowed to discuss the mission with anybody but me. Do you understand?"

Ollie said, "Frankly, no I don't understand. Do you mean I won't even be allowed to call my wife, who, by the way, is expecting me to be home in two hours?"

"That's all been taken care of. Your wife has already been called by your CO and told that you are going to Misawa for a few days of training. You will be back here in five days max. Now let's get going. In order to maintain security we intend to get this show on the road right now."

The colonel gestured toward the door and the group moved through the door and within minutes was boarding a blue Air Force King Air executive size transport plane. Several minutes later they where air borne and heading north. There was no conversation during the flight. From the terrain, Ollie knew that their destination was not Misawa. The long flight ended and they started a decent into a small, single runway landing field. Ollie had been intently looking out the window, trying to get his bearings. He thought he recognized some terrain that registered as being Hokkaido, the most northwest point in the Japanese Island chain.

The King Air taxied to the entrance of an earth sided revetment. The pilot killed the engines and the passengers deplaned and helped the small ground crew push the plane into the covered revetment. The incoming crew and the ground crew loaded into Jeeps and made the short run to a Quonset hut set back in a group of scraggly trees. Once inside the incoming group assembled in a small conference room. The colonel removed a map from his brief case, unfolded it, and spread it out on the table.

Ollie quickly observed that the map was a commercial Atlas of the northern part of Japan, the Sea of Japan, North Korea, China and South Eastern Russia. There were no marks on the map.

The colonel looked at Ollie and said, "I'll give you the short version of the mission. The Strategic Air Command wants us to determine the location, type, and competency of the Soviet radar in this area," pointing to the general area around Vladivostock.

"They have on ground intelligence data but need to know technical data that they can only get by sending a specially equipped plane into the area. That will be your job. You'll be flying a specially equipped F94 to the edge of the International Russian Boundary under the direction of an airborne controller who will direct you to the target areas. The controller will receive and record information that your special equipment will be transmitting."

"Two questions," Ollie said, unable to mask his skepticism. "It must be over six hundred kilometers to Vladivostock. Round trip that is well beyond the range of an F94. Second, what is the special skill that I have that is required for this mission?"

"Both good questions," the colonel answered confidently. "We have modified the plane to mount two extra, disposable wing tanks and since you won't have an RO we have added an extra fuel tank in that compartment. We have taken every ounce of unnecessary weight out of the plane, including the fifty caliber guns. We haven't flown it a full twelve hundred kilometers but we have flown it partially loaded with fuel and our estimate is that you will have plenty of fuel.

In answer to your second question, your radio school training in Morse code gives you superior training in that type of communication. All of your directions will be transmitted in a special code and will require precision navigation based on the orders received by code. Any other questions?"

"Not at this time, sir." Ollie responded.

"Good, I'll show you to your quarters. Early tomorrow we will start the dry run through of your mission in a practice facility we have set up. You will have only two days to get ready. You probably have figured this out by now but this whole mission is based on as few as possible people being involved in as little time as possible to maintain secrecy."

The next two days were long and strenuous for Ollie and the crew of the control plane communication team. Ollie was isolated in a dark room and the communicators, in a separate room, provided him with navigation and timing instructions in code. When Ollie received an instruction he repeated the instruction out loud so the controllers were sure that he had understood correctly.

On the second day Ollie inspected the specially outfitted F94. The technicians from the control plane showed Ollie how to turn on the special electronic package, mounted in place of the normal on board radar. The special package would record data on any Soviet Radar impulses that bounced off the F94 and transmit the data to the control plane.

On his own time Ollie had been running his own calculations on the weight of the plane and thrust that the engines could develop on take off. With the help of booster rockets that would be jettisoned as soon as the plane was airborne, Ollie concluded that getting off the ground would be marginally probable.

He remembered his father's advice that he was not to volunteer for anything. He couldn't remember volunteering. He hadn't even been ordered. These people just told him what he was going to do and hadn't asked his opinion. He doubted if they had even discussed the possibility that he might not want to participate.

After dusk on the third day, Ollie sat in the cockpit of his plane and checked the operation of the electronic gear in his plane while the control plane crew checked their equipment. When they were both satisfied that all systems were operating correctly the control plane, a modified four engine Constellation with commercial markings, took off and headed south and after an hour flying time reversed course and assumed a northeasterly course normally followed by commercial traffic on the way to Alaska. As the plane headed north it began to drift slightly off course toward Russia. The intent was for the Russian Radar to think that the plane was slightly off course but no threat.

During this early maneuver, Ollie had retired to the Quonset hut, had a light meal and at the last possible moment, put on his rubber survival suit. Now he was sitting at the very edge of the runway, running the engines up near full throttle, trying to ignore the rivulets of perspiration that quickly saturated the flight suit under the survival suit. He got the green light for take off, full throttled, released the brakes and as the plane sluggishly started to roll, lit off the boost rockets and started to accelerate down the runway. He watched the airspeed carefully and as he approached rotation speed gently pulled back on the stick and felt the plane stagger into the air. He immediately retracted the landing gear and jettisoned the booster rockets and started to breathe easy as the ground began to slip away. In what seemed like minutes he picked up the strobe lights of the control plane. He keyed the code signal to the airborne radar and instrument observers in the Constellation to indicate he was in position. Almost immediately he received a compass heading to execute. He began to leave the Constellation and headed west. A few minutes later he received instructions to turn on his special equipment and received a message back that the equipment was functioning properly. Twenty minutes later he received instructions to change course and start a slow decent from his 30,000 feet maximum to 10,000 ft.

During the next half-hour he received two more changes of course and changes in altitude. Ollie was starting to be concerned about his fuel and his location. He was quickly approaching the point of no return and knew that he was much further west of the position that he had been during the practice runs.

To the south he could see the lights of a large city that was probably Vladivostok. He knew that he could not break radio silence and was trying to determine a course of action. Nervousness had caused him to start to sweat profusely, dampening his flight suit and fogging the visor of his helmet.

CHAPTER *6*

Near Moscow, Russia, 1937

Tamara Krasnov bounded through the front door of the small family apartment outside the Podluk Air Force Base. Her cheeks were bright red from excitement, her blue eyes flashing happily.

"We did it! We did it!" She shouted.

"What did you do?" Her mother asked. When she saw the sheepish grin on the face of her husband, as he followed Tamara into the apartment, she knew.

"Oh no Yuri," she exclaimed. "Don't tell me you took her up in the airplane. She is only nine years old. How could you do such a dangerous thing?"

"Now, now Sasha," Yuri said as he slipped his arm around her waist. "There is less danger riding in an airplane than riding on a horse and you let her start riding horses when she was five. Besides, I had to do this. I have been promising I would let her fly with me since the first time she saw a plane in the sky. You know that. This was inevitable. Maybe now I can have some peace."

"How did you make sure she would be safe?" Sasha said, shaking her head in disbelief.

"I put a pair of goggles on her and strapped her on my lap. She loved it. At first I thought she was screaming because she was frightened. Then I realized that she was really enjoying the ride."

Sasha turned to Tamara who had been standing nearby, jumping from foot to foot, and asked, "were you not frightened even a little bit?"

"I didn't want it to ever end." Tamara said. "Now I want daddy to teach me how to fly the airplane. I watched him and I think I can learn."

"See what you have done." Sasha moaned. "You have created a problem bigger than the one you thought you solved."

Later Yuri would have to admit that Sasha was correct. Tamara hounded him until he promised to teach her to fly. He started the ground instruction part of her training when she was ten and was amazed by her comprehension of even the most difficult parts of the training. When he could no longer deny her the chance to actually fly he had a trainer specially equipped to fit her small body. He had a large pillow fastened to the rear seat of the open cockpit bi-wing trainer and had special extensions mounted on the rudder pedals and control stick. They practiced the communications they would use while in flight and after what seemed like an eternity to Tamara, took their first training flight. Tamara's handling of the plane amazed Yuri. From the first moment that she took the controls she was in command and smoothly moved the plane through all the maneuvers they had practiced while the plane was on the ground. When Yuri turned around to look at her he had expected to see her face in deep concentration. What he saw was a smile that would light up Moscow. While he was looking at her she held up her left fist and shook it in a victory salute. From that day on she lived for the few minutes a week her father could take her flying. For Sasha it was a constant worry but she did now have leverage over her small daughter. If Tamara didn't do her chores or homework Sasha would just show her the flight books and tap them. Tamara knew what that meant. Get busy or you don't fly.

G. B. Mooney

Growing up in the Stalin era had been difficult for the entire Russian population. Marx, Lenin and Trotsky had successfully driven the revolution that deposed Nicholas II and his autocratic oppression and police control. Unfortunately for the people, Stalin forced his way into power. The leaders of the revolution had for the most part been intellectuals who wanted to socialize Russia for what they considered as being good of the people. Stalin was a cruel, manipulative schemer who plotted and bulled his way to power, trampling and eliminating anyone who opposed him.

Tamara was born just after Stalin gained control. By the time she was ten Stalin's control was total. Purges had eliminated any opposition and a single totalitarian party that was both fractious and chaotic controlled the country. The new government was struggling with lack of food and consumer goods production. First a five-year plan and then a seven year plan were initiated to strengthen production. In the process the population, who had expected some relief, were again subjected to oppression and total government control of their daily lives.

Tamara's father was conscripted into the new Army Air Corp. Because he had been in university for two years he was promoted to officer status. After completing his flight training he was assigned to the Air Force Defense Ministry and stationed in Podluk, just outside Moscow. Because of his position, Tamara and her mother enjoyed the benefits of adequate food, clothing and housing. The family, however, was never without fear of falling from favor. Even as a small child Tamara could sense that her parents lived under continuous stress.

Her father transferred back to active flying in the new Soviet Air Corp when Tamara was twelve. By the time she was thirteen she had grown nearly to the height of her father and could fly a plane without special equipment. Over her mother's strong objections, her father allowed her to fly solo in the old bi-plane that the air force allowed him to use on weekends. The experience of flying in an open cockpit plane would have frightened most girls her age, but Tamara loved the feeling of speed and soaring above the city and farmlands.

When Germany invaded Russia, Tamara's father went off to war. He participated in the design and testing of the new, sleek YAK fighter and then assumed command of a squadron of recently graduated pilots. Yuri, who had no combat flying experience himself, could only teach his pilots what he had read in books. They practiced flying as two plane teams to protect each other and spent time on aerobatics, combat maneuvers and gunnery. The new YAK fighter proved to be nimble, sturdy, and rather simple to fly.

Fortunately for the Russian Army, Yuri's squadron was ready by the time of the Battle of Kursk. The Russian army was extended in a salient that reached southwest from Moscow. Despite the advice of his top officers and his intelligence reports, Stalin refused to withdrawal his troops to Moscow. The German army had launched an offensive from the north and the south of the salient and was threatening to cut off the supply line for the Russian Army. The Germans were being very deliberate, knowing that when they cut off the supply line they could destroy the entire Russian army at their own pace.

Yuri's squadrons of YAK fighters disrupted the German plan. The Russian fighter planes proved superior to the German Messerschmitts and Stukas and gained air control over the salient. The little YAKs were rugged enough to land on bumpy airstrips near the front, re-fuel and re-arm and take off. The German planes had to fly from improved fields to the west and wasted time and fuel getting to the combat zone. The Russian flyers knew the area and flew visually based on well-known landmarks. The Germans would try to fly by compass heading and were continuously getting lost. The iron deposits in the area destroyed the accuracy of their instruments. The Russian pilots would let the German fighters chase them east and when the Russian pilots took evasive action the Germans would break off the chase and head for their own air strips. Unfortunately for them, the errors in navigation, caused by erroneous compass readings, caused them to get lost. Many crashed without getting close to their home bases.

After a month of being pounded from the air by the strafing YAKs, the German army withdrew and the Russian army was saved. Yuri was promoted to General and was awarded every medal created for the Soviet military.

Unknown to their parents, Tamara and her cousin Helena volunteered for the Russian Air Force. They told their mothers that they were going to work in a war production plant safely east of Moscow. Both mothers had protested at first but had finally capitulated.

When the Germans surrounded Stalingrad the Soviet started using woman pilots to harass the enemy troops. For some unknown reason the women had superior night vision. Even on moon-less nights they had the ability to find the German encampments, hand drop incendiary bombs from their open cockpit bi-planes, and find their way back to their airfields. Tamara and Helena became a top rated team. They were flying almost every night for two years. The girls lived in primitive camps in the make shift airdromes with little food and had to fight off continuous amorous advances by the men in the camp. Both the girls obtained large revolvers and wore them conspicuously when they were out and about and kept the revolvers under their pillows when sleeping. It was a difficult life for the girls but Tamara blanked out the hardships by looking forward to the nightly flights.

When the war ended the girls returned home to their civilian life. Helena was admitted to the Moscow State University. Tamara was also accepted and entered the University but after two years in aeronautical engineering school told her parents that she wanted to enlist in the Air Force for flight training.

"I want to fly airplanes, not design them." She declared passionately.

Both Yuri and Sasha objected but agreed when Tamara convinced them that she would enlist right after graduation. With Yuri's help Tamara was admitted into the pilot training program in 1949 and graduated with top grades in her class a year later. She was ecstatic when she was assigned to advanced jet fighter school.

She did not always find life in the military to the liking of her free spirited thinking. At first there had been disciplinary action and then finally the threat of dismissal. Her father had a long discussion with her and she finally realized that to fly she would have to comply with the doctrine of Soviet Military life. There were times when the non-flying part of her service became unbearable. She was rotated to every air base in Russia. Some bases were tolerable, some were outstanding, but the majority of the bases were remote, dusty and lonely. She was usually the only female pilot on the base and often, after arriving at a base for the first time, would be harassed by the men looking for sex. Things would improve when the word spread that her father was a high party official. The loneliness never went away.

Tamara had been assigned to a high tech secret air base in southwest Russia, near Vladivostok in early 1951. She had really wanted to be assigned to a Russian squadron that was flying advanced MIG jets on combat missions against the Americans from China, just north of the Yalu River. The Russian Air Force had been systematically rotating its' highest rated pilots into the squadron for combat experience. Since Tamara was always the highest rated pilot in any squadron where she was assigned, she could not fathom why her request to join the combat group had been repeatedly denied. Her present assignment had not been very interesting. Occasionally she would be on ready duty and in the short time she had been at her new post she had only been scrambled once to chase an off-course commercial airliner that was heading toward Soviet territory.

She was on ready duty again, fighting boredom and sleepiness when the scramble alarm sounded. *At least I will get to fly tonight,* she said as she bolted for her plane. The ground crew had started the engine before she arrived and the crew chief helped strap her into the cockpit and connect her radio and oxygen mask. Within minutes of the alarm she was airborne and climbing to altitude on the heading provided by the radar controller.

Tamara squirmed uneasily in the seat of her old MIG. Rivulets of perspiration were running from her armpits down her side, and down her back, soaking her flight suit. For the third time she tried to adjust the cockpit temperature. The heater shut off and she immediately began to shiver. Another attempt brought the cockpit temperature back to oppressively hot. She had reported that the heating and cooling system was not functioning reliably and in typical Soviet fashion she was told to do her job and quit complaining

Even though her father was an important member of the Communist Party and an Air Corp war hero she knew that she was always in a precarious position. Women were barely tolerated in the Russian Air Force. She was flying a MIG because of her father's position.

Tamara had found the intruder quickly. As she suspected when scrambled, it was an American, commercial Constellation. She had overtaken the larger plane, slowed down and flown up along side the pilot side of the commercial airliner. The pilot of the American plane veered off to the east as soon as he sighted the fighter. Tamara smiled, *I'll bet that pilot will have to change his underwear,* she said to herself.

If she had been more observant she would have noticed a pod that covered a special antenna array installed on the bottom of the fuselage, just aft of the wings.

She flipped on her radio and reported in. After orbiting the Constellation that was apparently turning around and heading south, she was ordered to return to her base. She was also told that there had been two radar indications on the screen when she had scrambled, a large one and a smaller one in line with the large one. Control ordered her to remain observant and gave her a heading to return to the base.

Now she was sweating inside her flight suit. She concentrated on maintaining alertness, not allowing herself to think about her discomfort and her unsuccessful attempts to wiggle her way into the Soviet 64th Aviation Corp fighter squadron that was flying into North Korea from China.

The hair at the base of her helmet suddenly stood on end and an electrical shiver went down her spine. She had caught the slight movement of something below and in front of her; just a quick, silvery glimmer, highlighted by a partial moon. She started to activate her radio to ask for advice and stopped. The intruder might pick up the signal. She also thought that it might be a decoy put up by her own command to test her proficiency. She discarded that quickly as being stupid. She had standing orders to take the initiative if she clearly recognized a potential enemy in Soviet Air Space. With her keen night vision she quickly tracked the intruder and identified it as an American F94 that was already at least thirty kilometers into Soviet territory.

I don't know what you are doing here, Tamara said to herself as she lined up for a deflection shot, *but your dead.*

She depressed the firing button on the stick and the three slow firing cannons on her plane thundered, temporarily slowing her air speed. Her first pass burst took the tail section off the F94 just behind the cockpit. She applied her air brakes and turned sharply and picked up a visual of the falling plane that was in a tumbling spin, rotating toward the ground like a giant falling leaf. She saw the pilot eject. Just before the plane hit the ground it exploded in a huge fireball.

She continued to orbit the area while calling in on the radio. Ground control advised her that they had the crash area pinpointed and ordered her back to her home field.

Her commanding officer met her in his staff car when she climbed out of her MIG.

"We are going to a de-briefing. I don't want you to say anything to anybody, not even me, until Air Commander Yeshkov debriefs you. Understood?"

Tamara smiled and silently mouthed, "Yes sir."

How could they now turn down her request to join 64th in China

Chapter 7

Northeast of Valdivostock Russia, 1951

Ollie had just made up his mind to abort his mission. He had not received instructions from the controller in the last five minutes.

The rest of the world accepted a three-mile offshore limit as international air space. The Soviets insisted on twelve miles. It was a moot point for Ollie. He knew he was over land in Soviet territory in violation of International Law.

His fuel was so low that it was questionable that he would be able to return to his base. He reached for the throttle and applied power and was just starting an upward left turn when a violent shock jolted the plane, slamming Ollie against the side of the cockpit. Reaction to the shock and the sudden change in direction was automatic. Without thinking he applied pressure to the controls to correct his heading and attitude. Nothing happened for an instant and then he realized that he was in a wild, tumbling spin that he could not correct. He had a quick recollection of something ripping past his plane just as the shock hit. It quickly registered that he had been shot at and hit. The centrifugal force of the spin made it nearly impossible for him to move his head. He managed to twist his head slightly, enough to see that the entire rear end of his plane was gone. Still fighting the mounting G force caused by the spinning plane, he struggled to get his hand on the ejection lever. From the rapidly spinning altimeter he knew that he had only a few more seconds to eject. He barely got his fingers on the ejection lever and then pulled as hard as he could. The next several seconds were a blur. He was conscious of the ejection explosion and the impact of the air smashing into his body. He could not breathe and almost instantly became unconscious. When he revived he was floating toward the earth below his parachute and occasionally caught a glimpse of a MIG that was orbiting him.

Off in the distance he first saw and then felt the blast of his plane blowing up just before it struck the ground. A delayed self-destruct signal, triggered by his ejection, had blown up the plane and its special equipment.

Ollie peered down into the darkness, trying to see the landing area. Before he could get his bearings he hit the hard ground with a bone-jarring thud. Fortunately there was not much surface wind to propel the billowing chute so he had time to move his arms and legs to see if he had been injured. There was considerable pain in every portion of his body but he knew that he had no broken bones. After a few moments he disengaged himself from the seat harness and stood up and started to walk around, flexing his arms and legs.

"Now what?" He said out loud.

It took several hours but eventually Ollie could see headlights approaching his general area. The headlights would stop moving and somebody in the vehicle would sweep the area with a searchlight.

Ollie started walking toward the light. Since he had no idea of where he was he decided that escape was impossible. He had decided to play stupid and act surprised that he was not in Japan, claming instrument malfunction.

It took another hour before the lights from the truck illuminated Ollie. There was a great deal of shouting in Russian from the truck and Ollie was surrounded.

In the glare of the truck lights and flashlights shining in his face he did his best to look bewildered and asked, "Where am I? Who are you? Does anyone speak English?"

The troops grabbed him by both arms and dragged him to the rear of the truck and helped propel him into the back. The rest of his greeting crew climbed into the truck, talking loudly in Russian and gesturing toward Ollie. They did not harm him but made him lie on the bed of the truck as it started a long, bumpy ride.

It was light when they reached their destination. When the truck came to a halt Ollie was dragged out. He looked around and realized that he was in a military base; judging by the familiar smell of jet fuel, it was an air base.

The Russian leader of his captors grabbed Ollie by the arm and started toward the steps leading into a gray, drab building with metal barred windows and a thick metal door. Ollie was steered into an empty cell and the barred door was clanked shut behind him. The cell had one window, too high to look through, a steel cot bed, a hole in the floor that Ollie figured must be the toilet, and a water spigot.

Ollie stripped off his survival suit and sat down on the cot. About an hour later a guard opened the front door and carried in a tray with food and slid the tray into Ollie's cell through an opening in the bars. Ollie spooned the luke warm cabbage soup into his mouth and tore off chunks of the hard brown bread and within minutes had finished his meager meal. He washed the meal down with a strange tasting tea. He had been awake and under stress for over twenty-four hours and began to nod off and gradually slumped onto the cot and fell into a deep sleep.

When he awoke he was surprised to find himself in a different place. He was not in a cell but was in a room that looked like it might be a room in a mental hospital. There were no windows, the walls were padded and the steel door had a small opening at eye level. Ollie tried to sit up on the bed but was so dizzy that he immediately lay back down. He drifted off to sleep but was awakened by somebody roughly shaking his arm. He opened his eyes and tried to focus on the person who was now forcing him to his feet and half dragging him toward the open door. Another guard seized his other arm as he entered the hall. The guards half carried, half-dragged Ollie into a room that was empty except for a desk and a few chairs and a single light bulb hanging on an electrical cord from the ceiling.

Ollie was directed into a straight backed chair and a few minutes later a stocky, middle aged Russian officer, with a prominent cheekbones, small dark eyes and a prominent chin, opened the door, entered the room walked around the desk and sat down in the chair facing Ollie.

"Good afternoon Lieutenant Miller. Did you have a nice sleep?"

The Russians perfect English, with just a hint of accent, alerted Ollie to the fact that he was more than likely facing an officer of the Russian Committee for State Security, the Komitet Gusudarstueivnoy Bezopanosti, KGB.

"Where am I?" Ollie asked, not having to try to act dazed.

"Let's not play games," the officer said with disdain. "We know who you are, everything there is to know about you, militarily and personally, and what your mission was. Please don't waste my time. All I want you to do is confess that you deliberately broke international law and flew into Russian territory."

"I have no idea what you are talking about," Ollie said with some hostility. "I was on a simple instrument check out flight in a plane that had just had its instruments repaired. The Instruments must have malfunctioned. As far as I know I was on a heading for my base in Misawa."

"You are already starting to annoy me," the Russian said, his voice intense with anger. "You were flying a specially modified F94 designed to check our air defense system. Just a few days ago you were assigned this special mission and were flown to Hakkadio from Johnson Air Force Base. Incidentally, neither your wife nor any of your friends know where you are or what you are doing. The US Air Force has already forgotten that you ever existed. They got their data and you are expendable. I will type up a confession and you will sign it and this will be over. Don't take up any more of my time or I will ship you off to the coalmines in northern Siberia today."

Ollie was stunned by the Russians outburst. The only possible explanation was that he had been drugged. *How long had he been drugged and how much had he told them*, he wondered. For all he knew, they may have had him drugged for days and may now know every detail about his life.

"All I really have to tell you is my name, rank and serial number." Ollie said defiantly.

"I have heard enough," the KGB Officer shouted. "I am sure you won't like Siberia. You will never see your wife or son again and most likely won't survive the first year in the work camp."

He stormed out of the room and the guards picked up Ollie by his arms and steered him back to his padded cell.

Ollie was sitting on the cot when he heard a female voice saying, "Hey, American; I want to talk to you."

He walked to the door and looked out the slot into the clear, brilliant blue eyes of a young woman with short blonde hair, a narrow attractive face with high, prominent cheekbones. She was almost as tall as Ollie. Despite the ill fitting uniform and the absence of make up, she was extremely attractive, in a tomboy sort of way.

They looked at each other for a few seconds and the women said, in slightly broken English, "I shot you down. Why did you start to accelerate and turn just as I shot? Did you see me coming? Why didn't your radar operator know I was coming? I didn't see your radar man eject. What happened to him? I have to know."

Ollie continued to study the woman and did not answer.

"Come on," she said with a disarming smile. "What would it hurt to tell me?"

Ollie was going to ignore her but he decided it would not do any harm to talk to her. Besides, he speculated, he might learn something about his future.

"My name is Ollie Miller. What's your name?" Ollie said, extending his hand through the small opening in the door.

He was surprised by the strength of the delicate hand that grasped his extended hand.

"My name is Tamara. I shot at you and you start to move away before I shoot. Why did you change course?"

"It had nothing to do with you," Ollie said. "I didn't see you coming. I just saw the lights of a city to the south and thought I may be off course so I was changing course to see if I could figure out what city was there."

"It was good for you that you changed course. If you had not you would be dead. The rest of what you say is…" she hesitated for a few seconds, trying to come up with the right word and then, looking him directly in the eyes said, "Bull Shit. I know range of your plane. You were on some kind of a suicide mission weren't you? Why you do that?"

Ollie looked at her and smiled, "Been flying since you were a young girl haven't you?

Tamara hesitated and then looked at him curiously and said, "Yes, since I was nine. My father was in Air Corp and taught me to fly. Why do you ask that? "

"Remember the first time you saw a plane flying. Remember the chill that ran down your back, knowing some day you had to fly? "

"Yes I do remember," she said wistfully, recalling the memories of her early youth.

"Do you remember the first time you flew in a plane? The first time you flew by yourself? Do you still get that warm feeling every time you climb into a plane and take off? And are you sad that a flight is over, even if you are dead tired? "

"Yes, it is as you say," Tamara said, nodding her head affirmatively.

"Me too," Ollie said. "Now I will probably never fly again and it makes me very sad."

"Now I know why you do it," Tamara said with a sad smile. "We are alike. We would do anything to fly."

The smile left her face and her changed facial expression portrayed her concern, "I am sorry for you, Ollie. I know how I would feel if I thought I would never be free or fly again. You are going to a very bad place. I wish I could do something to help but I can't. What you did was serious and I am afraid that even though you where just doing what you were ordered, you will be punished. Is there anybody at home waiting for you?"

"Unfortunately, yes." Ollie responded sadly.

"Too bad." Tamara said as she turned to leave. "Good-bye Ollie."

Northeast Siberia, Russia, 1952

Ollie looked at the reflection coming out of a dirty unwashed window and shook his head in disbelief. His hair, a tangled, greasy mess, had grown to below his shoulders and a bushy black beard covered most of his face. The beard was a necessity; it protected his face from the harsh Siberian winter while he was working outside, clearing forest for a railroad track right-of-way. His bulky, filthy, putrid smelling work clothes covered a body that hadn't been bathed for months. Ollie was starving and at least forty pounds under his normal weight. His guards didn't care about his physical problems. They just rousted the prisoners out of their moveable sleeping quarters and started them working every morning. The forced laborers received two small meals a day, consisting of vegetables, usually in a totally bland soup, hard bread and tea. The meals didn't provide enough calories to replace the calories burned by the strenuous work. By the end of each workday Ollie's legs and arms were shaking so violently from exhaustion that he could barely make it back to his bunk.

Nearly every day someone died. The guards just stripped the clothes off the body and dragged it into the forest where it became a feast for the emaciated animals that followed the work crew. When he could sleep he had nightmares about the animals ripping him to shreds while he was still alive.

Ollie didn't know how long he had been in the moving work camp. He had numbly lost track of time. For the first several months he really expected somebody to show up and free him. As he dragged through the months he began to lose hope. It was the worst of his childhood dreams. He felt abandoned, lost and alone with his fears. The only thing that was constant was his despair. Not only for his physical torture but also for his deepening mental depression. *What was happening to Mary and his child? Had his mother and father been notified that he was missing? Would his mother blame his father for the loss of another son? Would they ever know what happened to him?* He was sure that he would not survive much longer. He had already lost the will to live and had been considering just walking out into the forest in the middle of the night to lay down and die. The only thing that kept him alive was knowing that he had to survive to get back to Mary. During the months of deprivation he had constantly thought of the things he had never told her. He longed to hold her and tell her that she was the only woman he would ever love and that he would be there for her forever, to protect her and their son. At night the loneliness and realization that he would probably never see her again forced silent tears to run down into his beard and freeze. Every time he thought he had reached the end of his endurance he just concentrated on the image of Mary until his resolve returned.

As near as Ollie could figure, he had been working on the railroad project nearly a year when a Russian officer walked into his sleeping quarters and asked in English, "Which of you is Oliver Miller?"

When Ollie raised his hand the officer said, "Come with me."

The Russian led Ollie to a truck and motioned for him to get into the back. The officer got into the front of the truck and they started a bumpy ride down the railroad bed. In half an hour they reached the part of the line to which the track had been laid. The supply train was nearly unloaded and Ollie and the officer climbed up the rungs of a ladder into a crude caboose.

In time Ollie was taken off a train and taken to a cold, damp building. Once inside the building he was led into a room without windows and ordered to strip. He was led through another door into a shower room and had a short hot shower, his first in over a year. He was given clean clothes, a haircut and a shave and then taken to a clean room with a bed, toilet and sink. He had not been provided with a toothbrush so he used his fingers and the harsh lye soap and attempted to clean his teeth. He shook his head in wonderment. Never in his life did he think that just being clean would make him feel so good.

He had been in the room for about an hour when the door opened and a Russian enlisted man carried a tray of food into the room and placed it on the bed and left the room. Ollie, who had only been fed sporadically on the trip, devoured the beef, potatoes, vegetables, bread and coffee. A short time later the same orderly came back and removed the tray and dishes. Ollie sat on the bed for awhile and then, for the first time in what seemed forever, lay down in a comfortable, warm bed and went to sleep with a full stomach.

CHAPTER 8

Faintly, in the distance, and then getting closer and louder, Ollie heard a male voice saying, over and over, "Lieutenant Miller, wake up."

Gradually the grogginess left him and he sat up on the edge of the bed. *I wonder if they drugged me again?* He thought to himself.

The man standing in front of him was looking at him with an inscrutable gaze. When he was sure the prisoner was awake he said, "Follow me", turned and started out the door. Oliver followed at a fast gait, barely able to keep up with the Russian.

After several twists and turns they arrived at the door to an open office. A Russian officer was standing inside the office, looking out the window at people milling around in the prison yard below.

When Ollie entered the Russian turned from the window and motioned for Ollie to sit down in the straight back chair facing a desk. When Ollie was seated the middle-aged officer, average sized, with black hair and broad weather beaten facial features, seated himself behind the desk and said, "My name is Yegor Rutsky, I am the commandant of this facility. I trust that by now you have been fed and have had some sleep and are wondering where you are and what has happened. Somebody interceded in your behalf and most likely saved your life. I can tell by your physical appearance that you would not have survived much longer where you were. Fortunately for you, you have been transferred here to Irkutsk in southeastern Russia. This is a minimum-security prison. I advise you not to cause any trouble and not to try to escape. Give us even one problem and you will be back on that railroad building crew. One of my staff will indoctrinate you in our procedures and schedule."

The officer left and another, younger Russian entered the room.

"As the commandant has told you, this is a minimum-security detention center. You will receive continuing education and will be on a rotating work schedule. The schedule is always the same, one week in the laundry, one-week in the kitchen and one-week in a factory. One day a week will be totally devoted to education. If you do try to escape you will be severely punished. Even if you did try to escape, you would have no place to go. The nearest foreign country is China and their border guards would shoot you on sight. Follow me and I will take you to your education advisor."

Valeriy Zorkin was sitting alone in his Spartan office. He had requested some pictures or wall coverings to cover the harshness of the room but had been scoffed at by his old-line superiors in the KGB. He was aware of their suspicions of him because of his many years studying psychology in England, Switzerland and the United States. The "Old Boys", as he thought of them, were more into torture and drugs to break their subjects. Valeriy used the newer, subtler approach to mind control that broke the spirit but not the body.

He had been assigned to Irkutsk when several American Air Force crews had been captured after being shot down when flying over Soviet Air Space. Valeriy's assignment was to break the prisoners and with the help of an Air Corp officer, dig out all the technical data that they could obtain. Once the technical data was obtained, he would be free to steer the subjects into becoming tools of the Soviet Propaganda Ministry.

This assignment had come at an opportune time. Valeriy was had become tired of Moscow and what he silently called the three *P's*, paranoia, persecution and pasmurno, the Russian word for dull, dreary weather. Like all Muscovites he lived in perpetual fear of being purged because of some one reporting him for some slight comment or action viewed as detrimental to the Party. At least in Irkutsk he was out of the main stream but he knew he could not let his guard down. The KGB especially liked to spy on the KGB.

When Ollie was ushered into his office, Valeriy stood and with a pleasant smile, extended his hand and introduced himself to the gaunt American.

"Welcome to Irkutsk," he said with apparent warmth and sincerity. "I'm so pleased that you where transferred here. Please be seated while I review your dossier."

Ollie sat down and studied the young man sitting across from him. To Ollie, all Russians that he had met to date had been stern, devoid of personality and in his view must have been perpetually constipated. This one, taller and less stocky than any other Russian he had encountered, had a coarse peasant face with broad features, a pleasant smile and blazing red hair. An internal voice warned Ollie to be careful. He thought of the old American saying, "Good Cop, Bad Cop". This Russian was probably the good cop who would try to gain his trust. *What could they possibly want from me?* He wondered.

The red haired Russian looked up from the dossier. *They must have had this man drugged for a week,* he had concluded. The typed notes covered at least fifty pages and chronicled Miller's life from his childhood up until he was shot down and captured.

"Well Oliver, how did you like growing up in Greenwood Pennsylvania?'

Without blinking an eye Ollie responded, "Probably the same as you liked growing up in Saint Petersburg."

The young red head laughed heartily, "I am glad you haven't lost your sense of humor. That is one thing I really liked about the Americans. Our folks have to have a considerable amount of vodka before they loosen up. Your countrymen seem to be in good spirits most of the time."

"Maybe we have more to be happy about than you do." Ollie replied.

"I think you may be right." The Russian replied with a smile. "Although our leaders consider your life style decadent."

"From your excellent English, I would guess that you have spent several years in the US. Do you think we are decadent? Or do you envy our life style?"

This is going to be very interesting, Valeriy thought. For the last two years he had been dealing with Russians and political prisoners who would be frightened if they had a thought of their own. This young American would be an interesting challenge.

In answer to Ollie's question Valeriy answered truthfully, "A little of both."

"Could you tell me more about where I am and where I have been?" Ollie asked.

The Russian sorted through the papers in his dossier and after finding the correct place said, "You were shot down about sixty kilometers north of Vladivostock and were sent to work on a railroad gang building a new line from Magadan to Murmansk.

Now you are in Irkutsk in southeastern Russia near the China and Mongolia border. Irkutsk is near Lake Baykal, the largest, deepest fresh water lake in the world. When I get time off I like to go there to fish."

"How long will I be here?" Ollie asked.

"I really don't know, I guess it depends on you and your progress."

Ollie became silent and mulled over the Russians last statement. *What did he mean by progress?*

"Is it possible that my wife and parents be notified that I'm alive?"

"That is very unlikely. Our military seems to enjoy keeping your country in the dark when it comes to captives. Let me see what I can do. I have to go through my superiors you understand. Otherwise I would be with you in a cell or worse." Valeriy confided.

The first session with the KGB officer continued for another hour.

"That's enough for today." Valeriy said, rising and extending his hand. "I will see you tomorrow."

An enlisted man led Ollie out of the building and into the prison compound. Ten gray drab three-story detention buildings surrounded the compound yard. A double chain link fence surrounded the entire facility. There was one gate that was heavily guarded. Ollie observed guards patrolling outside the fence and in the space between the two fences. There were also groups of guards patrolling inside the compound.

Ollie was taken into one of the buildings and shown into a room with four bunks and four open clothes closets with shelves. Ollie's change of clothes was already in the closet. The escort handed Ollie a sheet of paper that contained instructions for the next week. Each day he would work in the laundry from six am till noon and after lunch would continue his indoctrination.

The guard left and Ollie sat down on the bed in the empty room. Just after dusk the prisoners began to return to the buildings. The three other occupants of the room arrived together and stared at Ollie without saying a word. Ollie tried his little bit of Polish, then the little Russian he had picked up and then finally English. The English caused a response and one of the men motioned for Ollie to follow him. He led Ollie to the wash room and Ollie joined the rest of the men after they cleaned up and followed them to the dining room. After dinner the men walked back to their room were they wearily dropped into bed. Within minutes the room was filled with the snoring of all three men.

Before the sun came up the men were up, dressed, had breakfast and were on their way to their assigned work. Ollie found the laundry and was assigned the task of folding the dried clothes and sheets. After lunch he was led back to the administration building and into a classroom. The indoctrination for the day was a movie about the reign of the czars and why the excesses of the royalty led to the revolution that had freed the peasants.

Ollie looked around and found that there were only two other people in the room. Since the movie narration was in English he assumed that the two other people spoke English. When the movie was over he tried to catch the other two as they left the room but they quickly moved down the hall, ignoring his call to wait. A guard stopped him at the door and took him to Valeriy's office for his second session

As soon as he was ushered into Valeriy's office Ollie looked the Soviet in the eyes and asked, "Will my wife and parents be advised that I'm still alive and where I am?"

"Nice to see you again Ollie." Valeriy said with a broad smile." I'm working on that. My superiors didn't say no right away and that is a good sign."

Valeriy had plans for using Ollie's strong desire to have his wife informed of his location. He knew that his plan would be devastating to Ollie, but he wanted to gain his confidence before dropping his bomb.

"Let's continue with your indoctrination. What did you think of the movie?"

"I don't much like propaganda films," Ollie replied flatly. "I prefer a good action movie. Will they show any John Wayne movies?"

"It's okay for you to talk to me like that," Valery said softly as concern showed in his face. "Be careful when you are outside this room. My friends take their indoctrination very seriously. Just nod like you agree and you won't get into trouble. Now lets talk about your entering the Air Force and your training."

The rest of the week was a repeat of this day. Work, indoctrination and "counseling". Ollie was aware that it was all the same; propaganda to bend his mind.

After the first week Ollie was on the full workday cycle for six days and then all day indoctrination the seventh day. He liked the factory rotation the best. His work in the factory was menial labor but at least he got out of the damp, dreary compound and got a glimpse of the city and its people when being transported to and from the factory.

G. B. Mooney

Working in the kitchen was the worst rotation. By the end of the six days he was sure that he would never get the grease out of his hair and pores of his body.

Ollie had been vigilant when near the other prisoners. He kept searching for a face that might be that of a fellow American. The other men in his room and on his work crews had indicated, mainly by gestures, that there were other Americans in the compound. One evening when returning to his room from the laundry Ollie was startled when he almost ran into a tall, gaunt man, walking in the other direction. Despite a radical change in appearance, he instantly recognized Bill Snelling, his crew pilot when he was in MATS. He had aged and looked like an old man. He looked directly at Ollie, winked and mouthed the word "later". Ollie continued to walk toward his room, uncertain of what to do. Bill had been flying B29's over North Korea. *How had he ended up a Russian prisoner? How could he talk to Bill and how many other Americans were in the compound?.*

His "education", as Valeriy called it, up until the last month had become tedious and repetitive. The last two sessions had included another officer who asked a hundred questions about Ollie's training and equipment. Ollie's stock answer to the training question was, "Probably the same as yours". His answer to equipment questions was, "You probably know more about that than I do."

The Air Corp Officer got perturbed after the second session and started yelling at Ollie. Valery predictably played the good cop and calmed the Air Corp Officer.

When Valeriy tried to convince Ollie to cooperate Ollie said, "I am not trying to be a smart aleck. I know you have our planes for research and we had your planes. I was at a field in South Korea when one of the Chinese pilots defected and flew in your latest model MIG. Why waste your time trying to get technical information from me that you already have. I just flew the planes. I didn't design them."

Occasionally Valeriy would give Ollie an English newspaper to read. Ollie noticed that the papers that he got always contained bad or negative news about the war. The armistice talks were in process and in addition to news about the armistice there was disturbing news about the American prisoners of war. According to the news reports the morale of the UN prisoners was low and the defection rate was high. Attempts to escape were nonexistent and the death rate in the camps was high. An uneasy armistice was signed on July 27, 1953. When the American prisoners started to be released the stories about brainwashing and collaboration increased with reports that one third of the American prisoners cooperated with their captors.

When Ollie stated his doubts about the reports Valeriy began to bring him copies of the Los Angeles Times. Most disturbing to Ollie was the story about the two dozen Americans who refused to be repatriated and remained in North Korea. This was beyond Ollie's comprehension and he silently questioned the authenticity of the newspapers.

"Now that the war is over," Ollie asked hopefully, "would I be sent back to the States?"

"I can't lie to you Ollie," Valeriy said. "You're not a prisoner of war. Your country is not at war with us. You are here forever so please, for your sake, start thinking about yourself and resign yourself to your new life."

Two weeks later a subdued Valeriy had Ollie brought to his office, "Sit down Ollie, I'm afraid I have some very bad news."

He had a copy of the LA Times on his desk. He turned the paper around toward Ollie and pointed to a story about a Commercial plane crash in Alaska. Toward the end of the story it listed the casualties including the name Mary Callahan Miller and her son Kevin.

Ollie read and reread the story. Tears streamed down his face and eventually he began to sob and buried his face in his arms. Valeriy walked around the desk and tried unsuccessfully to console him. He offered Ollie a glass of vodka but Ollie only shook his head disconsolately, unable to accept this latest blow. The reasons for living were now diminished by two.

Ollie stumbled around in a daze for the next three months, thinking seriously of doing something stupid like attacking a guard or climbing over the fence. He decided to die. While working in the factory, just after dark, he bolted for the door and made it to the front gate before being felled by the butt of a guard's rifle. He regained consciousness in the compound hospital. The first blurry faces he saw where the commandant's and Valeriy's.

"Why didn't they shoot me?" He asked weakly. "Why don't you just put me out of my misery!"

After a few days in the hospital Ollie was moved into solitary confinement. When Ollie's time in solitary was over, Valeriy met him when the guards half carried him out of the cell and returned him to his room.

"I explained to the commandant what had happened and that you wanted to be killed. He understood but said that you would have to be punished so that the other prisoners would not think we are soft. Originally he was going to send you back to a work camp. I talked him out of that. Maybe we can do something to make your life more interesting."

While Ollie was in solitary the KGB had decided on a different approach for dealing with the Americans. Rooms wired for monitoring had been prepared and the Americans were moved in together in their new barracks. At first the prisoners where almost paranoid in their approach to their new roommates. They treated each other with suspicion and were guarded in their conversation.

The prisoners started to meet secretly after dark in the halls outside their rooms. Ollie realized that in addition to American Air Force prisoners there were American civilians in the group. There were four who had voluntarily moved to Russia in the 1920's and 1930's to help the communist revolutionaries establish their new country. They were particularly bitter since they had been caught up in the paranoia of one purge or another and had been separated from their families for years. None of them knew the status of their wives or children. All of them had been arrested and jailed when they had tried to return to the United States.

Ollie learned that Bill had been involved in what the Air Force called a "Ferret" program. After several attempts like Ollie's, the Air Force had equipped a number of B29's as reconnaissance planes. They where designated RB-29's and were tasked to probe Soviet Air Defense and radar. Bill's plane, with its twelve-man crew, had been shot down deep in Soviet territory. Bill didn't know the fate of the rest of his crew. None of them were in Irkutsk. From nosing around he had determined that there were members of at least five other RB-29 crews in the compound.

One day Bill disappeared. He was gone and not even Valeriy could tell Ollie what had happened. Ollie began to memorize the names and hometowns of the other airmen. He insisted that they all do the same and pledge that if anyone ever got out, they would contact the Air Force and try to contact the families.

Valeriy had been carefully monitoring Ollie's moods and behavior. When Ollie was starting to come out of depression Valeriy would push another button. His latest action was to show Ollie copies of Mary's letters to the Air Force, at first asking and then latter pleading for information about Ollie. He even produced a copy of a letter from Mary's Senator and Congressman to the Air Force demanding information about Ollie's disappearance.

"Look at your Air Force answers to these letters," Valeriy said with disgust. "All they will say is that you were on a mission and didn't return. Look at this letter. In response to your wife's direct challenge that she knew that you weren't at Misawa when the Air Force said you were. The Air Force in effect tells her to quit bothering them. Here is another Air Force letter to Mary's senator that has at least three lies. What kind of people are these that would force your wife into such despair. Why would you risk and then essentially give up your life for these kind of people. They are probably glad that Mary was in the plane that crashed. Now they have one less person questioning them about stupid programs like the one they sacrificed you for or for the ferret mission that your friend Bill was sent on."

The last statement caught Ollie off guard and he looked at Valeriy with obvious incredulity.

"Yes," he said, "We know all about your secret ferret program and the RB-29's that your country has foolishly sent into our air space. So far we have shot down ten of these suicide planes. What a shame, over a hundred of your fellow Americans lost in an undeclared act of war. And your government makes pious statements about how good they are and how bad we are! I think you are loyal to the wrong country. In our country you would have been revered as a hero and the state would have taken care of your wife and child forever. Your government lies to your people and is controlled by greedy capitalists. A lot of your fellow Americans figured that out when they were in Korean POW camps."

Valeriy stopped and then contritely apologized to Ollie, "I am sorry, Ollie, I know you have enough problems without my ranting, but it is frustrating for me to see you suffer and know your government is,...I am sorry, I am doing it again."

A few weeks later during their regular indoctrination session Valeriy casually remarked to Ollie, "I finally found out what happened to your friend Bill. He signed a confession and was returned to the US."

"I don't believe that at all," Ollie said with complete disdain. "Bill would never have done anything like that. He would never want to be classified as a traitor."

Valeriy handed some type written papers to Ollie and said, "I couldn't believe it either until I saw these."

Ollie took the papers and started to read the confession that Bill had apparently signed. Ollie recognized the signature.

The Russian smiled. He was pleased with himself. His program was moving along quite well. He already had signed confessions from over half the American airmen. He had obtained their signatures after telling them that Bill Snelling had been released after signing a confession. He had instructed each of them to maintain secrecy or lose their chance for freedom. It had been so easy. Now he was avoiding the airmen and in awhile would show them a bogus note from the American Embassy denying the existence of the Americans and denying repatriation.

He had plans for Ollie and soon his work in Irkutsk would be over. He wasn't looking forward to returning to Moscow but with the work he had performed he hoped that he would be rewarded.

A few days later Ollie was summoned to the commandant's office. When Ollie entered the office the commandant remained seated.

"I wanted to tell you this myself," he said solemnly." It has been decided that we are going to return you to your embassy in Moscow. Arrangements are being made and as soon as they are completed we will make travel plans."

It took awhile for the commandant's statement to register in Ollie's brain. *Was it possible that he would soon be free?* He was afraid to think about it for fear he would jinx the release. He went back to his room and was unsure whether or not to say anything to the rest of the American airmen. Finally he did tell them and promised that the first thing he would do would be to contact the Air Force and their families to tell them where they were. He noticed that a few of the men looked at him with some hostility.

Ollie waited impatiently for two weeks and heard nothing. When he walked into Valeriy's office for his regular weekly session he knew immediately that something was amiss. Valeriy was standing behind his desk with a disconsolate look on his face, holding papers with the embossed seal of the United States government.

"Read this," he said, handing the papers to Ollie.

Ollie read the letter and shook his head in disbelief and reread the letter again from the beginning.

"How can they say that their records do not show that I exist! This is stupid. Just take me to the Embassy and I will prove to them that I do exist."

"Read the last paragraph again," Valeriy said. "They accuse us of trying to insert a KBG agent into the US. And the world says that we are paranoid!"

Ollie felt like he had received a severe blow to the stomach. He sat down hard and for the second since being captured, completely lost his composure in front of a Russian. Ollie began to sob uncontrollably. Tears streamed down his face, dampening his shirt. There was a tremendous pain in his chest and he literally thought his heart had broken. He could not breathe and after few minutes collapsed and fell hard to the floor, banging his head against the concrete with a sickening thud.

CHAPTER 9

Tokyo Japan, 1951

Mary was not concerned when Ollie didn't return from his training mission. She was used to his being away for long periods of time and she just went about her normal routine. When two weeks had gone by she started to become concerned.

When Bill Thomas called and asked where Ollie was, her concern turned to panic. She had assumed that Bill was with Ollie. When Bill heard the fear in Mary's voice he tried to calm her and said, "Let me see what I can find out and I'll call you back."

Bill headed toward the squadron commander's office and waited impatiently. After a few minuets the commander's orderly allowed Bill to enter.

"What can I do for you, Lieutenant Thomas?" The commander asked.

"Sir, I'm here to inquire about my pilot, Lieutenant Miller. I haven't seen him for two weeks. I thought that maybe he had taken a furlough without telling me. I couldn't imagine him doing that but I was assigned to help train some new people and really did not think too much about it until I called his wife. She thought that both of us had been sent to Misawa for a few days training. Now both of us are worried. Can you tell me what has happened?"

"I would like to know myself," the squadron commander said. "I have been calling Wing for the last week to find out when he will be back so I can schedule your rotation. They have been giving me the run around. I know when I am being brushed off."

"I'm sorry sir, but what did Wing have to do with Miller?"

"They called and told me they wanted Miller for a special project that would last about a week. I called Miller in to my office and sent him to a meeting. That is the last I have heard."

"This may just be a misunderstanding, but as you can imagine, his wife is really concerned. Could you call wing again and forward her concern?"

The Squadron Commander picked up the phone and said, "Get me Colonel Johnsen at Wing."

A few seconds later he was talking to the wing commander, explaining his problem. After listening for a few minutes he hung up the phone and turned to Bill with a perplexed look on his face.

"They said that any information on this subject is classified and that I was not to discuss it with anyone. I think your pilot may have been tapped for some sort of secret project."

"What do I tell his wife?" Bill asked.

"They said to tell her that he is on a special assignment and that she would soon be hearing from her husband."

When Bill called Mary to tell her about his inquiries he omitted the part about Ollie's mission being classified. She didn't buy the explanation.

"This is BS," she said with disgust. "Even when Ollie was in Korea he called me at least once a week. You know that. He would never go this long without trying to contact me. I began to worry when he didn't call me himself to tell me he was going to be away. I will get to the bottom of this even if I have to get MacArthur involved. I know how the military operates and I will not let them alone until I get the truth. Give me the names and phone numbers of Ollie's chain of command."

Bill tried to calm Mary but he knew he was wasting his time. He did promise to ask around to see if anyone could remember anything unusual about the time when Ollie had disappeared.

Mary was relentless. She was on the phone daily with the officers in Ollie's chain of command, demanding information and answers. She didn't like the standard answer, "Your husband is on a special mission and will call you when he can."

After months of frustration Mary solicited the help of a few of her friends in the military government. They got the same response from the Air Force. In desperation she started writing to the federal senators and congressmen from her home state, and to her father's friends in the State Department. She also wrote letters to the Air Force chief of staff and to the Department of Defense. Some attempted to help but eventually told Mary they could not spend any more time on her problem.

All this activity was draining time from her regular job. Her boss was sympathetic but advised her that he was not satisfied with her performance and advised her to decide what she wanted to do; either work for him or to resign and try to find out what had happened to Ollie.

She received another blow when the day care facility advised her that she could no longer send Kevin to day care while she worked and she could no longer live in the Enclave. They said that she was no longer in the WAAC and was not a civilian employee of the military government, and therefore was not eligible for the service or the housing. She tried unsuccessfully for weeks to make arrangements for Kevin's care while she was working. The day care center had extended their time to allow her to make other arrangements but at the end of two weeks she had not been able to find help. A few of her neighbors volunteered to help her on a temporary basis but she could not find a permanent solution. Finding a new apartment was also proving to be a serious problem.

She was really getting desperate when another blow was delivered. One afternoon, when she had taken her lunch hour, she returned to find a note on her desk asking her to report to her boss. When she asked her fellow employees if they knew why, one of them said, "I don't know what has been happening but some American civilians came in right after you left and went right into the bosses office. After a few minutes they came out and went through your desk. Then they left after talking to the boss. They took some of your stuff with them."

Mary quickly went through her desk drawers and could not find the file folder containing her letters about Ollie's disappearance.

The secretary outside her boss's door knocked on the door and after saying a few words motioned for Mary to enter.

"What's going on?" Mary asked. "Who were the men that took my files on Ollie?"

"I have been advised not to discuss anything with you. I'm not at liberty to tell you who they were but I can tell you that effective immediately you have been fired. I want you to remove your personal belongings from your office and leave immediately."

"This is incredulous!" Mary exclaimed. "What really is going on and who were those men?"

"You have known for some time that I have not been happy with your work. I'm sorry about your husband but I have a business to run and I can't pay you when you are devoting most of your time to things other than your job." He turned his back and over his shoulder said, "Please get your belongings and leave."

Mary was stunned; she tried to tell him that she would not spend any more of his time working on her personal problems. He just motioned to the door and shut it behind her when she left. *Well,* she thought, *with what I have saved I should be able to live for awhile. It's really going to be difficult, looking for a new place to live and trying to find a new job and taking care of Kevin.*

That evening Bill Thomas called. Concern was reflected in his voice. "Mary, I was visited by some Military Intelligence types this afternoon. They knew that I had been asking a lot of questions about Ollie. Their message to me was cease and desist or I would be in a lot of trouble. They also told me to break off contact with you. What is going on?"

"That's what I would like to know," Mary said with apparent frustration.

She told him about the civilians visiting her boss and her subsequent dismissal. Bill was really agitated. "Why can't they tell us what happened? What are they covering up?"

"I don't know," Mary replied, "but I'm going to spend full time on this until my money runs out."

Bill said, "If they do sign an armistice I don't know how long I'll be in Japan but I'll keep in touch. Call me when you have relocated."

When the Korean War ended and the prisoners of war started to return, Mary's hopes soared and then were dashed when Ollie's name didn't show up on any of the lists. She was still hopeful when the papers began to carry stories about the North Korean government failing to provide information on Americans listed as Missing in Action. Occasionally a name would surface and Mary would be encouraged. Her positive attitude was tested when after three more months she had no news about Ollie.

Mary, with the help of her friends in the Military government, finally found a one-room apartment. The rent was so high that she figured that she would be only able to live for three months before she was totally broke.

Just when she was about to give up, one of her business contacts referred her to the president of the biggest bank in Tokyo. He wanted a personal assistant with contacts in the American military and business community. The first three interviews with his vice presidents went exceptionally well. There was some concern about her last employment. The fourth interview was with Shurio Yamagutshi, the bank president. Their meeting was fascinating for Mary. The job he was offering was an exceptional opportunity. Shurio did not speak fluent English and although he was taking private tutoring in English he wanted an assistant who understood all the nuances of the English language and American business.

Mary's impression of Yamagutshi was favorable. His charm and modern attitude toward women impressed her. Unlike some of his countrymen, he acknowledged that women could function as well as men in business. Although he was small in stature, Mary easily discerned a superior intellect. She was sure that he would be a major factor in Japan's economic reconstruction. There was a major drawback. Yamagutshi wanted his assistant to live full time on his estate. When Mary questioned a vice president on this point she was told that it was not negotiable. She was also told that she could not keep a child on the estate. With regret she turned down the job offer.

The next day she was summoned to Yamagutshi's office. A driver picked her up and when they arrived at the bank she was directed into the president's office. He rose when Mary entered and motioned for her to sit.

"It was with deep regret that I learned of your refusal of my offer," he said. "I understand your reasoning but I have a suggestion. If you have relatives in the US, perhaps one of them would be willing to accept your son for a few years until you get established. I would be willing to pay for his transportation, and you could visit him on vacation or when you are in the States. When he is older I will consider having him move on to the estate. Also, if you accept this position I will use my influence to help you determine what happened to your husband."

The offer caused Mary to wander emotionally. She had never considered sending Kevin back to the States while she stayed in Japan. The option had never even occurred to her. At first she rejected the idea and then began to wonder if anyone in Ollie's family would help. She left Yamagutshi's office in a state of confusion but said that she would explore the option.

Late that evening she called Ollie's mother and father in Pennsylvania. Like Mary, they had been applying pressure, trying to get

CHAPTER *10*

Irkutsk, South East Russia, 1953

One by one the American Airmen drifted away from Irkutsk.

Ollie had reached the end of his perseverance. The helplessness, monotony and the lack of direction in his life were increasing his periods of depression. He would go for weeks without talking to anybody, moving from place to place like a zombie.

Valeriy knew that Ollie was in a state susceptible to the suggestion that he had been preparing. During the last three weekly sessions with Ollie he had just sat in the chair, in a daze, not responding to Valeriy's conversation. This week he had a surprise for Ollie. He walked around the desk, patted Ollie on the shoulder and said, "Come with me. We are going to do something different today. I am sure you will enjoy the change."

He led Ollie to the front entrance to the compound where a car was waiting. The driver, an armed Russian guard, opened the back door of the car. The driver started the car and exited the compound. Ollie had only ever seen one part of the city on his way to and from work in the factory. They left the city and its narrow streets and ancient buildings and headed out into the country. The scenery was fascinating to Ollie. For the last year his view of the world had been limited to dreary buildings. After driving for over an hour they entered a village that was built along the side of a lake.

"This is Lake Baykal," Valeriy said as Ollie breathed the fresh air deep into his lungs. "I think I told you before that this is the largest fresh water lake in the world and that I sometimes come here to fish. I stay at a friend's cabin here. We are going to stay here for a few days. It will do you good. You can relax and get away from the routine that you have been in. Come; let's go in."

The car had stopped in front of a rustic log cabin that sat a hundred feet from the lake. The cabin was set in a forest of pines that emitted an intoxicating balsam fragrance. When they walked through the cabin door, Ollie stopped and admired the primitive opulence of the furnishings. The main room was large and furnished with comfortable over-stuffed chairs, sofas and a huge dining room table. The kitchen took up the rest of the first floor. An open staircase rose to a balcony that led to four bedrooms.

"Very bourgeois," Ollie said. "Do the peasants know that you live like this?"

"My friend, who lets me use this cabin, is a high Party official. I'm sure that the peasants, as you call them, would not mind if they knew how hard he works for them." Valeriy said as he showed Ollie around the cabin.

The staff for the cabin, a cook and her husband caretaker, lived in a small village near the cabin. After Ollie had been shown to his room, where he found clean clothes and toilet items, he bathed, shaved and dressed in the clean clothes. When he started down the steps to the living room he could smell and see the wood fire that had been started in the fireplace. The cook had prepared a light supper for Valeriy and Ollie. By the time they had finished eating it was dark and Valeriy suggested that Ollie retire.

"I have some special plans for tomorrow so why don't you go to bed." Valeriy said, "I am going to stay up for a little while and do some reading."

Ollie returned to his room and within minutes after getting into bed was in a deep sleep. Being in a room alone, without snoring roommates, was luxury that his mind quickly accepted, rewarding his body with total relaxation.

He awoke after uninterrupted sleep, stimulated by fragrance of breakfast being cooked in the kitchen below his room.

"Did you sleep well?" Valeriy asked with a smile, as Ollie descended the staircase. "Or did the peace and quite keep you awake?"

"It was the best night's sleep I have had in years," Ollie replied. "Why are you doing this?"

"I was concerned about you," Valeriy replied, patting him on the shoulder. "I could tell that you were deeply depressed and I thought a change would do you good. Let's eat some breakfast and then do some fishing. Do you like to fish?"

"No, I have never been fishing so I can't say that I do."

"Well at least come with me and give it a try. We won't be out for long; I have some other guests coming in for lunch. Let's get going," the Russian said cheerfully. "I have been looking forward to this for weeks."

Ollie wasn't much of a fisherman, as it turned out. As they were docking the boat Valeriy asked if he had enjoyed the morning.

Ollie replied, "Well I didn't catch anything but I did enjoy the clean air and the boat ride."

While Ollie was cleaning up for lunch he heard a car drive up and Valeriy greeting the newly arrived guests. When he walked down the steps he was surprised to see Tamara Krasnov, dressed in tailored, feminine slacks and a sweater, accompanied by an older, gray haired man, also in civilian clothes. The mans rigid bearing, aura and stature, was an immediate flag that this was a military officer of high rank. An attentive younger man, also dressed in civilian clothes, viewed Ollie with interest. Ollie recognized the look; the young man was an aide.

Valeriy introduced Ollie to the new arrivals; "You already have meet Tamara."

The young Russian woman smiled and extended her hand and said, "I am happy that you are still alive. Later we will talk about flying. Yes?"

Valeriy then turned to the distinguished older man and said, "Ollie this is General Aleksandr Gaidar. He has traveled all this way to talk to you."

Ollie accepted the bear grip handshake and the Russian general said in heavily accented English, "Lieutenant Miller, I am happy to at last meet you. I am sorry for the treatment that you have received in my country but I am sure that you know our position on your mission. I am more deeply concerned by your countries refusal to accept your repatriation. I want to talk to you about something that might interest you and at least give some meaning and pleasure to your life."

They seated themselves at the dining room table and as they consumed their meal the general continued talking. "I will be completely candid with you. I want you to become a member of my staff. I need someone who is knowledgeable about the English speaking countries to provide me with input on many areas, both military and non-military. We are living in dangerous times and I need help in dealing with the western mind. I will not be asking you to do anything that would cause danger to the United States. In fact you would be in a position that may help our relationship with your ex-homeland.

The events of the last two days literally had Ollie's head spinning. It was impossible for him to instantly analyze the statements of the general or make a decision. The general had anticipated this and said, "I don't need your response this minute but I would like to have your decision by tomorrow morning. We would train you in Russian and other languages and you would have your own lodgings near my headquarters. You would be free to come and go, within reason, as you desire. I am offering you a job that will allow you to become more than a prisoner the rest of your life. Think about it and tell me your answer by tomorrow."

Ollie left the cabin and wandered down to the dock and sat down on a bench that overlooked the lake. His mind was churning. It seemed that accepting the offer would make him a traitor. Then again, his own country had disclaimed his existence and refused to even investigate the Russian offer to set him free. He had often, in his mind, questioned the authenticity of the documents he had been shown by Valeriy. *Was anything the truth? Were the Russians manipulating him for their own advantage? If he accepted he might have the opportunity to find the answers to these nagging questions. He might even have the opportunity to escape. But escape to what? His parents probably thought he was dead so returning to the States would allow them to stop grieving about another son lost to war.* His final decision was to accept the offer. It was far superior to the alternative; spending the rest of his life in prison without possibility of escape.

He had just made up his mind to accept when Tamara joined him on the dock.

"Is very difficult for you," she said, taking his hand. "I think about you often when I am flying and what you said when we first meet. Think much and make up your own mind. But now I have a surprise for you. Come with me."

She led him around to the front of the cabin where an uniformed driver was waiting in a car. They got in the car and in a short time were at a small, grass strip airfield.

An old Polikarpov biplane, two-cockpit trainer, was sitting on the strip.

"Is it not beautiful?" Tamara said, climbing up on to the wing. She reached into the rear open cockpit and removed two leather helmets with goggles. She tossed one set to Ollie and pulled the other over her short blonde hair. She got in the rear cockpit and motioned for Ollie to get into the front cockpit. "Get in, we are going flying."

Ollie climbed in and Tamara motioned for the ground crewman to spin the prop. On the second attempt the old engine sputtered and then settled down into a competent roar. Tamara started to taxi and then turned into the wind and applied full power. The little biplane jumped forward and was quickly climbing. Ollie felt the exhilaration of being airborne. It was as thrilling as his first ride in the old Jennies when he was a kid.

Tamara skillfully flew the plane back toward the lake and gave Ollie a beautiful view of the lake side community. She flew along the lakeshore, gradually gaining altitude and then reached forward and tapped Ollie on the shoulder and motioned for him to take the controls. Ollie placed his feet on the worn rudder pedals and lightly gripped the stick and then nodded his head to signal that he had the controls. He felt Tamara releasing control pressure and the plane was his.

The joy of flying again made him, at least for the moment, forget where he was. He was in the element he loved, flying a plane. All the memories of his youth came flooding back. The vision of his first flights in the old Jennies led him to images of his family and friends, bringing tears to his eyes. *What were they doing? Did they think of him often and were they trying to contact him? Would he ever see them again?*

Ollie removed the goggles and ducked down beneath the windscreen and wiped away his tears with the sleeve of his shirt and replaced the goggles. He continued flying putting the plane through gentle turns, not wanting to put stress on the old airframe. After what seemed like minutes Tamara tapped him on the shoulder and he reluctantly gave up controls.

Tamara was not as gentle with the old plane. She put the plane into several aileron rolls and then into a steep dive and buzzed a fishing boat. Too soon for Ollie, they where back on the ground.

On the way back to the cabin Tamara said, with exuberance, "You have a good time, Yes? I learned how to fly in that type plane. I have one of my own that my father gave me on my birthday. Come with us and I will let you fly it whenever you want as long as you help me service the plane."

Valeriy and the general greeted them at the door of the cabin.

Ollie looked at the two men and said with conviction, "I have made up my mind. I'm going to accept your offer."

Both men smiled broadly and extended their hands. Valeriy said, "I'm going to miss you but I know you made the right decision."

Tamara smiled warmly and grasped both Ollie's hands.

"I am happy for you Ollie, we will have lots of good times flying."

Ollie left Lake Baykal, with the general, his aide and Tamara, in the general's plane. When they landed in Podluk, outside Moscow, Tamara accompanied Ollie to his new quarters within the confines of the Russian air base. She spent the rest of the day with him, touring the base, showing him the important buildings and the office where he would be working. She arranged for him to be issued uniforms and then they had dinner in the officer's mess. She took him back to his quarters and told him that the general's aide would pick him up the next morning to complete his indoctrination.

"I tried to get you in the same building that I live in but it is full." She smiled. "When somebody leaves I will try again. I am so happy for you. Now you can get back into the sky where you belong."

Early the next morning the general's aide picked up Ollie at his quarters and escorted him to Air Command headquarters and waited until Ollie was issued a security badge and then showed Ollie to his new office.

His next stop was at the supply depot where he picked up his new, blue Air Corp uniforms and a complete issue of underwear, flight gear and toilet articles. Ollie wasn't exactly sure what his rank would be but the uniform and epaulets where that of an officer.

When Ollie was dressed the aide took him to the aide's office, adjacent to the general's, and began instructing Ollie on his duties and schedule.

His duties, to start, were simple. He was given English newspapers and magazines to read and prepared a summary of the items he thought would be of interest to the staff. For the first six months his life was relaxed and his duties light. As he became proficient in conversational Russian he was invited to sit in on staff meetings.

After a few months the gaunt American was no longer a curiosity and the people he passed stopped staring at him when he passed by. He did know, however, that to the Russians he was "The American". When he asked Tamara why they didn't call him by his name she laughed and said, "Your name is foreign to us. We will have to think of a good Russian name for you. I know, I will call you Olieg Millerovic. That is close to your American name and I can still call you Ollie."

Soon, all the Russians were using his new name.

Ollie's first excursion off the air base was an adventure. Tamara invited him to visit her father's dacha estate just outside Moscow. She picked him up at his quarters and drove into the dwindling light to the estate. Ollie could see, from the lights of the car, that the dacha was a two story, rustic building surrounded by trees. Tamara parked the car and as they approached the front door it opened. A large masculine version of Tamara stood in the doorway. The bear of a man embraced his daughter, lifting her off the ground. After talking to Tamara for a few minutes he turned to Ollie and extended his hand, "In case you hadn't guessed," he said while crushing Ollie's hand, "I am Tamara's father, Yuri. Tamara has told me much about you. Would you prefer that I talk in English?"

Ollie withdrew his hand from the vice like grip and said, "It's an honor to meet you sir, I would prefer Russian. I need the practice."

"Good, come in and I will show you around our country home while Tamara puts your bag in your room."

Yuri took Ollie on a tour of the warmly furnished home.

The house was built similar to the cabin Ollie has visited in Lake Baykal but was much larger and more opulent. The wall decorations were warm oil paintings of the Russian country, ranging from flat farmland scenes to mountain rivers, interspersed with tapestries and wall hangings.

"My wife Sasha decorated this home. You can feel her warmth and vitality in every room. Unfortunately she did not live many years after to enjoy her work," Yuri said sadly.

"I am sorry. I lost my wife and son at an early age so I can appreciate your sadness." Ollie said, patting Yuri on the back.

"Enough of the past," Yuri declared. "Come; join me in a drink before dinner."

They sat down and enjoyed a simple meal of beef, potatoes, cabbage, and brown bread with ample portions of vodka, served by Yuri's live in housekeeper and her husband.

After dinner they sat in front of the fire and Yuri questioned Ollie at length about his incarceration and his new duties.

"General Gaidar is a good man," Yuri said reflectively. "He is tough and demanding but is also an intelligent and fair man. You will learn much from him. Always tell him the truth, no matter how bad it might be. I know how much he detests people who are not completely honest."

The next morning after breakfast Tamara said, "Come, I want to show you something that will make you very happy."

She led him to the car and after he was seated in the passenger seat drove around the back of the house and started down a dirt road toward a barn like structure. She stooped the car and started to open the barn doors. When they got the doors open she steeped back and said, "What do you think of my baby?"

Ollie started to walk around the Polikarpov biplane, examining every inch of the plane.

"I take it that this is the plane your father gave you for your birthday."

"Yes, and if you will help me push it out, we are going to go flying."

Ollie scampered around to the other side of the plane and started to push. It took some effort but they soon had the plane positioned on the end of the grass landing strip.

They both performed a walk around inspection, checked the gas tank to make sure it was full and then cracked open a petcock valve at the bottom of the tank to drain out any accumulated water. Tamara climbed into the rear cockpit and operated the controls, checking out the ailerons, rudder and elevators. When she was satisfied she signaled Ollie to spin the prop to start the engine. Ollie spun the prop and the engine started immediately. He ran around the back of the plane climbed up on the wing and stepped into the front cockpit. Tamara handed him a pair of goggles and as soon as he was strapped in he gave her the go signal. Tamara applied throttle and the plane started down the strip and almost jumped into the air. They spent the next hour darting around the clouds, first climbing to maximum altitude and then skimming the treetops, taking turns flying the plane.

When the fuel was getting low they reluctantly returned to the airstrip. Tamara effortlessly landed the plane and taxied up to the door of the barn and cut the engine.

When they climbed out of the plane Ollie exclaimed, "That was great. I am happy that I have a friend that likes flying as much as I do."

They pushed the plane back into the barn and drove back to the house.

"The next time you come we will service the engine and check the airframe and control cables." Tamara said, her eyes flashing with happiness.

"Any time you say will be fine with me," Ollie replied. "Is next week too soon?"

They had lunch with Tamara's father and then left to return to the air base. Tamara had ready duty that night.

Ollie kept all the papers and magazines he was given until he had read every word on every page. It kept him abreast of world events and the progress of what the world was now calling "The Cold War".

The Soviet Air Force was developing new long range bombers and more advanced MIG fighters. Ollie accompanied the general on inspection trips to the aircraft design, manufacturing and test facilities. He was often consulted about the placements of instruments and controls. They would let him sit in the cockpit but of course would not let him fly the warplanes. At times he considered asking to be allowed to fly but rejected the idea. He knew some still called him "The American" and he had nothing he could offer to convince them that he would not bolt. They had good reason. Ollie was continuously plotting ways to escape.

Ollie and Tamara spent as much time as they could at her father's country estate, servicing and flying the old bi-plane. As the Russian winter approached their flying trips diminished. The weather was too uncertain and the open cockpit was freezing cold even when the sun was out.

Two dreary winter months passed and Ollie was starting to get bored. When he got tired of his cramped quarters he would dress is his warm winter gear and venture out into the cold. It usually only took a few minutes for the blues to disappear. The biting cold reminded him of the days spent on the Siberian railroad gang. His present situation was so much better that he soon would forget about his boredom and loneliness.

CHAPTER *11*

Tokyo, Japan, 1956

Mary was deeply immersed in her new job. Her new employer, Shurio Yamagutshi, was both demanding and benevolent. She had an office on his estate, adjacent to his. Every working day she rode with him in his chauffeur driven car to the main office of the Bank of Tokyo.

Her lodgings at the estate where sumptuous. She had a large sitting room, a bedroom with modern American furniture, and a private bath. A maid and chauffeur driven car were available by picking up the phone. The servants treated her with respect and without a trace of rancor.

At first her duties were limited. One of Yamagutshi's vice presidents was responsible for her training. Gradually she began to help in the analysis of bank loan applications, the sources of bank funding, and the day to day operation of the bank. Yamagutshi began to have her attend all meetings with department heads, potential recipients of bank loans and representatives from foreign banks. Her main area of focus at first was funding companies that wanted to start new ventures or acquire other companies. As Yamagutshi's trust in her increased he broadened her duties and responsibilities and delegated some of his decision-making functions.

Each evening after dinner, they would retire to the sitting room for warm saki and tea. It was this part of the day that Mary enjoyed most. In addition to discussing bank business they had lengthily discussions about world events and the news of the day. It was also during this time that Yamagutshi would inform her of the latest information he had obtained about Ollie.

Yamagutshi had important friends in the North Korean government who had been painstakingly having POW records searched for any mention of Ollie. Their four-year search had been fruitless and they came to the conclusion that Ollie had never been a prisoner of the North Koreans.

Yamagutshi was relentless in dealing with the American government. A representative of the Air Force came to the bank and gave Mary an official looking report that concluded that Ollie was flying a training mission over the Sea Of Japan and had not returned and therefore was assumed to be Missing In Action and presumed to be dead. The report also said that at the conclusion of five years the Air Force would consider Ollie officially dead and would process papers providing Mary with any money due. Mary did not accept the report. She has been down this same road with the Air Force before and had punched many holes in their previous reports.

Yamagutshi tried to calm Mary before she further abused the Air Force representative. "Be calm, Mary. I will not let this die. We will find somebody who knows the truth."

Shurio Yamagutshi's financial empire was expanding at a rapid rate. He had invested heavily in the emerging Japanese electronic manufacturing companies and in several automotive manufacturers. Mary had played a key role in evaluating his new ventures and because of their success she was promoted to vice president of the bank. When Shurio opened Yamagutshi Investment Company and started to apply most of his time to the new Brokerage Company, Mary took over as chief operating officer of the bank. At first his fellow Japanese business friends derided Shurio for his non-traditional appointment of a foreign female to a top position in his business. They began to see the wisdom of Shurio's daring move when the foreign companies moving into Japan preferred to do business with an attractive American woman.

It was exhilarating for Mary to be at the center of the redevelopment of the Japanese business complex. She thrived on her sixteen-hour workdays. Her work schedule gave her little time to agonize over Ollie's disappearance or to miss Kevin.

She wrote often to her in-laws, keeping them advised of her activities and continuing search for Ollie. She sent a check with every letter. The amount of her checks increased as her responsibilities and salary grew. The grandparents faithfully answered her letters, often including pictures. They also repeatedly told Mary that Kevin was continuously asking when he would be with his mother. The first letters she received were pitiful and drove Mary to tears. Her son had arrived in Pennsylvania in a near catatonic state. It had taken his grandparents weeks to get him to talk or eat. Now he was out of his shell and was playing with his cousins, but he was still asking about his mother on a daily basis.

By the second anniversary of Kevin's departure Mary had stopped writing as often. She still sent money but because she had little of interest to report she started to write once a month, then every other month and then only on birthdays and holidays. At first the grandparents pleaded for Mary to either come back to the States or to have Kevin return to Japan. Later they began to demand action, but now seemed resigned to the possibility that Mary was never going to take direct responsibility for Kevin. Being removed from Kevin became less and less strained. Mary really only felt remorse on Kevin's birthday. Submerging herself into her work quickly dispersed the remorse.

The Bank of Tokyo and the Yamagutshi Stock Brokerage were both prospering with the influx of foreign money to finance industry. The economy was doubling every year, driven by the world demand for consumer goods. The electronics industry could not keep up with the foreign demand for low cost television sets, radios and cameras. Mary's daily meeting schedule looked like the sign in log at the United Nations. The wealth of the world was drifting to Japan and its hustling businessmen and workers.

Work was so hectic and interesting that Mary was slowly loosing her guilt over shipping Kevin back to his grandparents. The frequency of the letters diminished to a trickle. She did have periods of regret and guilt. Each time she felt guilt she increased the monthly amount she invested in a brokerage account earmarked for Kevin's trust fund.

Her personal life now included Shurio Yamagutshi as her par-amour. What had started as a business partnership had grown into a platonic relationship. Since Mary was living on Yamagutshi's estate she became his defacto hostess and then his mistress.

Mary found no romance in the relationship. Shurio was attentive and generous and treated her with uncommon respect. As the years passed she began to enjoy his companionship. Her feelings never came close to the love she had felt for Ollie but she did recognize a growing, deep affection. A generous salary and no-fee investment of her money in Yamagutshi Stock Brokerage repaid her faithfulness. Each month she was provided with a statement of her account that was rapidly appreciating under Shurio's watchful direction. She was firmly entrenched as the president of the bank and was a director of the new Yamagutshi Corporation that was a conglomerate of Shurio's financial and manufacturing holdings.

Shurio's wife had died during World War II. Although Shurio never discussed the death of his wife, Mary deduced that she died from a severe, prolonged medical problem. Before the start of start of World War II Shurio had sent his two young sons to Switzerland. A man and his wife who became their surrogate parents while the sons attended school had accompanied them. The boys stayed in

Switzerland until the war ended and then, after a summer in Japan, were sent to the University of California for college and then to the Harvard School of Business. When they returned to Japan they both started working in their father's business. The boys had assumed American first names. James, the youngest, started as a trader in his father's brokerage and was quickly promoted to managing director. Robert, the eldest, started in the bank as a teller and quickly moved up the ladder to Chief Loan Officer.

The young men were only home a few hours when Mary became aware of their animosity. In the presence of their father they were respectful to her. When their father was not around they were arrogantly and pointedly hostile. Mary met with them alone and together and tried to determine the cause of the problem. Both the men advised her that they knew she was trying to position herself to inherit their father's estate and that they were not about to let that happen. Mary tried to assure them that she had no intentions to ingratiate herself and receive any of their father's estate. She volunteered to prepare a written document to that effect and asked them to discuss their problem with their father. Although she had never seen Shurio's will she was sure that she would not receive any part of the estate. She knew how much Shurio loved his two sons and how much he had missed them when they were away. Mary never did know if they went to their father. They didn't change their attitude and if anything became more distant.

When Shurio began to complain of pains in his lower abdomen, they took him to the hospital for tests. On the way home from the hospital Mary stopped in the brokerage and transferred her financial holdings to a trust fund she had established with a Tokyo law firm that was independent of the Yamagutshi Empire. If anything happened to Shurio she was sure that the two sons would take legal actions to seize her funds. Switching the funds would at least protect what she had earned and set aside for Kevin.

G. B. Mooney

Six months later Shurio died. Mary had spent every evening after work and every weekend in the hospital with Shurio, trying to comfort him and ease his suffering. His sons visited occasionally, always explaining that they now had to spend more time protecting the business interests.

Mary was surprised to learn that she had inherited one third of Shurio's business holdings. As anticipated, the sons contested the will and won. Mary received nothing and the two sons called a special board of directors meeting, voted her off the board and removed her as president of the bank. Once again she was out of a job, but this time she was independently wealthy and within a few hours of the son's press release announcing her dismissal, she started receiving job offers.

CHAPTER *12*

Podluk, Russia, 1954

"You need a break from your work," Tamara declared, brushing the snow off her parka and stepping into Ollie's quarters. "I know you haven't had any fun for months. This weekend you are coming to the ballet with me. A friend who is away is going to let us use his apartment in Moscow."

Tamara picked Ollie up in her car after lunch on Friday. She had appealed to the general for Ollie to have three days off. The general had immediately approved. Ollie threw his traveling bag into the back seat with Tamara's and climbed into the passenger seat. She chattered away on the short drive to Moscow, relating stories about her flying and her father. They stopped in front of a rather bleak, red brick apartment building just a few blocks away from the Bolshoi Ballet Theater.

The two carried their bags up to the third floor and began to explore the apartment. It was extremely small with barely enough room for a couch and a chair in the living room and a bed and dresser in the bedroom. The bath had a tub, toilet and sink that looked like they where a hundred years old. The kitchen, a part of the living room, had a stove and an ancient refrigerator with the condenser coil mounted on top. The contents of the refrigerator and the food pantries were meager.

"Is there any place to eat out in Moscow? Are their any restaurants?", Ollie asked.

"Don't worry, we will not starve," Tamara replied confidentially. "I know where to get supplies. Anyhow, we have an invitation for dinner tonight."

They spent the next few hours rounding up a variety of foods. Tamara managed to accumulate a rear seat full of supplies from government-controlled stores and an Officer's mess. She also stopped at her father's apartment and picked up some ham, coffee, eggs, a bottle of Vodka and a bottle of French wine.

"Wait till he finds out what I have taken," she said as they left her father's apartment. "I will never hear the end of it, I am sure."

Back in the apartment Tamara picked up her travel bag and took it into the bathroom. Ollie could hear the bath water running and after what seemed to be an hour the bathroom door opened and Tamara stepped out and slowly turned around to give Ollie a complete view of her ensemble. She was dressed in a knee length, black velvet evening dress, with a high neckline, and long sleeves.

Ollie smiled at her obvious lack of confidence.

"You look fantastic," Ollie said with a smile. "This is the first time I have ever seen you in a dress and wearing make up. I'll look ratty in my baggy uniform, compared to you."

"I have another surprise for you," Tamara said. She went back into the bathroom and when she returned she was carrying an expensive looking dark blue business suit, a white shirt and a tie. "I had my fathers tailor make this for you. I hope it fits."

Ollie retired to the bathroom and after bathing and shaving put on the outfit Tamara had given him. The fit wasn't perfect but he had to admit it was much more presentable than the Russian issue military uniform. When he stepped out of the bathroom Tamara ordered him to turn around.

She looked at the outfit critically and said, "It's a good fit for not being able to measure. Don't you think?"

"I think we will be the best-dressed couple at where ever we are going. By the way, where are we going?" Ollie asked.

"We are going to my cousin Helena's house for dinner," Tamara replied, smoothing her hair with her hands. "You will like her and her husband Sergi. My cousin and I grew up together during the war when things were very bleak. She married a University professor. They both are a lot of fun. After dinner we are going to the theater at the university to see a student play. Bring the bottle of wine and we will leave."

They drove though the cold, foreboding city, occasionally waiting for bundled up pedestrians to cross the streets. Ollie had seen pictures of Moscow and was not impressed by the ornate lines of the building architecture. The round domes and pointed spires looked like the rendition of a bad dream. *Perhaps if the sun were shining the city would look more alive*, he thought to himself. *God knows it couldn't look more dismal.*

The apartment where they were staying was on the northern end of the city. Tamara drove past the Kremlin and through the massive, snow covered Red Square. She then turned toward Gorkiy Park and Moscow University, to her cousin's apartment in the southwest section of Moscow.

Tamara was right about her cousin and her husband. They were both energetic and brightly cheerful.

In contrast to Tamara's fair skin and blonde hair, her cousin Helena had dark brown hair and a light tan complexion.

"I know she has a lot of Muslim blood in her," Tamara joked. "I have heard family stories about how wild her mother was in her youth."

"Then your mother must have visited Scandinavia before you were born." Helena fired back.

Sergi, Helena's husband, did not look anything like a University Professor. He was lean and clean-shaven, and for a Russian had a light-hearted personality. During discussion Ollie learned that Sergi was an athlete and during sabbaticals trained with the Russian track team.

Helena confided to Ollie that Sergi, a sprinter, could probably make the Russian Olympic team.

For dinner Helena surprised Ollie by serving hamburgers, French fried potatoes, a salad with a light vinaigrette dressing and the biggest surprise, bottled Coca-Cola.

"How did you manage this?" Tamara said in complete surprise.

"I asked Sergi what he thought an American would miss after five years and this is what he came up with. Sergi lived in America for a short time. Since we don't have anything like this he thought Ollie would like it."

"This looks delicious," Ollie said. "Where did you get the Coke?"

"Sergi bribed an employee at the American Embassy. They have a machine there with cold drinks. I don't know what it cost and I don't want to know." Helena said as she patted Sergi on the cheek.

"It didn't cost me anything," Sergi said with a hearty laugh. "My friend from the embassy will be over next week to collect from you," pointing at Helena.

Ollie had been listening to the light banter and finally started to eating with great gusto. "This tastes even better than it looks," He said, wiping his face with a napkin. "I don't remember American burgers being this good. You should open a restaurant."

They all laughed heartily at the thought of an American food restaurant in Moscow.

"That will never happen in our lifetime," Sergi declared.

After dinner the two couples piled into Tamara's car for the trip to the university. The small theater was in a large gloomy building in the university complex.

The play was a rather serious tome that stressed the advantages of working for Mother Russia and the glory of sharing.

Ollie realized that it was propaganda, but then again, the USSR ran the university and the students were attending at no cost.

When they were back in the car Sergi said, "Not too many laughs in that play were there."

"Sergi, someday you are going to say the wrong thing at the wrong time and we are both going to end up in Siberia," Helena said with a note of sadness in her voice.

"Enough of that," Sergi said cheerfully. "Let's get back to our apartment and open that bottle of wine. I have been thinking about that all evening."

As soon as they were in the apartment Sergi opened the wine and started to regal them with stories about his students, the other university professors and then started on Helena. Soon they where laughing so hard they started grasping their sides, pleading with Sergi to stop.

Tamara made the first move to call it an evening, knowing their hosts both had to work the next day. Ollie thanked the couple a dozen times for their thoughtfulness and their company.

Ollie was very quiet in the car on the way back to their apartment.

"Why are you so quiet?" Tamara asked. "Are you sad? I thought you were having a good time."

"I did enjoy the evening," Ollie said, "but it did bring back a lot of old memories. I will admit I'm just a little sad. It was really nice of you to go to all this trouble. I'll be okay. Let's not spoil the rest of our weekend."

When they got back to the apartment Tamara immediately retired to the bathroom and Ollie prepared a place to sleep on the couch. When Tamara came out of the bathroom she was wearing a long robe. She motioned to the bathroom and said, "Your turn."

Ollie changed into his pajamas and when he came out of the bathroom noticed that the bed on the couch had been undone. He glanced into the bedroom and looked at Tamara questioningly.

She was lying on the bed in a nightgown.

"Tonight we sleep together," she said quietly. "Come to bed and I will make you very happy again."

G. B. Mooney

Ollie had been suppressing his attraction for Tamara since the first time she took him flying at her father's estate. He had tried to think of her as a sister but that had failed. He cast off his doubts and his inhibitions as he removed his pajamas. Tamara slid her nightgown over her head and slipped into the warmth under the blankets. Ollie followed and was quickly embraced by Tamara who began to kiss and stoke him tenderly. Ollie's heart began to pound and his breath became short. It had been years since he made love. For a moment he hesitated and then was overcome by the desire created by Tamara's touch and aroma. He started to reciprocate and soon Tamara was moaning and becoming more aggressive. She was obviously experienced and created an overpowering passion that they both swirled into.

The next morning they slept in. It was almost eleven before either of them made a move to get up. Neither wanted to leave the warmth and intimacy of their bed. They finally got up, dressed, and made a hearty breakfast of ham, eggs, fried potatoes, bread and coffee. After cleaning up the apartment they motored around the city with Tamara acting as tour director. She pointed out the Lenin Stadium, Tretyakou Gallery where Helena worked, the State Library and drove past the Kremlin and the imposing Red Square. Ollie admitted that the city looked better in sunlight, but nothing could help the ugliness of the buildings.

They returned to the apartment late in the afternoon and after a light dinner got ready for the ballet.

Tamara again surprised Ollie by putting on a blue silk evening dress that matched the color of her eyes.

"You look like a movie star," Ollie said admiringly. "I knew you were beautiful but that dress really does something for you."

Tamara smiled and slipped into a full-length fur coat and put a fur hat over her blonde hair, "Let's go," she said with a smile. "I think you will enjoy the ballet."

She was right, Ollie did enjoy the ballet. The dancing, even to his untrained eye, was graceful and athletic. The costumes were brilliant and the scenery was beautiful. He was impressed with the theater and the well-dressed audience. Most of all he enjoyed the music. He had never been that much interested in music but the magnificent orchestra rendition of Shastakovich music would be running around in his mind for weeks to come.

When Tamara asked if he had enjoyed the ballet he truthfully could answer yes. That brought an appreciative hug and kiss as soon as they were in the car.

The next morning they slept in again. When Tamara finally woke up she stretched sensually and said, "I could get used to this decadence."

Ollie rolled over and embraced her tenderly and they made love. This time Ollie grasped Tamara's arms and made her lie still while he made love to her. After Tamara's deep climax she rolled on top of Ollie and made love to him, stopping when he was near a climax, until he begged her to finish.

When they both lay exhausted, Ollie said, "I hope it isn't to long until we can do this again."

"I am sure it can be arraigned," Tamara said teasingly.

When spring arrived they started visiting Tamara's father's country estate at least twice a month. Even when her father was there, Tamara would wait till late at night and sneak down the hall to Ollie's room. The fear of detection added excitement to their trysts.

One weekend in the country in late June, during dinner, Tamara's father looked at them and said, "You two aren't fooling anyone. Why don't you just get married?"

Ollie and Tamara looked at each other in shock and then started to laugh, "How long have you known?" Tamara asked.

"The first time you two came out here I knew that this was going to happen. I am an intelligent person. I could see it was inevitable."

Both Ollie and Tamara where unusually silent on the return drive to their base. Ollie was thinking about Tamara's father's statement, "Why don't you get married?". Her father's statement was made without prejudice or rancor. The thought of marrying again was not distasteful. He enjoyed being with Tamara and looked forward with anticipation to any adventure that she planned. But marriage, that was something that he had never considered. He glanced at Tamara and could tell that she was also deep in thought. *Probably having the same thoughts that I have been having,* he thought.

Ollie was correct, Tamara was thinking about her father's statement. She did have strong feelings for Ollie but had not even considered getting married. It might interfere with her first love, flying. Men ran her command and although they were used to having women in the military she was not sure what the regulations were for married women. They just might kick her out. That possibility frightened Tamara. She could not imagine a life without flying her MIG.

Just before they reached the base Tamara pulled off the road and stopped.

"I think we should talk for a few minutes," Tamara said. "What do you think?"

"I think for the time being we should continue just as we are." Ollie said, watching Tamara closely to get her reaction.

Tamara reached over and took his hand and smiled broadly, "I agree. We both have a lot to lose if we get married and we are having so much fun now. I am afraid we would ruin it if we tried to get married. Who knows what the military might do?"

Ollie did eventually move into Tamara's building. Their quarters where just the length of the hall apart. Most of their fellow officers knew what was happening but considered it to be none of their business and seldom commented upon the activities of the two lovers.

They were sometimes apart for months at a time. Tamara was temporarily stationed at other air bases, sometimes to help train other new pilots and sometime for retraining with new equipment or new tactics.

Ollie made his first contact with English speaking people since leaving prison when he was assigned as an observer to a conference on Commercial Air Transportation. The Russians had limited foreign commercial aviation but several non-Russian air carriers were flying in and out of Russia. There had been considerable confusion on flying protocol and the conference was set up to resolve the communication problems and work out a system for electronic identification of aircraft.

The meeting took place in Paris. Although Ollie was always under the supervision of a senior officer, even at night, he did feel the spirit of the city and the vibrancy of the people.

He did not sit at the main table during the conference. He sat along the wall near his delegation, taking notes and offering comments when asked.

On the second day of the conference, as he was leaving for lunch, a member of the English delegation bumped into him as they both started out the door. The Englishman apologized profusely and offered his hand. When Ollie accepted the apology and reached to grasp the Englishman's extended hand he felt a small piece of paper being pressed into his hand. The Englishman withdrew his hand and quickly exited the door. Ollie palmed the note and stuck his hand into his pocket. Later when he was in the cubicle of a men's room he withdrew the note. It read, "Lt. Miller, 5th. Air Force, I want to meet with you. Will advise you how."

Ollie studied the note for a few minutes trying to decide what to do. This could be anything, even an attempt by the KGB to see how he would react. He decided that it was probably a test and during lunch showed the note to his immediate superior.

His superior looked at the note and then put it in his pocket and said, "I will take care of this. Tell me immediately if anybody else tries to make contact with you."

During the rest of the conference Ollie caught the Englishman looking at him several times but no further attempts at contact were made.

When Ollie returned to Moscow he related the incident to Sergi. They were walking around the university track cooling down after a run, while the women sunned themselves behind the bleachers that surrounded the track.

"Why didn't you try to make contact with him? His next note was going to say "Bill Snelling asked me to look you up," Sergi said softly in English.

Ollie stopped walking and Sergi immediately lightly grasped his arm and said, "Keep walking."

Ollie was totally taken back, "How do you know that? Who was the guy and how did you know about it?"

"For now I will just say that some people would like to make contact with you. I have been asked to make contact and have been waiting for the right opportunity for months."

"For what purpose?" Ollie asked, in obvious confusion.

"Come on Ollie, you are an intelligent man, I am sure you can figure this out if you just think about it."

"Who are you representing?" Ollie asked, turning to look into Sergi's eyes.

"I am trying to help my people here in Russia," Sergi replied. "I believe in the purpose of the revolution but I think our present rulers are too dictatorial and repressive. The people are living in fear. At least once a month there is a purge and people disappear. I knew some of the people who have been arrested and I know that they were not a threat to the country."

"These people," Ollie asked, "are they Russians or foreigners?"

"I really can't tell you at this time. Perhaps someday I will," Sergi replied.

"You have really put me in a precarious position," Ollie said, starting to pace nervously. "How do I not know you aren't KGB? How do I know you aren't part of a scheme to test me? If I turn you in I might be hurting Helena and Tamara. If I don't I could be on my way to Siberia in the morning."

"Suppose I tell you a few things that I have been told about you that only somebody from your family would know. Would that help you make up your mind?" Sergi asked.

"Hell no, it would not," Ollie said with disgust. "When I was first captured I was drugged for a long time. My indoctrinator knew every thing about my personal and military life. If he had a complete dossier I am sure you could have one."

"What would it take to convince you?" Sergi asked. "You tell me and I will do it."

"That's the point," Ollie said. "I don't know what all was pried out of me while I was under drugs so I can't tell you. Also, I don't want to get Tamara involved in something like this. I'm really in trouble here."

"Who do you think Tamara works for?" Sergi asked.

"She is an Air Corp officer so she works for Russia." Ollie replied.

"Do you really think that it was an accident that she was at Valeriy's cabin at Irkutsk when he took you there or that there wasn't a reason she befriended you and took you flying? Think about it Ollie."

"Are you telling me that Tamara is KGB!" Ollie asked, surprise and disbelief registering on his face. "That is hard for me to believe."

"No, she isn't KGB, but she does work for them. You know that you are under constant surveillance and it is not just when you are in public. Tamara has been your watchdog off the base since day one."

They were approaching the end of the walk and the women were moving toward them.

"Don't do anything foolish," Sergi said as they approached the girls. "I will try to think of something to convince you that I'm telling the truth."

Ollie found it to be extremely difficult to maintain the same attitude toward Sergi and Tamara. Occasionally Tamara would notice that he was depressed and would do her best to cheer him up. Two weeks after Sergi's bombshell Tamara asked again what was troubling him.

"I know its stupid of me but I can't help myself. I keep asking myself why you were at Valeriy's cabin and why you were nice to me?"

Tamara reflected a few minutes before answering. After she shot down Ollie and talked to him she had called her father and asked him if he could help Ollie. A few months after that she had been assigned to China and the Soviet 64th Aviation Corp. While assigned there she had shot down two American Sabre Jets and had partial credit for shooting down two B29's. She had finished her tour in China and got orders to report to General Gaidar for a special assignment. She had reported to the KGB officer in charge of the project and had been instructed in her duties. Tamara was delighted when she found she was to help Ollie out of confinement. She had thought about him often, wondering if he was still alive and if he would ever be free to fly. The first part of the assignment went so well that she agreed to befriend Ollie and provide information on his activities to the KGB.

She hadn't planned to get romantically involved, it just happened. Not that she wasn't experienced in sexual activities. During her youth she had the normal experiences with her cousin Helena, who showed her the erogenous areas on her body, and with her cousin Yergy who still probably didn't know what happened when the two girls seduced him. She had been involved with several of her fellow pilots who were always challenging her femininity. Her lovers seemed totally intent on self-gratification with little regard for her.

Ollie had been different. Their first night together he had been tender and had brought her to an all-consuming climax the first time they made love. What started out as pity and concern had grown to love. The love was powerful but not stronger than her love for flying.

Tamara studied Ollie's face for a few minutes more and then said, "I thought you figured that out right away. The general must have been told, probably by my father, that I had talked to you after I shot you down. Then General Gaidar contacted me and told me you were very depressed. I was very happy to hear that you survived Siberia. They told me they were thinking about offering you a way out of confinement. I was very happy when they asked me to help and I have never been sorry that I said yes. In fact I have never been happier in my life. Before you ask, I was also assigned as one of your observers. The KGB is always asking me about your activities and what you say. They are so paranoid!"

Ollie had been watching her face and eyes closely while she talked and was convinced that she was telling the truth. He breathed a sigh of relief and said, "I guess living in Russia has made me paranoid too."

CHAPTER *13*

Virginia, USA, 1956

Norm Lynch climbed into his unmarked government car and started on a routine assignment, relishing the drive from the Central Intelligence Agency headquarters at the farm in Virginia to the western side of the Allegheny Mountains in Pennsylvania.

This would be a pleasant relief after his last two mentally exhausting tasks in Europe. At his old for spook work age of fifty-eight, he had asked for and received an assignment that was not as stressful as the usual games he had to play in the foreign espionage community. He was really starting to dread his role as a controller of foreign agents working for the CIA. The cat and mouse games and the constant worry about double agents were taking its toll. This duty was just what he needed to refresh his nervous system. Jack Daniel's, of late, had been letting him down.

He would have to be careful on this assignment. He had read the Air Force confidential file on his new subject. The parents of the Air Force officer that he was investigating had been told that their son was MIA and presumed dead. The file did not contain information on the activities of the missing officer but it was easy to surmise that he had been on some kind of secret mission. He would bet a month salary that the Air Force knew what had happened but they had been stonewalling the family for five years. His supervisor had discussed the situation with him and they had decided to approach the subject's younger brother

and tell him that the Air Force was collecting information to help identify MIAs on photographs that they had obtained from the North
Koreans. He would ask the brother not to mention his inquiry to the
parents. He did not want to raise hope.

The assignment was a little unusual. The missing Air Force officer
was evidently living in Moscow and was being recruited for CIA
work. The subject was evidently reluctant to trust anyone and had to
be convinced that his contact in Moscow was really friendly and not a
KGB agent.

Norm settled in for the drive through the lush valleys of Virginia.
After heading west to Winchester he headed north to the Pennsylvania
Turnpike and then west to the New Stanton exit then north to
Greenwood. He checked into an inexpensive motel and after unpacking
looked up the phone number of the subject's brother. He dialed the
number and after a few rings a woman answered.

"May I speak to Tim please," Norm asked.

A minute or two latter a male voice said, "Hello, who's calling?"

"Is this Tim Miller?" Norm asked.

"Yes it is," the voice responded, "Who is this?"

"My name is Major Joseph Barr," Norm answered. "I'm with Air
Force Military Intelligence. I would like to meet with you and ask you a
few questions about your brother Ollie. I would like you to keep this
confidential. We don't have any new information about your brother
but we are collecting information that may help us in the future. Where
and when can we meet? I would like to meet you somewhere other than
your home so that only you are involved. Is that agreeable to you?"

"I guess so," Tim said hesitantly. "I don't know what I can tell you but
I can meet with you this evening after dinner."

"I haven't had dinner myself," Norm replied. "If you can suggest a
place for me to eat I will meet you there after dinner."

"I would recommend Mountain View Inn. It's just east of town on Route 30. They have a nice dinning room and I can meet you in the lobby of the Inn about eight. Is that OK with your?"

"Sounds fine to me," Norm replied. "I will be the old guy with gray hair and glasses. I'll be wearing civilian clothes, a blue sport jacket and gray slacks. This won't take long. Not more than a half an hour. See you at eight."

Norm found the Inn, just off the main road and had an adequate meal in the main dining room. The food was average but the warm ambiance of the room and the outstanding view of the mountains made up for the bland food. He carried his coffee out into the large meandering hotel foyer and found a seat with a view of the front entrance. Promptly at eight a tall dark haired young man, dressed in dark slacks and a sport shirt, entered the front entrance and immediately spotted Norm.

As they shook hands Norm said, "I didn't have any problem spotting you, you look just like the picture of your brother."

"Do you have any identification?" Tim asked. "This certainly is unusual."

Norm opened his brief case and removed an Air Force picture identification badge. He also removed his wallet and produced a driver's license.

"I don't blame you for being skeptical," Norm said. "I would be to in your position."

"Tell me again what you are here for." Tim said as he studied the ID.

Norm removed a few eight by ten photos from his brief case and gave them to Tim.

"We have had a number of photos like this come into our hands. Some from the North Korean government and some from sources that I can't disclose. What we are doing is enlarging the photos to make large copies of each person on the photo. Then we compare it to photos of POW's that have been returned to the States. We go out and talk to the person we have identified and have them tell us as much as he can about the other people in the photo. Eventually we wind up with a few on each photo that we can't identify. Then we try to match the unknowns up with men who are still listed as MIA. If we can ID an MIA then we can go back to the North Koreans and ask them to provide information. If we can return even one MIA it will be worth the effort or expense."

"How can I help?" Tim asked, returning the photos.

"I have a questionnaire," Norm said. "I'm going to ask you some questions and I want you to think about each question and only answer if you are sure you know the answer."

Norm started asking questions, recording the answers on the forms. Most of the questions were about items that would produce identifiable physical signs.

"Did your brother have any physical deformities?"

"Not that I know of."

"Did he ever break any bones?"

"Not when he was at home."

"Did he have any physical scars?"

"Yes, a few that I can remember"

"Tell me about the scars."

"He had a scar about a half-inch long on his forehead just between his eyes."

"How did he get the scar?"

"When we were kids he was standing up on the back of a wagon, facing away from me. He thought that he lost his balance and fell out and hit his head. I had pulled the handle on the wagon and made him fall. I remember that it bled a lot and I never told anyone that I had pulled the handle."

"Any other scars?"

"He had a scar on his right side. He got it swimming at a place we called the Rocks. He dove in to some shallow water and really banged his side on one of the rocks. That one required stitches."

"Any other scars?"

"I remember one other. He was messing around with a chemistry set trying to push an "L" shaped glass tube through a rubber stopper and the tube broke. It went through the part of his right hand between the thumb and the first finger. It bleed for awhile after he pulled the tube out but fortunately didn't do any damage. I haven't thought about any of these since I was a kid."

Norm had enough information to complete his assignment but he continued asking questions until all the answers had been recorded. He collected his papers and put them back into his brief case.

"Thank you for taking the time to talk to me. I don't know if we will ever find your brother but I want you to know that we are still looking. Don't give up hope but don't tell your Mom and Dad. I don't want them to have any false hopes."

"I won't," Tim said, starting to leave. "I don't know if you know this but Ollie was the second from our family not to come home from a war. My older brother was killed during World War II, flying over Germany."

"I was aware of that," Norm said with genuine sympathy. "I hope that someday we can tell you for sure what happened to your brother. Can I buy you a drink?"

"No, I have to get going. I told my wife I was going to find an open hardware store to buy a part I need."

Tim shook Norms extended hand and left. Norm wandered back to the quaint bar that overlooked the dinning room, ordered a drink and spent a pleasant evening drinking and listening to an excellent musician playing the piano in the dining room.

The assignment had been easier than he expected. He had three bits of information that the KGB, no matter how competent, could not possibly have. All he had to do now was get it into the hand of one of the operatives in Russia.

CHAPTER *14*

Sergi had been watching for his drop pick up signal for weeks. This morning Sergi was relieved when he found the signal in his mail slot. After his final class he took his normal route to his apartment. As he rounded a corner near his apartment he had a slight collision with an elderly lady who was hurrying along the sidewalk carrying a few bundles of clothing. When they collided she dropped one of the bundles and Sergi stopped to help her pick up the bundle. As he picked up the bundle he palmed a small container that had been carefully attached to the bundle with a thread. The thread broke easily as he palmed the container. He apologized to the woman and then started down the street. He continued to hold the container in his hand, prepared to discard it at the slightest sign of trouble. He walked the remaining blocks to his apartment and did not even look at the container until he was safely inside his front door. He hurried to the bathroom and withdrew the microfilm from the container and placed it in front of the bathroom light and read it with the help of a magnifying glass. He re-read the message again to make sure he would remember the contents and then lit a match, burned the film and its cardboard container, and flushed the residue down the toilet. He was now ready to talk to Ollie and hoped that information he had just received would convince Ollie that he could trust him.

Tamara and Ollie picked up Helena and Sergi at their apartment on Friday evening and drove out to the country house, arriving after dark. Ollie had been living on the edge for months and the strain showed in his face and voice when he talked to Sergi. At any moment he expected the KGB to appear and arrest him.

While the women were preparing dinner Sergi slipped Ollie a note, telling him that he had some information of interest and that he would talk to him the next day when they were outdoors away from possible recording devices. Ollie read the note, nodded his understanding, and then placed the note into the fire they had started in the fireplace.

They had a pleasant dinner with sparkling conversation and then had an after dinner drink in front of the fireplace.

Tamara started to yawn and stretch sleepily and Helena laughed and said, "Come on Tam, I know you are not sleepy. You just want to start making up for lost time because Ollie has been away. Please do us a favor and keep the moaning and screaming at a reasonable level. Sergi and I would like to get some sleep tonight."

Tamara and Ollie tried to look innocent as they walked up the stairs to the bedrooms. They were in each other's arms before the door closed.

The next morning the men begged off when the woman wanted to go horseback riding.

"You two go," Sergi said, "Ollie and I will just take a walk and enjoy the clean air."

When they had walked a short distance from the house Ollie stopped and looked at Sergi and said, "What do you have to tell me?"

"What I am going to tell you was recently provided by the American government. This is a message from your brother Tim. He said that you had a scar on your forehead that you got when you fell out of a wagon when you were a child. He said that you always thought that you had fallen out but that he had pulled on the handle of the wagon. He was afraid to tell your mother that he had caused the accident. He also said that you had a scar on your right side from an injury that you got swimming at someplace called "The Rocks" and that it required stitches.

One other thing, you were trying to push a glass rod through a rubber stopper during a chemistry experiment and ended up by pushing the broken tube through your right hand near your thumb. I have looked very closely at your forehead and right hand and can't see a real prominent scar and I don't know if there is a scar on your right side. Since I can't see any scars I am sure whoever questioned you while you were under drugs didn't see them either. Even if they did how would I know that your brother caused you to fall out of the wagon? You would be the only one to know he was there when it happened. I know the KGB is good but I know they are not that good. What do you think? Do you need more proof?"

Ollie digested the information for a few minutes and then said, "I don't know that I am one hundred percent convinced but what you have told me does make sense. I have grown out of the scars but I did have them when I was a kid. What if I do believe you? What do you want from me? If you tell me that you are working for the CIA I will probably tell you to go to hell. If you are, you are working for a country that had a chance to get me out of Russia years ago. They denied that I existed and said, even if I did exist, they didn't want me back."

"How do you know that?" Sergi asked.

"They showed me a letter from the State Department," Ollie replied. "I know I wasn't really mentally competent at the time but I know what I saw."

"Don't tell me you believe the KGB. They have been telling you lies since they first captured you. These people are experts. They can make fake documents that would fool even the CIA. How do you know for sure what has taken place? If you want to believe them that is your choice but believe me, these people will do anything to get what they want."

"If the US State Department believes that I exist why don't they just help me get out of Russia?" Ollie asked heatedly.

"If that is what you want I will ask them," Sergi said. "They think you are a valuable asset and could do a lot of good for your country."

"Which country?" Ollie asked angrily. "The one who sent me on a no return mission and to the best of my knowledge considered me expendable and could have cared less about me until I was in position to help them again. Or the country who legally shot me down for violating International Law and then gave me something to do with my life?"

"Ollie, I am going to tell you again that you don't have any idea what your country did after you were shot down. I do know that you have been very carefully brainwashed and now are working for an evil government. You have been living the life of the elite few. Try to spend some time with the people who live in fear every day. They are afraid to say or do anything that could cause them to disappear without a trace. If you want to continue working for Russia or want me to try to get you out, it will be your choice."

Ollie was silent for a few minutes and then said, "I will ask you again, what do you want from me?"

"All you have to do is tell me what you are doing and what you see and hear. You don't have to actively look for anything or write anything. You will just tell me and I will get the information to the correct people."

"There has to be more to it than that," Ollie said skeptically. "What happens if you are discovered or just disappear? What do I do?"

"We will establish a protocol that will give you advance warning if any thing is about to happen to me. I have an escape procedure and so would you. We have established various safe places where we can go for pick up and extraction. I will tell you that I have contacts inside the KGB that will give advance warning. I can't give any guarantees but I trust my life to the escape procedure everyday."

"If the US won't get me out now, and that is my first preference, what do I do a year from now when I am tired of playing spy and want to get out? Also, what is happening to my Air Force pay and time served?"

"I don't know but I promise to find out." Sergi truthfully replied.

"I will think about it while you get the answers to my questions. I am also going to give you the names and addresses of some fellow American airmen I knew in Irkutsk. I want to know what happened to them."

Ollie went back to work and in his spare time reviewed his options a hundred times. He could stay status quo and live his life in Russia with Tamara sharing his destiny.

He could also join Sergi and be a spy while still maintaining the life in Russia.

Or, if Sergi could arrange it, he could leave Russia and go back to the States. This was his first choice; he still had family in the US. They probably thought he was dead so it would be a source of joy for his family if he returned.

His only regret would be leaving Tamara. Beside the deep affection that he had developed he knew that she would be in danger the moment he defected. It was the hardest decision he had ever had to make and each day he changed his mind.

He knew that information he provided would be helpful to any enemy of Russia. He was right in the middle of new technological developments and the politics of dealing with foreign governments who were buying aircraft and training from the USSR. His relationship with Tamara's father also provided an insight into the Russian political process.

A month after their last discussion Sergi and Ollie had time alone while watching a soccer game at Sergi's university. The women had decided to stay home and talk while the men watched the game.

There weren't many spectators at the game so it was easy to pick seats away from other people.

"I have answers to your questions," Sergi said while looking straight ahead at the game in progress. "They will not jeopardize me and my network to get you out. They feel that the KGB would surely launch a full investigation of your activities that would flush my network and me. They didn't say this but I think it would also put Tamara in danger. The only way they would take you out would be if they took me out at the same time and they are not willing to do that. I hope you understand their thinking. I knew your leaving would be a problem for me and possibly my network.

They also guaranteed that you would be continued as active in the Air Force. They have already notified your family that you are presumed dead and have paid them your death benefits and insurance. If anything does happen to you, they will make a lump sum payment to your family. I would depend on circumstances at the time as to whether or not they disclose what you have been doing."

"That limits my choices to two," Ollie said sadly. "I don't have much enthusiasm but I guess I'm in."

"I'm pleased with your decision," Sergi said, patting him on the knee. "Let's get started with procedures."

"What did you find out about the American airmen?" Ollie asked.

"All I can tell you is that they are listed as MIA," Sergi said apologetically.

"Is that all? Did they at least get somebody to ask the Russians why they are in prison in Russia?"

"Think about that for a minute," Sergi said. "What if the US starts demanding answers about a bunch of Americans that were at Irkutsk when you were there? How long do you think it would take the KGB to deduce that you may have had something to do with the inquiry and start to wonder how you got the word out? I am sorry, Ollie, you are going to have to start thinking like the KGB, otherwise we will both be dead and gone in no time."

Sergi spent the next hour discussing operating procedures and answering questions. When he had completed his instructions he started asking Ollie questions to make sure Ollie had completely understood. A lack of knowledge could be fatal to both of them.

At the end of the session Ollie asked, "How did you get started in this messy business?"

"I will give you the short version," Sergi said, rising and stretching to relieve the muscle tension in his arms and legs. "I spent World War II in Washington D.C.. My father was a Russian rep for the lend lease program. After the war ended he stayed in the US for five years and was listed as an importer/exporter. Actually he was still in the business of trying to get all kinds of help to Russia after the war.

When Senator Joe McCarthy started his hearings we headed back to Russia.

The entire time I was in the US I attended your schools. I came back to the US and got a teaching degree. What I didn't know till just a few years ago was that my father was very active in back channel politics. Many problems where worked out to our mutual advantages by people like my father, who were not identified as emissaries, and unusual people like news paper reporters, taking the time to try to understand and resolve problems by unofficial negotiations.

To get on with the story, I became friendly with a well-known news personality who had been a friend of my father. When I went back to school in the US he sort of looked after me. During summer breaks I would go back to Russia. While I was here I became more aware of the harshness of our government as compared to your free society. During my senior year in college I was discussing events in Russia with my patron and he asked if I would be willing to help normalize life in Russia. I said yes and the next thing you know I am back here teaching English and American History in Lomonusov State

University and providing information to your country. I can't see how I have contributed anything as yet. I just hope I live long enough to see some democracy in Russia."

"I don't see how I will be contributing anything either," Ollie said. "I'm not the least bit interested in politics. All I ever wanted to do is fly. I guess the only thing that will motivate me is knowing that I may help some kid to do what he wants to do without the government being involved."

Life did not change much for Ollie after his decision to help Sergi. He kept focused on his duties and kept his eyes and ears open when around the staff officers and foreigners.

The late 1950's were troubled times for the free world. Ollie had passed on information that was already known in the US. The Russians had perfected the nuclear bomb and had developed the hydrogen bomb. What the US probably wasn't totally aware of was the progress the Soviets were making for delivering the bombs. Ollie had passed on information about long range bomber production and the new Soviet developments in inter-continental ballistic missiles. He was sure the Soviet successful launch of Sputnik into orbit had placed fear into the hearts of the non-Soviet world.

Ollie had been lobbying to get into the space program. He knew that the Russians were planning to place a man into orbit in the early sixties and he wanted to join in that ultimate flying adventure. Instead he was assigned to the Soviet Arms Control team. General Gaidar, learning of Ollie's disappointment in not being selected for space cosmonaut training, called him into his office and explained how important it was to have him on the arms control team. He would be invaluable in observing the Americans, particularly when they were socializing in the evenings.

When Ollie first read the Soviets Arms Control Plan he started to shake his head in disbelief. He asked to see the general and when he was admitted to his office said, "I don't think the Americans will take this proposal seriously. We are going to ask them to reduce their nuclear arsenal to nothing and we are going to promise to do the same. The first thing they will ask for is witnessing and inspecting our disarmament activities. Are you willing to let them in to witness and inspect our secret facilities?"

"Of course we are not going to let them in. But who knows what the Americans will accept. They are not very adept at negotiations. Look at what Stalin accomplished with Hitler and later Roosevelt and Churchill. They all thought Stalin was an ignorant peasant and they literally gave him millions of square miles of land and all its potential. Believe me, our negotiators aren't stupid. Also, we have a lot of influential Americans convinced that they are facing nuclear destruction."

It took months to set up the first meeting. Just as Ollie predicted, the Americans insisted on inspection to verify compliance with treaty terms. The Russians ignored the request and focused in on disclosure of assets. The negotiations quickly broke down and the meetings were terminated. After many months of negotiations by mail and telephone another attempt was made to have face to face meetings. This time the conference was held in Paris, France.

One evening after dinner he found himself exchanging small talk with a young, pale blonde member of the American team. The man, George Plankton, was an extremely nervous person. Ollie had noticed that he had little to say during the talks. Anytime either side said anything about the dangers inherent in both sides maintaining a growing nuclear arsenal, Ollie observed George nodding in agreement. During a discussion with Ollie the American actually said, "I couldn't believe what they are making my children do in school. They have actually shown them movie pictures of a nuclear bomb test and made them practice getting under their desks if their is a bright flash.

They have my kids scared to death. They are smart enough to know that if a bomb goes off they will be dead or worse. Somebody has to put an end to this madness."

Ollie had to suppress a smile, Talk *about negotiating from a point of weakness. This guy would totally surrender tomorrow and be happy if he and his kids were slaves as long as they were alive.*

The next evening a chill went up Ollie's spine when an American he had talked to a few times said, "Do they play much baseball in Russia?"

It was the month's recognition code, given to him by Sergi before he left Moscow.

Ollie gave the correct response, "No; it's not one of our sports. What team do you like?"

The correct answer came back, "I'm a Yankee fan."

They continued to discuss sports while they walked around the room and finally stopped where they were away from walls and furniture.

"Notice anything interesting?" The American asked.

"I think George would surrender tomorrow. Also I have noticed him talking to one of our team who I know is KGB. Better keep an eye on him. Also, my people think you are weak. They respect strength and all you people have projected so far is wishy-washy weakness."

They continued their discussion for a few minutes more and then parted and sought others to talk with.

At the debriefing the KGB officer in charge asked, "What were you and the American talking about?"

"Just small talk." Ollie replied easily. "He wanted to know if we played baseball in Russia. I am afraid he didn't find me too interesting."

At the third series of meetings George was missing from the American team and Ollie noticed a definite stiffening of the American posture.

After the third series of meetings Ollie had a long discussion with the general. He convinced him that he was not contributing anything to the process and asked again to be transferred to the Space Program, where he thought he could contribute something. He refrained from saying that all the useless talk was boring.

The Air Marshall knew the real reason for his request and said, "I didn't think you were destined to be a diplomat. You are more interested in hardware than talk. I will see what I can do."

Ollie was at the Baikonur Cosmodrome, the Russian space center in barren, dusty south central Kazakhstan, on April 12, 1961, when they launched Yury Gagarin, the first man into space. Ollie had stared east into the disappearing cloud of smoke until the smoke disappeared, marveling at the intestinal fortitude necessary to sit on top of a rocket.

In the early sixties the Russian space program launched a three-man space capsule with Komarov, Yegorov and Feoktiston aboard. They landed after fifteen orbits.

Komarov became the first Russian cosmonaut to die when a Soyuz parachute line twisted and his capsule crashed.

During the same period Valentina Tereshkova became the first woman cosmonaut and Aleksei Leonov became the first man to walk in space.

Valentina was a close friend of Tamara's. Both were notified on the same date that they had been selected to join the space program. Tamara had her father intercede on her behalf. "I don't want to be passenger on a computer controlled flight," she told her father, "I want to fly. If they ever want somebody to actually fly something in space I might be interested." It took some diplomatic maneuvering by her father but Tamara got her way and did not enter the space program.

Ollie was assigned to the Cosmodrome periodically during the space program, first staying in Tyuratam and then in the bleak, dusty new town of Leninsk that sprung up outside the space facility.

The Cosmodrome was in an area of low lying plains in south central Kazakhstan. Most of the Russian nuclear testing had been conducted west of the Space Facility near Semey and the Caspian Sea. Visitors avoided that area of the state.

On the rare occasions when Tamara could visit Ollie when he was assigned to the space center, they would spend their free time in Almaty, the capital of Kazakhstan, near the states eastern border. In contrast to the bleakness of the Space Center, Almaty was a visually delightful, cosmopolitan place to visit. The city had an opera and Ballet Company, a symphony orchestra, state university and an Academy of Science.

A major part of the Soviet Nuclear Arsenal was stored at the Space Center. Few news people were invited to the center and security was extremely heavy. Ollie did not make direct inquiries about the nuclear weapons stored there but he was very observant when he had the opportunity to travel through the storage area or when he was talking to the military in charge of the arsenal. He relayed the meager amount of information he was able to obtain to Sergi when he returned to Moscow.

When Russian intelligence reported that the Americans were installing ballistic missiles with nuclear warheads in Turkey, Khrushhchev was livid with anger. His advisors soon came up with an answer, send Russian missiles to Cuba.

When the Cuban missile crisis started in 1962, life became hectic for both Tamara and Ollie. Tamara's squadron was at full time alert in the east and Ollie was working twenty hours a day helping to get the Ballistic Missile Command to peak readiness for either a pre-emptive strike or a quick response. He was kept so busy that he had little time or opportunity to tell Sergi what was going on. He only hoped that Sergi's other assets were providing information and that clearer heads would prevail.

He knew that the Americans were blockading Cuba and that several Russian vessels were being kept from unloading. He was also aware that the young American president was talking very tough and threatening to attack Cuba and Russia. In the back channels a deal was cut. Russia would remove the missiles from Cuba if the American missiles were removed from Turkey. The world was only advised of the Russian removal of missiles. To the world the tough American president had won. The Russians laughed themselves silly as they hoisted their vodka. It had been so easy to remove a real threat.

Their joy was short lived. The Americans developed another weapon that neutralized the Soviet missile threat. The US started launching one ballistic missile carrying nuclear submarines a month. Soon the Russians were surrounded by enemy nuclear subs with nuclear tipped missiles that could strike anywhere in Russia. The subs were virtually undetectable and constantly on the move. The Russians recognized the stalemate and began to develop nuclear powered attack and missile subs to counter, but the immediate threat of nuclear war diminished.

CHAPTER *15*

Tokyo, Japan, 1962

Yoshida Makoto, CEO of Makoto International, met Mary Miller at the front door of the modern Makoto building in Tokyo on her first day of work. He personally guided her to her new office and then to the office of each of his vice-presidents. He gracefully introduced Mary to her new peers, carefully smoothing the feathers of each of the men as he introduced his new vice-president. After returning her to her new office he introduced her to Ruth Longware Shigeru, Mary's new assistant.

After Yoshida departed Mary and Ruth, a petite redhead with a charming array of freckles, sat in Mary's office and became acquainted. Ruth had been a secretary at UCLA when she met Saito Shigeru, a student at the University. They had married just after Saito received his Masters in Business Administration. After Saito's service in Italy with the US Army during World War II, Saito and Ruth had moved to Japan and worked for the post war Redevelopment Council. When Shigeru was promoted, Ruth and Saito agreed that Ruth's working for Saito would be considered inappropriate so she applied for a job at Makoto.

The two women formed an instant friendship that carried out of the office environment.

On that first day Ruth walked Mary through the entire complex, introducing her to the people who, as she put it, really got the work done in the banking, development, manufacturing and brokerage business of Makoto International.

Like most businesses, the Table of Organization and titles of the workers did not reflect who ran the business. People who worked in small cubbyholes or offices made sometimes-major decisions. As Makato grew larger in size and scope, managers were hired and the staff was continuously reorganized. The only thing that made the business successful was the sometimes-clandestine communication across organizational lines on the organizational chart. Ruth knew the real movers and decision-makers in the organization and provided Mary with a real chart of the way Makoto operated and then introduced her to the power managers. The lesson was invaluable.

Back in his office Yashida Makoto was gleefully arranging a dinner party for his new vice president. He had met Mary when she was president of the Yamagutshi Bank and had admired her talent and dignified good looks. When he learned that Shurio's two sons had cashiered Mary out of the business he could not understand their stupidity. Even though Shurio was a competitor he had been a friend and Yashida had praised Mary's contributions to Shuiro's company. The day Mary was fired at Yamagutshi, Yashida had called her at her apartment and offered her a vice-presidency. Now she was working for him and he was delighted.

Makoto's perception proved to be correct. When the business community learned that Mary was working for Makoto, they started moving business from Yamagutshi to Makoto. Makoto, who was known to be a very serious man, smiled broadly every time he passed Mary or her office. *How wise I have been,* he congratulated himself. *This stroke of luck makes up for a lot of stupid things I have done in the past.*

Within a year the banking end of Makoto International had increased twenty five percent, a number that surprised even Yoshida.

He had another ploy that he was exploring. He had two of the most respected lawyers in Tokyo reviewing the legal aspects of Mary losing her one-third share of Yamagutshi's holdings. So far the results were positive. If he could get the court ruling reversed, Mary would profit financially and he would have a vice president who owned one third of his biggest competitor's business. The possibilities were exciting.

Mary had forgotten the bitterness she had felt when Shurio's sons unceremoniously dumped her. At first she dreamed of revenge, not so much because of the money. She was proud of the contribution she had made to the success in Shurio's business and the reputation she had developed. Her quick hire by Makoto had let her forgive and forget. Each succeeding year brought increasing success and recognition to Mary. Her life had stabilized to the point where she had begun to think about a reunion with Kevin.

Contact with her son had diminished to an occasional note from Ollie's brother who was now Kevin's guardian. Mary had intensified the communications with Kevin's uncle and had started to receive friendlier letters in return. The pictures she received showed a maturing Kevin. Her son was starting to look just like Ollie when they had first met.

From Uncle Tim's letters she learned that Kevin was an excellent student and athlete. She also knew that Tim was having a difficult time providing for his family so she restarted sending monthly checks to help with expenses. Mary was in the process of arraigning for Kevin's college tuition and a possible trip to Japan.

She was aware, from her correspondence with Kevin's guardians, that Kevin had grown into a self-sufficient young man who still deeply resented his mother's abandonment. Kevin had not written her for years and in his last letter, when he was twelve, had bitterly stated that he would never forgive her. At first the letter had been very distressing to Mary. However, after deep thought she realized that Kevin's position was justifiable. She had indeed abandoned him to pursue her own life after it was obvious that Ollie would never be found. *If he won't come here to see me,* Mary thought, *I will ask for a leave of absence and go back to the States and try to make up for my mistakes.*

Mary's social life had improved. In addition to the many company functions she attended, with the help of Ruth, she was developing a new circle of Japanese and American friends. They were fond of partying and traveling. Mary had moved into an upscale apartment building in one of the best sections of Tokyo.

Mary let herself into her apartment, returning from the second party she had been invited to on the weekend. She made her way to her bedroom and debated on taking a shower before going to bed and then wearily decided to wait till morning. She undressed, set her alarm clock, and fell into bed. Within minutes she was sleeping so deeply that she did not hear her front door opening. Two intruders made their way cautiously to Mary's bedroom.

Before Mary knew what was happening one of the men jumped up on the bed and pinned her to the mattress. The other forced her arm upward and slipped a syringe into her armpit and forced the fluid from the syringe into her body. There was a second of fear on her face and then it contorted in pain and her body started to convulse and she was unconscious.

The men waited for a few minutes and then the man who had made the injection felt Mary's pulse and then nodded to the other man. They carefully retreated from the apartment, checking to assure that they were not leaving anything behind. One of the men cracked open the front door and after checking for clearance, both men departed down the internal fire escape and were back on the street undetected. The entire efficient operation had been completed in five minutes.

When Mary did not show up for work on Monday Ruth started calling her apartment. When she had not reported by lunch time and still didn't answer her phone Ruth Called Yoshida Makoto and asked if he had sent Mary to a meeting somewhere. When he answered negatively she really began to worry. She called Mary's apartment for the twentieth time just before the close of business. When she didn't answer Ruth called Yoshida and he told her to meet him in front of the building in ten minutes. When she arrived at the front door, Yashido's car and driver were waiting. As soon as Yashido arrived she directed them to Mary's apartment.

Ruth located the building manager and the trio entered the elevator and exited at Mary's floor. Ruth rang the front door chimes and when she didn't answer the manager opened the door. As soon as the door opened they knew from the odor that something terrible had happened. They searched the apartment. Yashido placed a handkerchief over his mouth and nose and was the first into the bedroom. He quickly retreated and picked up the phone and called the police.

Ruth hesitated at the bedroom door and then entered apprehensively. Mary was lying in the bed; her dead eyes open in her contorted blue face. Her sphincter had released her body fluids and the odor was overwhelming. Ruth began to sob and gag and ran from the room. The group moved to the hall outside the apartment and the manager went down in the elevator to meet the police. The police arrived and started taking information from a shaken Ruth and Yashido. They stayed in the hall until Mary's body was removed.

The doctor who performed the autopsy ruled that Mary's death was caused by a massive heart attack; a conclusion that befuddled both Ruth and Yashido. Ruth thought that Mary had been in excellent health. Yashido knew she was. He had personally reviewed the results of her management pre-employment physical with the examining doctor. At Yashido's insistence, he was allowed to hire another doctor to perform an independent autopsy. The conclusions were the same; death caused by a heart attack.

When the Makoto lawyers, acting for Mary, opened her safe deposit box, they found her will. It named a lawyer in the law firm where she had placed Kevin's trust fund, as executors of her estate. Following the instructions in the will, Mary was cremated and her ashes strewn in the park near her apartment where she and Ollie used to walk.

The executor started the process of delivering Mary's estate to Kevin.

If either of the doctors who had performed the autopsies had been more observant they would have found the needle mark in Mary's armpit. The discovery could possibly have led to an investigation into who would have benefited by her death.

The combination of the cremation and incompetence of the medical examiner and the police would forever disallow an investigation that would have provided justice. Yoshida suspected foul play but could not convince the police to start an investigation. If the police had been competent and investigated the scene they may have discovered evidence that would have led them to the two men who entered Mary's apartment. They were members of Jakuza, the Japanese Mafia backed Jiken crime specialists, for hire to anyone who had money. That trail would have led them to the Yamagutshi brothers who were no longer threatened by the potential loss of one third of their empire.

CHAPTER *16*

North Vietnam, 1967

When the new American president, Lyndon Johnson, assumed office, after John Kennedy was assassinated, the Americans got more deeply involved in Vietnam.

The Russians, as expected, backed the North Vietnamese, providing conventional weapons and ammunition.

When the American increased their participation and started flying aircraft over North Vietnam, the NV asked the Russians for anti-aircraft weapons and instructors. When Russia started sending Surface to Air Missiles to NV, with radar tracking and firing control, Ollie was sent as a technical advisor.

Of all the woebegone places in the world where Ollie had been stationed, as an American and as a Russian, Ollie despised Vietnam the most. He had lived in dusty, barren, hot hellholes and rock cold frozen outposts, but Vietnam, in his view, was the nadir of the world. He hated the heat and the humidity. It was almost impossible to breathe. When you sucked in the damp air you also sucked in the putrid smell of the jungle and untreated sewage.

The food was abominable and you could almost see the amoebae swimming in the water. When he first arrived he made the mistake of drinking the water and was rewarded with a month long bout of dysentery.

It was not as bad when he was in his apartment in Hanoi. He could buy local vegetables and cook them and drink wine instead of water. He also found a source of bottled water that he could use for tea and after a year of pleading finally got a portable water distillation device for his apartment. His apartment was a one-room efficiency near what was once the living area of diplomats. The furnishings were aged and decrepit and the plumbing was unreliable.

He spent the major part of his time in the jungle, setting up surface to air missile sites and radar equipment. Life in these remote camps was primitive and dangerous. Aside from the distinct probability of dying from food poisoning or dysentery, poisonous and dangerous vermin and insects inhabited the jungle camps. Worst were the huge river rats that nested near the brown water creeks and rivers. He hated being awakened from a light sleep by one of the rats crawling over some part of his body. Like most of the jungle villagers he kept a stick within easy reach while sleeping, to club the rats.

All of these discomforts were minor compared to his dealings with the Vietnamese military. They where crude and cruel. After four hundred years of domination by Europeans, they hated all white people, including people like Ollie who were in their country to help. They were disrespectful and haughty and openly resented being put in a position where they had to take instructions from him. They took every opportunity to make him as uncomfortable as possible.

After two years of hell with few days off, Ollie was contacted by his superiors in Moscow and was relieved of his duties as a technical advisor. He remained in North Vietnam as an investigator, interviewing American airmen who had been shot down and captured and then moved to Hanoi prisons. He made occasional trips into the jungle to interview prisoners being held in primitive jungle prisons.

When he was in the prisons he interviewed the prisoners, prying information out of the battered and distressed Americans. Most of them showed complete deference to his questioning and told him to take a hike or worse. His primary source of information came when a prisoner lapsed into temporary periods of mental discontinuity. Ollie would cajole and sympathize and sometimes secured information that would not have otherwise been obtained.

He had been recording the names and serial numbers of every prisoner that he interviewed. He wrote the information in code and hid the information behind a loose brick in the apartment.

Three years after his arrival in North Vietnam a Vietnamese agent of the CIA contacted him. He was walking in the park that surrounded Hoan Kiem Lake in the center of Hanoi when he was bumped into by a slight Asian of indefinite age. The man apologized profusely in Vietnamese and during the exchange pressed a note into Ollie's hand. As he started to leave he said in a barely discernible whisper, "Your friends in the Fifth miss you"

It had been so long since Sergi had given him the recognition code that he almost forgot the response. Also, the sudden contact had caught him off guard. The slight Vietnamese man hesitated for a minute and was about to break off the contact when Ollie recovered and said, "Even Bill?"

The correct response, "Yes, and Bob too." came back instantly and the man turned and rapidly walked away.

Ollie walked a few blocks, palming the note before he thrust it into his pocket. He was relieved that he had been contacted. He had three years of information to transfer. For the first time since being recruited by the CIA he had information that would be of immediate help to the US. He hated the Vietnamese for the inhumane treatment being imposed on their American prisoners.

When he was safely in his apartment he took the note out of his pocket and carefully unfolded the paper. It was a simple note containing only a place, date and time.

On the day and time written on the note, Ollie was apparently out for his usual nightly walk near the old Great Buddha Pagoda. He spotted his contact just ahead walking away from him at about the same pace. After several changes in direction the Vietnamese man stepped into an alley and waited for Ollie. As soon as Ollie turned into the alley the contact opened a door and motioned Ollie into a dark courtyard.

"It's very good. My men say you have not been followed. Come with me."

The slim man opened a door into a first floor apartment and after closing the door turned on a single, low wattage light bulb. He extended his hand and smiled.

"Lieutenant Miller, it is good to meet you at last. It's best if you do not know my real name, Just call me Ti, okay?"

"I'm glad that you have contacted me. I have been collecting information for three years and have been afraid that I would never get the information out." Ollie said, grasping the outstretched hand.

"We have much to do then," Ti said as he sat down at a table. "We have to establish the usual procedures for contact and drops. Any time we have to meet either of us can initiate the request and I will make the arrangements for where and when. We also have to establish emergency procedures for immediate requests and transfers and for bailout if either of us is discovered. I will be your only face to face contact but we do have quite a large network here and we are capable of major actions if required."

They spent the next hour establishing procedures and recognition signals.

Ollie made plans for a major drop of information in three days. That would give him some time to prepare the information. For the next few evenings on his walk Ollie made it a point to buy the Nhan Dan newspaper and sit in Hoan Kiem Lake Park while he read the paper. The night of the drop Ollie folded sheets of paper and placed them inside his jungle fatigue jacket. He had been transcribing the location of SAM and radar sites and the type of equipment installed. He also tried to identify the strengths and weaknesses of the operators. The information was in a simple code that had been provided by Ti.

The evening of the drop he started on his evening walk, purchased his newspaper and sat on a bench in the park to read. While he was rear-ranging the papers, getting ready to leave, he slipped his notes inside the paper. He got up and continued his walk, observing Vietnamese with identifiable clothing to pick up their "go" signals. They were monitoring for possible surveillance. Just as Ollie turned a dark corner a Vietnamese woman walking in the opposite direction removed a paper from her loose blouse, handed it to Ollie as he brushed by, as Ollie handed her his paper. The paper disappeared into her blouse. The exchange was made in less than half a second, in stride, and was not detectable to Ti who was walking on the other side of the street.

The information transfer was usually from Ollie to the outside. Ollie would leave a sign that he had information to transfer and the transfer was made, never in the same place or in the same way.

When they would have to change operations Ti would meet with Ollie and the next month's schedule and routines would be established.

Ollie transmitted the names, serial numbers and locations of each of the American prisoners that he interviewed.

Ti had obtained anti-biotics and morphine for Ollie. Ollie had a kit provided to him by the Russians containing the truth inducing drug and syringes. He used the truth serums on occasion but did inject antibiotics in prisoners with infections at every opportunity. When he could he injected severely injured prisoners with morphine to relieve their pain.

Ollie also started to pass on the locations of the jungle prison camps, hoping that some thing would be done to extract the Americans being systematically tortured before they died.

On his last visit into a new jungle camp he was surprised to find that there were only seven prisoners in the small camp. Even more startling was the rank of the prisoners. They were all Air Force officers with rank of lieutenant colonel or above. One of the prisoners was a one star general. Ollie had no idea how they had been captured but they were all in deteriorating health. He talked to the Vietnamese officer in charge of the camp who advised him that he suspected that the prisoners could provide important information that would be of interest to both of their countries. Ollie interrogated all the officers and did not obtain any information other than name, rank and serial number.

When he returned to Hanoi he passed the information on the prisoners, as well as the location of the camp and a rough map of the camp layout, to Ti for transmittal.

He wasn't surprised when he did not have any feedback on his transmittal. He never did. Occasionally he would be asked to provide additional information but he was never told what was done with his information. He assumed that the SAM locations would help save American lives. He was unaware of any attempts to extract prisoners.

On several occasions he observed people who looked like Americans in Hanoi. He would ask Ti to identify the "tourists". When Ti told him they were anti-war Americans who were leading the protesters in the States, Ollie could not believe him. It was so frustrating. He wanted to drag the Americans into the NV prisons and show them how Americans were being systematically tortured, starved and killed. Even though he had been away for almost twenty years he knew that the American military would not be mistreating prisoners. He wanted to expose the inhumane cruelty of the North Vietnamese military and was frustrated by his inability to provide direct help.

Two months after he had transmitted information about the camp with only seven prisoners, the commandant of the Hanoi Vietnamese prison, called the Hanoi Hilton by its prisoners, informed Ollie that the jungle camp with the high ranking American officers had been

G. B. Mooney

attacked. An American force had taken out the prisoners. They had captured one officer from the American removal team and they wanted Ollie to interrogate him to determine how the camp was spotted, the raid accomplished and the kind of equipment used.

The next day Ollie's Vietnamese driver picked him up at his apartment and they started the long, hot drive through the dank jungle to the camp. When they approached the clearing in the jungle he saw that the camp had been seriously damaged in the attack. The observation towers were down and there were many large holes in the camp buildings. The only building undamaged, except for the door that had been blown off, was the building that had housed the prisoners.

Terrific job, Ollie said to himself as he got out of the car to meet the agitated camp commandant.

`"The prisoner we captured was a US Marine officer," the commandant said. "He was taken up the river to the next camp. I could not get any information out of him. He was wounded and not entirely coherent. Maybe you can pry some information out of him. I wouldn't waste any time here. I don't think he will live very long."

The little Vietnamese officer dismissed Ollie with a wave of his hand and went back to haranguing the enlisted men that were repairing the camp.

Ollie got back into the car and gave his driver directions to the next camp. As they drove through the jungle canopy on a crude road that followed the Song Coi River Ollie considered the fate of the camp commander. *If I was in that mans position I would be heading south*, Ollie said to himself, *His boss will probably put a bullet in his head within a week*

After an hour of bouncing along the jungle trail in the stifling heat they finally arrived at the camp where the American prisoner was being held. Ollie presented himself to the camp commander and told him that he had been ordered by the Hanoi commandant of prisoner camps to interview the captured American. The commander rose without speaking and pointed to a hut across from his office.

Ollie walked across the dirt road and passed the guard outside the hut and entered the hut. After his eyes got accustomed to the damp darkness of the windowless hut, he saw a blood stained figure dressed in badly torn Marine jungle fatigues, laying in the corner, obviously unconscious and barely breathing. The back of his fatigues was coated with blood that was still oozing out of several wounds on his back and legs.

Ollie rolled the prisoner over and was shocked by the condition of his face. His nose had been crushed, probably by a rifle butt, and there was a festering wound in his cheek that had probably been inflicted by a knife.

The prisoner's face was contorted in pain, even though he was unconscious. Ollie tried to visualize what he would have looked like before his injuries. He had a slight frame, probably about six feet two and one hundred eighty pounds, short military cut coal black hair, a fair complexion that had been tanned by many hours in the field and probably, before having his nose broken, had been a very handsome young man. As Ollie was looking at the prisoner's face an unexplainable eerie feeling started to possess his body. He could not rationalize or describe the feeling, but it was so strong that he began to tremble. Finally he realized that the reaction had to be from being near the prisoner. This was unusual for he had seen many badly wounded Americans. Although he always felt compassion, the feeling he was experiencing was new. He reached inside the prisoners fatigue jacket and with trembling hands pulled out the prisoner's dog tags. He turned them over and held them so the light coming in the door would make the stamped name visible.

He blinked his eyes and squinted and read the name several times and then sank to the floor beside the prisoner.

The stamped name on the dog tags read "KEVIN O MILLER".

CHAPTER *17*

North Vietnam, 1971

It took a few minutes for Ollie to clear his head. He knew that the young marine was his son. The KGB had lied to him when they said his wife and son had been killed in a plane crash. He was furious. You son-of-a-bitch, Valeriy," he said out loud, "I'm going to track you down and kill you."

He pushed the thoughts of revenge from his mind. His son was near death and somehow he had to do something to save him.

The guard outside the door heard Ollie's outburst and came inside the hut.

"What's wrong?" He asked. "Should I go get the camp commander?"

"Yes, get him." Ollie responded.

It took a few minutes for the commander to arrive, giving Ollie time to formulate a plan.

"What is your problem?" The commander demanded as he stomped into the hut.

"This man is dying," Ollie replied calmly. "I think I can get valuable information from him if I keep him alive. I'm going to take him back to Hanoi."

"I can't let you do that," the commander said with authority. "Besides, you won't get information from him. I have already tried."

To himself Ollie said, yes, *and someday I will track you down and you will pay for this.*

To the commander he said, "I'm taking him. Call Hanoi if you want to. I'll sign a statement that I'm responsible for this man, but I am taking him with me."

Ollie turned and walked away and found his driver. They loaded the injured prisoner into the back seat of the car. Ollie got out his medical kit and gave Kevin a syringe full of antibiotics and a strong shot of morphine.

They drove back to the commander's office and Ollie signed a statement of responsibility.

Kevin was unconscious on the long trip back to Hanoi. They arrived in Hanoi just after midnight.

"Drive to you house," Ollie instructed his driver. "There is no use your being up all night. I'll drive to the prison and drop the prisoner off and take care of the paper work."

The driver thanked him profusely. It had been a long day and his new young wife would be happy to see him.

Ollie stopped at his own apartment and picked up a blanket and put it in the back seat. He gave Kevin another shot of antibiotics and morphine and then drove to the main gate of the prison. When the gate guard stopped him he said, "I have a prisoner to deliver from a jungle camp to the infirmary."

The guard walked around the car and opened the door and looked at Kevin.

"Wait here. I will get the papers for you to sign." The guard said.

He returned in a few minutes and had Ollie complete and sign a document and then opened the gate.

Ollie drove into the compound and stopped the car in front of the prisoner infirmary. He opened the door and found an attendant sitting behind a desk.

The attendant looked up and recognized Ollie.

"You are up late tonight," he said sleepily.

G. B. Mooney

"Just dropped in to see if anyone interesting came in today." Ollie said.

"Two pilots came in today. I think they were shot down a couple days ago. Both of them are in bad condition. I don't think you can question them but you can try."

Ollie nodded his head and started into the infirmary room and the attendant went back and sat down at his desk.

Ollie examined both the men. He knew that neither would live till morning. He reached into his pocket and retrieved the dog tags he had taken from Kevin earlier. Ollie walked around the bed so that he had a clear view of the attendant. He reached into the collar of the flight suit of the prisoner lying on the bed and removed his dog tags and replaced them with Kevin's.

As he passed the attendant he said, "You are right. I won't get any information from them."

When he got back to his car he rolled Kevin down to the floor of the car and covered him with the dark blanket.

The guard opened the gate and motioned him through without even glancing into the back seat.

Ollie breathed a sigh of relief as he drove back to his apartment. He had lots to do but so far all was going well.

He pulled up to the front of his apartment and sat for awhile, carefully checking each window and doorway for signs of people. When he was sure no one was watching he opened the back door of the car and with great difficulty got Kevin up on his shoulders in a fireman's carry. As quickly as he could, he carried Kevin into his apartment, cussing silently as he banged Kevin's head on the doorframe. He placed him on the couch and covered him with a blanket.

Next he had to contact Ti and make arrangements to transport Kevin out of the country.

The signal for an emergency meeting, this week, was leaving a broken pencil in a specific place, known only to Ollie and Ti, near the One Pillar Pagoda. Ollie drove to within a few blocks of the drop point and parked the car. He stepped out of the car and took a flask containing vodka from his pocket and took a small sip and then faked taking a long drink. He left the car and started to walk a little unsteadily, wandering aimlessly and stopping occasionally to take another swig from the flask. If any one was watching or noticed him they would think that he was a little tipsy. He made the drop and then wandered back to his car and drove, noticeably erratically, back to apartment and went to bed.

The next morning he checked Kevin to be sure he was still alive and then gave him another shot of anti-biotic and morphine.

He ate a light breakfast of fruit and bread and then got in his car and drove to the message point to see if his emergency message had been received. It had, so he walked to the assigned area and spotted Ti walking ahead of him. They continued walking in the same general direction until they were both advised that they were clear. Ti ducked into an alleyway and Ollie followed him down the alleyway and through a gate into a garden and into a house.

"What is the emergency?" Ti asked.

Ollie explained that he had to get someone out of Vietnam and deliver him to the American military.

Ti immediately started to object. "That is not our mission," Ti said. "Even if it were it would take a long time to work out the details and get approval."

"We don't have a long time. This man is going to die if we don't get him out right away."

"Why is this man so important?" Ti demanded.

"It's my son. I found him by accident in a jungle prison camp." Ollie said, looking into Ti's confused eyes.

Ti's expression changed to comprehension and he started to walk out the door. As he left, he stopped and looked at Ollie. "I'll see what I can do. Look for me in the next designated place tonight at eight. "

Saigon, South Vietnam

James Wilson had been running covert CIA operations from Saigon for two years. Before that he had been undercover in just about every country in Europe. The stocky, muscular Wilson, dressed in jungle combat fatigues, looked more like a tough combat commander than an administrative officer. The two years in Southeast Asia, starting in field operations, had toughened him both mentally and physically. In his job he had to be tough and disciplined. He made difficult life and death decisions daily.

He was quite pleased with the network he had established in North Vietnam. The information they had been providing, for the most part, had been highly valuable. His operatives were mostly catholic anti-communists Vietnamese who had been living in North Vietnam their entire lives. Because they hated the Communists they had been relatively easy to recruit.

He established network leaders first, sending in one of his personally trained operatives, and then having the network leader train his own people. A few of the recruits were later found to be communists. He has lost a few people because of infiltration but generally his networks were running smoothly.

Some reports were hand carried to Saigon, but most were transmitted by portable radios. Each network had a specific reporting time. If the network failed to report for five straight days, Wilson would assume that the network had been exposed. He would then contact the nearest other network leader by radio and have him investigate.

Luckily, to date, he had not lost anyone in Hanoi, his most important and prolific team. The team leader, Ti, a slightly built Vietnamese, was only twenty years old but was one of the most intelligent men that Wilson had ever meet. When Ti asked for something Wilson provided it without question. The information they were receiving on SAM sites had saved hundreds of pilot's lives and had allowed the Air Force to develop countermeasures and blocking techniques. The information coming from the north, listing American prisoners, would also be invaluable after the war.

The latest request from Ti was unprecedented. He was demanding a sea pick up of an American officer that somehow had been liberated from a NV prison. Ti did not identify the prisoner or submit a request. He only gave the date, time, and location and identification code for the vessel that would be delivering the prisoner. The only other information was that the prisoner was injured and nears death and would need immediate medical assistance.

Now Wilson would have to fight his way through the Military bureaucracy to fulfill the request. He called a meeting of the highest-ranking officers he personally knew in each branch of the US military in Saigon. Trying to go through channels would take too long. Also, the Military people thought the spooks where crazy and undisciplined and usually just gave them the minimum amount of assistance.

When the people he called arrived he read the transmission from Ti and then asked their help to accomplish the pick up.

"Who does he want us to pick up?" The highest-ranking Army officer asked, "This would be dangerous and very expensive. I am sure that nobody will authorize this unless we know who it is."

Several other officers expressed the same concerns.

Wilson got to his feet and walked to the door and said to the clerk outside, "Get me the director on the phone and let me know as soon as you have him."

He then walked back into the room and said, "I don't know who the prisoner is but I trust the judgment of my team leader in Hanoi. I can't tell you what kind of information he has been providing but I can tell you he has saved thousands of lives.

I also have a non-Vietnamese operative in Hanoi who has been in deep cover for nearly fifteen years. If these two people want somebody out, I want it done."

The clerk knocked on the door and advised Wilson that the director was on the line. Wilson picked up the phone and after a few brief statements repeated Ti's request, and advised the director that he wanted to act immediately. He answered several questions and then turned to the group and said, "The director will call us back in a few minutes. Can we spend the time making preliminary plans just in case this gets authorized? We aren't going to have much time to execute.

Fifteen minutes later the director called back. When he started to speak Wilson switched on the squawk box so that all the other officers could hear.

"The Joint Chiefs have approved the rescue operation and orders are being cut as we speak. I suggest that all of you contact your superiors on this immediately and give them a heads up.

The men in the room started back to their offices, formulating detailed plans as they moved.

Hanoi, North Vietnam

After Ti left, Ollie drove to the prison and reported in. He walked into the commandant's office and said, "I am not feeling well. I am going to my apartment to rest."

The commandant scowled and made a note in his log. He could smell the alcohol on Ollie and noted that information in the log.

Ollie arrived at the pre-designated meeting place precisely on time and followed Ti to a secluded house near the river.

"All the arrangements have been made. I had to tell my superior in Saigon that we were removing your son or he wouldn't give the final okay. We will have to get the passenger to the river here." Ti said, pointing to a location of the map. "We take the main road west out of Hanoi. Ten kilometers out of town there is a dirt road that turns off to the left. There will be two trees in a row that will have dead branches leaning up against them to identify the road. About two kilometers down that road there is a clearing. Two men will pick up your son there and take him to the river. Fishermen will get him to the pick up point in The Gulf Of Tonkin. Do you have any questions?"

"When is this to take place?" Ollie asked.

"Tonight," Ti answered. "I am going back to your apartment with you tonight and I will help you get him into the car. Some of my people are already in the area of your apartment to make sure we won't have any problems."

Ollie left the meeting place and walked back to his car and drove back to his apartment. He spent the rest of the day there and then, after sunset, started for Ti's pick up location. He drove a few blocks and then turned into an alleyway and slowed down. Ti appeared out of the shadows. Ollie stopped for a second while Ti opened the rear door and slid onto the floor in the back seat. He slowly drove out of the alley and made a turn onto the street that would take him back to his apartment.

As they approached the apartment Ti popped up out of the back seat and began looking for markers that would tell them to abort if a problem existed. Seeing none he told Ollie to park and the two men entered Ollie's apartment at a leisurely pace.

Ollie gave Kevin two more shots of antibiotics and morphine and then they wrapped him up in a blanket and carried him to the front door. Ti opened the door a crack and spotted one of his men across the street in a shadow. The man gave him the safe sign and they quickly carried Kevin to the back seat of the car. They laid him down on the seat and covered him with a blanket. Ti crouched down below the dashboard in the front seat and Ollie started the car and headed west.

As soon as they left the main part of Hanoi and started toward the jungle, Ti sat up and started looking for the turn off road. They located the road, turned into it, and quickly drove to the opening in the jungle. Ollie turned off the lights and for a few moments they sat there in the dark, inhaling the putrid smell of the jungle and the nearby river. Ollie startled and reached for his revolver when someone knocked on the back door.

Ti opened his door and said a few words and then motioned for Ollie to get out.

The men were already loading Kevin onto a crude stretcher.

Ollie started to follow them down the trail but Ti restrained him saying, "Come we must go. They will take good care of him."

The men disappeared into the darkness leaving Ollie to wonder if he would ever see his son again.

Ollie wrenched his arm from Ti's hand and started down the path toward the river.

Ti caught up with him and restrained him. "I know how you feel," Ti said, "If it were my son you would have to sit on me to keep me from going with him. They will take good care of him. You have to go back. I guaranteed Saigon that you would come back to Hanoi if they helped."

Ollie stopped and then reluctantly turned and walked back to the car.

"Get these to Saigon," Ollie said, handing the dog tags he had removed from the American pilot to Ti. "I traded my son's for these. These dog tags belonged to a man that was already dead."

During Ti and Ollie's next meeting Ollie asked Ti to tell the CIA in Saigon that he wanted out. The night they had moved Kevin out Ollie was awake all night. Prior to discovering that Kevin was alive he had little incentive to return to the US. Now he did and he had no reasons to continue to work for the Russians or the CIA and stay in the USSR. He would be unhappy not being with Tamara, but he hadn't seen her for three years. He did receive an occasional message from her through channels so he was always aware of her location. Now he was sure that he could defect without implicating anyone. He could just disappear into the jungle and with Ti's help, make his way to Saigon.

Ti told him that he would pass along the request.

Ollie had also been requesting Ti to ask Saigon about Kevin's status.

Two weeks after Ollie saw Kevin being carried down the jungle trail; a visibly shaken Ti told Ollie that Kevin had died before they got him to a medical facility.

The news was devastating to Ollie. Losing his son twice was unbearable. He had to maintain his composure when he was in contact with the NV but at night he just sat in his room, staring blankly at the ugly walls, allowing tears to flow freely. His son had grown into manhood without him. He would probably never know the details of his son's short life. The sick feeling in the pit of his stomach would not go away. Once again in his life, he had no direction and had little desire to continue.

Another week went past before he made contact with Ti and he received word that the CIA wanted him to stay in. They had plans for him. Ollie no longer cared about the CIA or their projects. He just wanted Ti to help him find and eliminate the jungle camp commanders.

Aleksandr Gaidar, who had just been promoted to Air Marshall, finally agreed to Ollie's pleas to relieve him from duty in Vietnam. Ollie had one last meeting with Ti to tell him that he was returning to Russia. Ollie made Ti vow that he would satisfy his request for vengeance.

Chapter *18*

Moscow, Russia, 1971

Tamara had been waiting impatiently for Ollie to return from Vietnam. She knew by reports from the air marshal's office that he had not been happy in Vietnam.

She had not been very happy either. Besides being away from Ollie, she had been spending time in places like Iran and India. Russia was providing military support to these countries and Tamara was supposed to be providing training. The Arabs could not accept her as an instructor of men and were continuously trying to involve her in controversy that would give them cause to have her removed. Her immediate superior finally requested that she be returned to Russia and not sent to any other Islamic countries. She returned to Podluk and was assigned as a test pilot for new fighters being developed.

The day after Ollie returned Tamara held a party at her father's country estate. Her family and Ollie's friends and co-workers were invited. The party was a warm success. Her father and the Air Marshall had provided an abundance of food and drink. After the party everybody but Ollie and Tamara left the dacha, leaving them to get reacquainted. They didn't leave the house for two days. During the two days Tamara finally extracted the reason for Ollie's melancholy. When he told her about finding Kevin in the prison camp she was shocked. He didn't tell her about trying to get Kevin out of Vietnam, he just told her that Kevin had died.

Tamara was sympathetic and tried to help Ollie dig himself out of his depression. By the end of the second day he was starting to return to normal and on the third day they got the old biplane out and went flying.

Sergi and Ollie finally found some time to spend together. They were walking along Arbat Street in Moscow while the two women were exploring the shops.

"The KGB lied to me about Kevin," Ollie said with disgust. "I want to know if they lied to me about Mary. Was she killed in a plane crash or was that a lie too? Can you ask your friends to find out for me? Also, can you have your friend in the KGB locate Valeriy Zorkin for me?"

Sergi was worried about Ollie's attitude. Ever since he had returned from Vietnam he had been distant and difficult to talk too. "Why do you want to locate Valeriy?" Sergi asked. "He was just doing his job. If you do anything rash you might be arrested and put back in prison."

"Just do it as a favor for me," Ollie requested, grimly. "I will take care of the rest."

It took awhile but Sergi did obtain information about Mary.

"She didn't die in a plane crash," Sergi reported. "She sent Kevin home to live with your parents and she stayed in Japan. She went to work for a Japanese banker and ended up as president of the bank. When the elder banker died, his two sons took over the business and bounced Mary out of a job. Nobody heard much from her for years but she evidently went to work for another bank. She evidently had a heart attack and died. She left a sizable estate to your son. That is all I have been told."

"I wonder how much of that is true," Ollie muttered sadly. "Mary would never have sent Kevin to the States alone. I am beginning to mistrust everybody, even you."

Sergi smiled and patted him on the shoulder, "Now you are starting to think like a spook. You may turn out to be a good operator after all."

"What did you learn about Valeriy?"

"My contact did some low level snooping. He thinks Valeriy is being sent to the United States, but he is not sure. Please, Ollie, just forget him. He was only doing his job."

"If he had ruined your life I would bet that you would feel the same as I do." Ollie replied passionately.

"Well Valeriy, what do you think?" The Russian KGB colonel asked as Valeriy entered the interrogation room at the KGB Moscow headquarters.

The KGB had picked up Ollie at his apartment on his day off and had taken him by car to their Lyubyanka headquarters. Ollie had immediately started questioning them about why they had picked him up. All the KGB officers would tell him was that it was just a routine questioning.

It took a great deal of control for Ollie to not over react to the situation. The first thing that occurred to him was that he had been discovered. He wondered if Sergi had also been picked up and what would happen to Helena and Tamara if his fears proved true. Inside his clothing sweat was beginning to dampen his underwear. He was sure that his questioners could see that he was distressed.

After three hours he looked at the lead interrogator and said, "What do you people really want? Do you want me to work for you? If you do just say so and tell me what you want and I will talk to the air marshall and we will consider it and respond."

For an instant a flicker of a smile started and then was quickly repressed by the lead KGB officer.

"We will talk to you again soon, but once again I will tell you that this is just a routine inquiry. We are finished. One of my men will take you back to your apartment."

1965. In 1971, India invaded East Pakistan and Pakistani troops eventually surrendered and India recognized a new nation of Bangladesh.

During and after the India-Pakistani incident Ollie and Tamara had found themselves in the middle of another armed conflict. They were both sent to India as technical advisors. The USSR had been backing India with support and weapons since India had become independent. The Indians, chaffing from years of British dominance had openly accepted communist help. The Americans backed the Pakistanis and once again Ollie found himself working for one side, the Russians, while passing information to the United States. The whole concept was wearing thin for Ollie.

Following the India-Pakistani conflict the USSR was forced into another conflict in Afghanistan to help a teetering communist regime. The three-year war was a disaster for Russia. The war seemed to be endless and without a point. Thousand of Russian military were killed and many more were injured and in the end nothing was resolved.

Tamara had been transferred to Afghanistan to assist the Russian pilots who were flying MIGs that she had helped develop.

Ollie, back in his office in Moscow, was summoned to Air Marshal Gaidar's office. When he entered he was surprised to see an obviously agitated Yuri Krasnov, Tamara's father, nervously pacing in front of the desk.

"Yuri, what a surprise to see you here," Ollie said as he approached. "What's wrong?"

Yuri turned to Ollie and said, "It's Tamara, she was flying in a helicopter from Kabul to Faizabag, through the mountains. The rebels shot down the helicopter in the mountains. Another helicopter flying with the one Tamara was in reported that the helicopter made a hard landing but wasn't totally destroyed. We don't know if the people onboard are dead or alive."

Ollie's face drained and he put his arm around Yuri and tried to console him and asked, "What can I do to help?"

"That is why I asked you to come in," the air marshal said. "We know that the Americans are providing support to the rebels. We have captured American equipment being transported from Pakistan to the rebels through the Kyber pass. We have operatives in the area and would like to send someone into the area to see if anyone on the chopper survived and if possible get them out."

"How can I help?" Ollie asked.

"We would like you to go into the area, with the help of our people, and try to make contact with the rebels."

"Wouldn't the rebels shoot me on sight?"

"Our plan is to set this up as if you are delivering supplies to the rebels. Since you speak both Russian and English we think you could work with our people and the rebels. What do you think?"

"If you can provide me with details about how the supply system works, including names and places, and develop a detailed plan, it might work." Ollie said with skepticism.

Afghanistan

Ollie had been camped out in the mountains northeast of Kabul for a week. His counterpart, a young Russian officer, seemed to relish the assignment, the rugged rocky terrain, completely devoid of vegetation, and the hardships. Ollie, on the other hand, was in continuing discomfort, impatiently waiting for a mule train coming in from Pakistan.

They had moved the supplies, seized from an earlier shipment intended for the rebels, by truck, from a warehouse in Kabal, to their present location in the mountains. When the mule train arrived they would load the supplies onto the mules and start into the mountains. Ollie was sitting on the ground with a rock at his back for support. He was sleeping uneasily when he was suddenly pelted and awakened by cascading rocks and dirt.

The young Russian officer had been on higher ground watching the trail. He slid down the hill and announced that the mule train was arriving.

Ollie got up and shook off the dust. A half-hour later the collection of motley mules and poorly dressed drivers stopped just below where Ollie had been sitting.

When Ollie got down to the animals, the Russian officer had already greeted the leader of the mule train and slipped him a wad of money. It took an hour to load the mules.

Ollie said goodbye to the Russian officer and the entire caravan moved out, heading due north into the mountains.

The caravan had been plugging along for a week without making contact with the rebels. Ollie, as usual, was walking in the front of the column with the leader. As they rounded a large rock formation armed men suddenly confronted them. They were behind the rocks on the high side of the road, pointing weapons at the travelers.

The pack train leader spoke to the rebels in their Pashto language and the apparent leader stepped out from behind a rock. Ollie instructed the mule train leader to tell the rebel leader that they had military, medical and food supplies for the rebels.

As soon as the message was given the rebel leader began to smile broadly and offered his hand to Ollie.

Ollie asked, "Do you speak English?"

The man looked at him and did not speak and then looked to the pack mule leader for a translation. He then answered in his own language and the mule pack leader told Ollie that the area rebel leader did speak English and that he would take them to meet him.

It took another slow day of foot travel to reach the main camp, located in a steep sided canyon, accessible through narrow passes.

They approached the camp from the south and were greeted by the rebel area leader. His English was rudimentary and halting but Ollie was able to converse.

The rebel leader thanked Ollie profusely for the supplies. They were almost completely out of armaments and food and evidently had been just lying low in the mountains waiting for supplies. The leader was delighted that he would be able to take some offensive action.

When they had concluded their business Ollie asked, "Do you know of any Russian helicopters that have crashed in this area? One of our American spies, a Russian woman, was on a helicopter that was shot down. I have been asked to find out if anybody knows anything about her. Do you know anything about this?"

"Yes, yes," the leader said. "We have her at another camp. We have been trying to decide what to do with her. We were thinking of trading her for supplies but haven't been able to determine out how to do that. Since you have brought us supplies you can have her. We will be glad to get rid of her. She is a problem to control. We almost shot her many times."

The next day the rebel leader took him to the camp where Tamara was being held. When they first walked into the camp Ollie saw Tamara, sitting on a rock, with a desperate, pained expression on her face. When she recognized Ollie she started to smile and speak. Ollie signaled her to remain quiet by slightly shaking his head from side to side.

The rebel leader walked over to Tamara and said, "This man is an American. He wants to talk to you."

"What is your name?" Ollie asked.

Tamara looked directly in his face and said, "Tamara Krasnov."

Ollie asked, "Is your contact in Moscow called Sergi?"

"Yes," She replied.

What is Sergi's wife's name?" Ollie asked.

"Helena." Tamara said with a slight smile.

Ollie turned to the leader and said, "This is the woman we are looking for."

He turned to Tamara and said, "I am here to get you out."

Tamara could no longer restrain herself. She threw her arms around Ollie and started repeating, "Thank you. Thank you."

Ollie took her aside and asked, "Are you all right?"

"I have some bumps and bruises and my ribs are sore. I don't think anything is broken. I will be fine now that you are here."

"Were there any other survivors?" Ollie asked, supporting her by putting his arm around her waist.

"There were no serious injuries," Tamara replied. "The pilot had time to go into auto rotation so we landed pretty soft."

"Where are the other survivors?" Ollie asked.

"I don't know," Tamara said. "We got separated immediately and I haven't seen them since."

Ollie asked the rebel leader what had happened to the other survivors.

"They were our enemies. We took their equipment and then disposed off them," he replied without emotion.

Ollie went back to Tamara and told her the fate of the other survivors.

She grimaced and was visibly distressed and said, "How soon can we leave? Let's get going before they dispose of us."

The rebel leader provided them with a guide to help them get back to the Kyber Pass and to Pakistan. As the mule train was preparing to leave Ollie thanked the rebel leader and promised to send another shipment to the area as soon as he could.

That night, as they snuggled under blankets trying to keep out the mountain cold, Ollie whispered in Tamara's ear, "We are getting to old for this. Why don't we retire?"

Tamara laughed softly and tried to get closer to his warm body.

When they were near the Kyber Pass road Ollie told the mule train leader to release the rebel guide, and called the Russian officer on the radio and set up a meeting place. They found the Russian officer waiting for them near the Kyber Pass road. After greeting the travelers the Russian handed the mule train leaded another wad of money and the train headed east toward Pakistan. Ollie, Tamara and the Russian started driving toward Kabul. All they talked about on the drive was taking a hot bath and sleeping in a soft bed. Every so often Tamara would squeeze Ollie's arm in silent thanks.

"I know they where going to kill me any day. I am sure happy that you found me in time."

Ollie said, "Don't thank me. Your father and the air marshal and our young friend," nodding to the driver, "did all the planning and work. I was just the messenger."

"I am still happy that you came for me," she whispered in his ear. "Tonight I will show you how happy I am."

Two weeks latter they were back to work in Moscow. Yuri Krasnov thanked Ollie by presenting him with an automobile. Ollie protested the extravagance; it was something that Ollie couldn't afford if he saved all his money for years. Yuri insisted that he keep the car.

"It doesn't begin to repay you for what you did," Yuri said with gratitude.

The air marshal rewarded them by assigning them to the Paris Air Show as part of the Russian Air Corp team.

"Hello again Captain Millerovic." The KGB officer said. "Please have a seat. I have something I want to discuss with you."

Once again Ollie had been summoned to the Moscow headquarters of the KGB. This time it had been a request that had come down through channels to the air marshal and then to Ollie.

The air marshal had called Ollie into his office and told him that the KGB wanted to talk to him. "They probably want you to do something for them at the Paris air show," the air marshall said. "They are always trying to get us to help them on one project or another. Just talk to them and see what they have to say and then get back to me if there is something you think I should know."

When Ollie arrived at KGB headquarters he was ushered into the office of the colonel who had questioned him the first time. The colonel motioned for him to be seated.

"All right," Ollie said, "what do you want to discuss?"

The KGB colonel looked directly at Ollie, to observe his reaction, and said, "We know that you are have been assigned to the Paris air show and we would like to enlist your help in several projects that we will have in operation there. Will you help us?"

"That will depend on what you want me to do," Ollie replied. "I won't kill anybody for you if that is what you want."

"No, no, we don't want to do anything that drastic. We just want you to contact some people from other countries and ask them if they will help us with certain programs. That is all."

"Are you trying to buy information?"

"Yes, something like that."

"Can you be more specific?"

"I will try to give you the general idea without being to specific." The colonel replied. "It will require you to develop friendship with certain people and then see if they are willing to accept money for either providing us with information or helping us to steer certain negotiations in a certain way."

"What you are asking me to do is recruit traitors!"

"Yes, you can say that."

"Don't you have people who have experience and training to do this type of thing?"

"Yes we do, but we want you to talk to people from several countries. You will have better access to them then our normal people. By midday on the first day of the show both sides will have identified all the espionage agents at the show. We always try to have a few people not associated with the KGB helping us."

"What countries will the people be from?" Ollie asked.

"Does it make any difference to you?" The colonel asked.

"If you are asking me if I would try to recruit somebody from the US I don't know what I would say." Ollie responded. "On the other hand they didn't want me so I guess it doesn't matter who you want me to talk to. It will be okay with me."

"Excellent," the colonel said with a smile. "We will start training you immediately. I'll call the air marshal and tell him that you will be spending considerable time with us before you leave for Paris. We will be telling you everything we know about your potential contacts and familiarizing you with our operating methods and personnel. We will also be setting up procedures to help you transmit questions and receive help while you are in Paris."

The colonel stood up and walked to the door with Ollie. "Report here tomorrow morning and we will get started."

"Can I call the air marshal from here?" Ollie asked. "I want to let him know where I am. He will want to give me instructions on what he wants me to do in Paris."

The colonel walked back into his office and put a call in for the air marshal. When the he answered the colonel identified himself and then explained that Ollie would be at KGB headquarters for a few days receiving instructions. When he finished talking he listened to the air marshal for a few minutes and then handed the phone to Ollie.

Ollie listened to the air marshal and then said, "That will be fine with me, sir." and hung up.

Ollie turned to the colonel and said, "It's all set, I will be here tomorrow morning for as long as it takes. The air marshal has a few things to discuss with me, but he says that it will only take a half-day before I leave."

Ollie reported to the KGB headquarters the next morning for training. As soon as he learned who he was to attempt to recruit, he passed the information to Sergi.

Two weeks later Sergi gave him his instructions, passed on by the CIA. The instructions were very simple. Just do what the KGB asked and keep his contact advised.

The two weeks before the Paris Air Show were hectic for Ollie. He had to catch up on some late technical and mechanical changes that had been made to the electronic gear on the planes they would be showing. He was also involved with the planning and rehearsal for the show and for becoming intimately familiar with the background of the people he would be talking to.

He and Tamara were working sixteen-hour days preparing for the show. Finally the officers in charge said, "We are ready." Everybody take two days off and get some rest and report back here. Don't report back with hangovers or you will be taken off the team."

Ollie and Tamara spent their two days at Tamara's father's dacha; resting and taking leisurely walks and then reported back to the base for transportation to Paris.

CHAPTER *19*

Paris, France, 1981

Assignment to the Air Show team was one of the most coveted assignments in the Soviet Air Force. The team traveled throughout world demonstrating and selling Soviet equipment.

The Russians loved having Tamara on the team. She would put her MIG through dazzling aerobatics and then taxi to the display area and cut her engines. The prospective buyers would be astounded when the beautiful, mature woman climbed out of the cockpit, removed her flight helmet, ran her fingers through her blonde hair and then worked her way through the foreign buyers. The implication was obvious. *You have seen what this woman can do with this machine. Imagine what your men could do.* It was a very successful marketing device and one that Tamara enjoyed.

Ollie's job was more technical. While Tamara romanced the politicians, Ollie provided technical information to the people who made the technical decisions.

Ollie's KGB designated contact was a colonel in the American Air Force, a member of the US team. The two men had little reason to contact each other during the show since both where excluded from each other's display areas.

The first evening of the show there was a dinner at the Ritz hotel for the show personnel and visiting dignitaries. After dinner Ollie and

Tamara were wandering through the crowd, talking to potential buyers. Ollie recognized Rick Hellman, the American colonel he was supposed to contact. He steered Tamara toward the American, knowing that he would recognize her. As they drew near the colonel spotted Tamara and walked over and introduced himself.

The American colonel was in his Air Force dress blue uniform, showing a chest full of ribbons and the wings of a command pilot.

"Colonel Krasnov, I am Colonel Hellman. I am looking forward to seeing you fly again. I was stunned by the aerobatics you performed today."

Tamara gave the American an admiring once over, smiling as she grasped his outstretched hand. *Very attractive,* she thought to herself, *almost too good looking.*

"Thank you," Tamara responded, "I see from your chest that you must be an excellent pilot."

Another potential customer walked up to Tamara and started asking her questions. Tamara excused herself and said, "I will see you later near the entrance," smiling at Ollie as she departed.

Ollie introduced himself to the American colonel and they both started walking toward a quieter location in the huge ballroom.

"What is your association with Colonel Krasnov?" The American colonel asked.

"She is my...," Ollie hesitated, trying to think of the correct word. "I guess you Americans would say she is my woman, but that isn't really true. And she isn't a girl so she isn't my girlfriend. But she is my best friend and we do live together."

"That's what I was afraid you where going to say," the American laughed. "I guess I don't have a chance with her."

"You will have to ask her that yourself," Ollie smiled. "I could tell that she was really impressed by you."

"By the way Ollie," Hellman said pleasantly, "All the guys from the Fifth said to say hello."

Ollie was completely taken by surprise. He stood speechless, trying to clear his mind. The man he was supposed to recruit had just given him the first part of the CIA recognition signal that he hadn't heard in years. He looked at the Colonel, who was looking very nonchalantly over Ollie's shoulder. Ollie stammered the correct reply, "Even Bill?"

The American replied, "Yes, and Bob too."

"Forgive me if I seem confused," Ollie said with more than a little concern. "This is really a strange turn of events."

"Oh what tangled webs we weave," Hellman said with a chuckle. "I know how you must feel. I'm going to become a double agent, pretending to work for the Russians while I'm working for the CIA and being paid by the Air Force. You think you are confused!"

"What are you instructions?" Ollie asked.

"I'm going to let you corrupt me for money," Hellman replied. "The Agency has been documenting my indiscretions for a year so my record looks a little soiled. That made me a target for your side. So I'll take money from the Russians and pass on information that the CIA wants me to pass on as misinformation, and we will see how it goes."

"We should probably meet a couple of more times before I tell the KGB that I have been successful," Ollie said. "Otherwise my people will think it was too easy."

"I agree," Hellman said. "Let's make it a point to seek each other out at all the functions and the day before the show ends tell them that I accept."

"Sounds like a good plan to me. I guess we better separate. I will look for you at the next event."

Rick was clearly appreciative of Tamara. Tamara was flattered and Ollie wasn't sure if Rick was just playing the game or was serious. The challenge did force Ollie to realize how attractive Tamara was to other men. Tamara teased him about his newfound attentiveness. Alone in their room, she removed any doubt of her love for Ollie.

On the last day of the show Ollie advised the KGB that Colonel Hellman wanted to talk to them and the KGB advised Ollie that they would take care of the rest. The KGB did not volunteer any information about Hellman. All they would tell him was that he had been successful in his assignment and they would contact him for future assignments.

By the end of the show Ollie and Tamara were exhausted and reluctantly left the excitement of Paris and flew back to Moscow.

On a weekend when Helena and Tamara decided to attend the ballet, the men begged off to do what Sergi called "men things". They drove, in Ollie's new car, to the University. Ollie thought they were going to another play or to a sporting event. They drove though the university complex and then, at Sergi's direction, Ollie started to drive east into the country. About ten miles from the edge of Moscow Sergi told Ollie to slow down, and directed him to turn into a dirt road. About a mile down the road they came to a dacha, similar to that belonging to Tamara's father.

"Who lives here?" Ollie asked as they pulled up to the front door.

"You don't have to know. We are meeting some people here I am sure will interest you," Sergi said as he left the car.

As they approached the front door Ollie noticed two other cars parked along side the house.

Sergi opened the front door and two men who had been sitting in the living room stood and started toward them.

Ollie recognized one of the men, Andrei Malenkovich, an intense, dark complexioned young man with jet-black hair and face that always looked as if a shave had been forgotten for the day. Ollie recognized him because Sergi had pointed him out as a close aide and advisor to Chernenko. He did not recognize the other man, a mid-forties, short, stocky, fair skinned man with brown hair. Both men were dressed in Russian cut business suits.

Sergi introduced Ollie to Malenkovich and then turned to the other man and turned back to look at Ollie and said, "This is James Lang. He is the bureau chief for the CIA in Moscow and is stationed at the US embassy as a member of their staff."

Ollie was somewhat taken back. *What would a top Soviet political operative and the bureau chief of the CIA be doing meeting secretly and why would they want to meet with me?*

The stocky American extended his hand to Ollie and said, "I'm pleased to meet you at last. We appreciate the work you have been doing. We are keeping detailed records of your activities and I can assure you that your full military pay is being deposited in a savings account."

Ollie acknowledged the two men and then turned to Sergi and said, "Isn't this dangerous for all of us to be in one place? At least three of us may be under surveillance."

"None of us were followed, if that's what you are worried about. We are all careful and have been meeting for years, but never in the same place twice." The Russian said.

"My next question is, why are we here?" Ollie said, glancing at each man in turn.

"Because something monumental will soon be happening in Russia and we will be right in the middle of the action," the American said flatly. "You explain it to him, Andrei."

"All right, please let's all be seated," the Russian said, motioning Ollie to a stuffed chair and then sitting in a chair opposite Ollie.

When they were all seated Andrei said, "It's not widely known yet but Chernenko is gravely ill and is not expected to live. Liberal members of the party, after careful preparation by many of us inside the party, will place a man in power. Our man will put an end to the long reign of communist power and fear. After he is in power the centralized government will be disbanded and we will eventually be a democracy. Many of us have been working for this all our lives. We are sick of the terror, the purges and the militancy of the party.

"Who is this man?" Ollie asked in disbelief.

"His name is Mikhail Gorbachev," Sergi replied. "He is a Party member and has been a Party official for many years."

"How do you know he will actually do what you say if he does become General Secretary?," Ollie asked skeptically.

"Because he wants to be the Secretary and can't do it without the help of the US," the stocky American replied. "He needs our money and our backing and he has pledged that he is going to normalize Russia."

"Even if I accept this as true, and right now I am having some trouble with that, what can the people in this room do?"

"After Gorbachev is elected both you and Sergi will be appointed to my staff. I will be Gorbachev's chief of staff." Andrei said, looking at Ollie. "Will that be satisfactory to you?"

"Just what will the three of us be doing?" Ollie asked, still shaking his head because of the incredulous statement that Andrei had made.

"Sergi will be the voice of the intellectuals. You will be the liason with the military and the American expert. I will be his chief advisor. We will be responsible for keeping him pointed in the right direction. Our friends in the CIA will be responsible for keeping money and business flowing into the country. Within a year all the satellites will be cut loose and the government will be decentralized. We will have independent states with free elections and independence with leadership in Moscow that is elected by the people. And we will welcome capitalism. I think you will recognize the model."

"How do you know Air Marshall Gaidar will let me go?" Ollie asked.

"That is not a problem," Andrei said. "The air marshall can't turn down a request from the Secretary. Also he will be delighted to have a former subordinate on the new Secretaries staff. I don't see any problem there."

"What could I possibly contribute?".

"We are going to bring about major changes that are sure to be resisted by the military," Andrei replied. "Your contacts in the military will be of tremendous help for determining hard line resistance and helping to modify that resistance. Gaidar will undoubtedly be a significant help. He always has been a fair minded and open man, always prepared to hear both sides of any problem. He just wants the best for the Russian population."

"When is this all to happen?" Ollie asked.

"Soon, and I guarantee that you won't miss it." The American said with a smile.

The men continued discussing plans and the meeting came to an end. Andrei left first. While they were waiting for time to elapse before Lang departed, Ollie took the American aside and said, "Eventually I want to return to the US. I want an official US document to be placed somewhere in the US where I know it will always be, like in a safety deposit box. I want the document to state my status and the guarantee that my military pay is in escrow with an identification of the bank and the account. I then would like the key delivered to me. Can you do that for me?"

"That won't be a problem. I'll advise you when it is done and give you the key," the American said as he was leaving.

On the drive back to Moscow Ollie said, "I'm still not sure I understand just what it is I will be doing."

"Don't worry," Sergi said. "I don't know what I'm going to be doing either. I'm sure they must have plans for us so we will just have to wait and see."

As predicted by Malenkovich, Gorbachev ascended to power. After the first wave of shock subsided new appointments were announced. It was a time of complete confusion for the people, the military and the secret police. The military and the KGB both thought that a bloodless coup had taken place. The people supported the new leader and were expecting instant resolution of all their many problems.

When the air marshal called Ollie into his office to tell him that he was being transferred to the Kremlin as a member of an advisory team, Ollie feigned surprise but was truthful when he replied, "I wonder what kind of advice they are expecting from me? I'm not the least bit interested in politics or world affairs."

"I didn't oppose the appointment," the air marshal replied. "I suppose they wanted a lower level military type who was not involved in the politics of the military to get an additional viewpoint."

"Well, I'll go, but you have to promise to extract me if I find that this new assignment is over my head or totally boring."

"They might also want you because you are an American." The air marshal said reflectively. "After all the US has Kissinger in a high office."

"I know who Kissinger is from reading the newspapers," Ollie said. "He is an educated man and a career diplomat. I sure don't fall into that category. I only have a minimum education and haven't had any contact with Americans for many years."

"In any event," the air marshal advised, "I want you to keep in touch with me. It will be helpful to the military if we have knowledgeable input from you so that we can best serve our new leader."

Ollie stood and shook the air marshal's hand.

"When I first met Yuri Krasnov he told me you were an honest, good man," Ollie said with sincerity. "He was correct. I have enjoyed working for you and I'll keep in touch. Now I guess I had better see if I can find an apartment in Moscow."

With the help of Tamara and her father, Ollie did find an apartment near Sergi and Helena, not far from Gorkiy Park. It didn't take long for Ollie to move his few belongings into the modestly furnished apartment.

For the first time since his tour in Vietnam he was on his own, having to buy groceries and cook his own meals and take care of his own laundry. Starting his new assignment and coping with the new responsibilities of taking care of himself brought his working day to twelve hours. After a few weeks he had developed a new routine and had found a woman in his apartment that would do his shopping and cook his evening meal and take care of his laundry. He paid for her service and shared the extra food allowance he was granted because of his new position.

His new apartment was in one of the newer buildings built after World War II. Although newer than most of the buildings in Moscow it had the typical lack of style and somber exterior. Ollie's two-room apartment was on the second floor facing a park in back of the building. It was comfortable and with Tamara and Helena's assistance he found some furnishings that brightened up the interior.

At first his new assignment was confusing and humbling. He had never felt so inadequate. During staff meetings he tried to keep a low profile, hopping that his opinion would not be solicited. Eventually the uneasiness slipped away and he found it simpler to attend to his duties. He would bounce the ideas of Andrei's staff and the top men in the military and get their reactions and input. Ollie did not limit his discussions to military matters. He also presented the military staff with Gorbachev's ideas on reorganization, economics and world diplomacy. For many of the military, discussion of these areas was new and stimulating. From past experience Ollie knew that there were some brilliant minds in the military. He brought some on that brilliance to Andrei by passing on the military comments and suggestions. Some of the suggestions where self-serving and self-promoting but mixed in were some gems. He could also sense that even the hard-liners were starting to think about life in a new Russia.

G. B. Mooney

The Americans didn't know what to think about the new Soviet leader statements. The liberals were delighted and the conservatives were suspicious. *Was this another colossal Russian attempt at misinformation?*

The policies of Pestroika [restructuring] and Glasnost [openness] got mixed reception in Russia. The hard-line party members still viewed Gorbachev as a weak traitor and immediately began to plot his overthrow. The civilians were more receptive, hoping for less government control and more consumer goods instead of military equipment.

The military people did not react until Gorbachev started to talk about dis-armament. Gorbachev and Regan, the American President, met at a summit meeting in Reykjavik, Iceland to formalize a bold arms reduction program. Gorbachev was convinced that the US Strategic Defense Initiative, called Star Wars by the American media, had placed Russia in an inferior posture. Successful deployment of SDI would swing the nuclear power balance to the US. Andrei and Ollie, using technical information provided by James Lang, had been subtlety pushing the line that the SDI was being readied for immediate deployment. This misinformation was also coming into Russian intelligence through Colonel Rick Hellman, the double agent Ollie recruited during the Paris air show.

In 1987 the US and Russia came to an agreement on the elimination of medium and short-range missiles. Most of the world breathed a sigh of relief. The cold war, that had placed a tremendous strain on the minds of thinking people, and had decimated the finances of the world powers, might finally be coming to an end.

The thought of giving up a position of power was an aberration to the Russian military hard liners. Ollie job was to identify the military opposition for what Malenkovich called re-education. Ollie spent many hours with his old boss, the air marshal, explaining the benefits of arms reduction, soliciting his help in convincing his friends in the military upper echelon. Ollie recognized that he was putting the air marshal at risk but he needed him to help pacify the hard liners.

In June of 1988 Gorbachev called a special Party conference and pro-posed sweeping constitutional reforms removing power from the Communist Party and giving it to elected legislatures. He also proposed a reduction of Party control in economic management and increased the powers of the president.

Andrey Gromyko retired as president and Gorbachev assumed the office. In March of 1989 the first free election since 1917 elected a Congress of Peoples Deputies and Gorbachev as President for a five-year term. Following the reorganization Gorbachev requested a meet-ing with the American government in the United States.

Gorbachev's visit to the United States was a triumph. The American media accepted him with open arms. His plans for disarmament, open-ness and the acceptance of non-government controlled business in Russia was accepted as the first step to normalization. American and other world business and financial people started to visit Russia, look-ing for places to invest.

These were exciting times for Ollie and Sergi. Sergi was particularly happy about the new normalization of living that was bringing peace to the people. Although there was still some paranoia, the people were beginning to view their government with less fear.

American capital and know how was starting to make its' presence visible in Moscow.

Despite the hype, the shift from government control of industry to privatization was slow and painful. The infighting and treachery was disconcerting to the foreigners attempting to take advantage of a large potential market for civilian goods. Advancement was stop and go, mostly stop unfortunately, causing distress to those Americans whom had invested large sums of money.

One evening while Ollie was having dinner with Sergi and Helena, Sergi asked, "What do you think about McDonalds coming to Moscow?"

"Who are the McDonalds?" Ollie asked.

Sergi and Helena started to laugh. "Remember the first time we had dinner and you said we should open up an American restaurant in Moscow? Well it's coming. McDonalds is an American restaurant that specializes in hamburgers. It will be constructed in Pushkin Square. You are going to get your wish. It will be open in about six months."

Ollie eagerly awaited the opening of the new restaurant, driving by almost every day to check the progress of the project. When it finally opened Sergi, Helena, Tamara and Ollie were one of the first customers. Standing in line to order, paying and then immediately receiving food was a new experience. They took their food to a booth and consumed it with gusto.

"What do you think?" Sergi asked.

"I like Helena's burgers better," Ollie said, licking his fingers. "But the French fries and the Coke are really good and I like all the condiments. What do you think?"

The consensus was that the food was a nice change from their regular diet. They became regular customers, working their way through the menu.

CHAPTER *20*

Commonwealth of Independent States, formerly the USSR, 1990

Gorbachev continued with his program to reconstitute the USSR as a Commonwealth of Independent States, with the armed forces controlled by a Military Command of the CIS. Soon independent armies were being formed by some independent states.

The free world was astounded when Gorbachev did not intervene when Poland, Hungary, Czechoslovakia and East Germany ousted the communists.

The Soviet economy continued to deteriorate and the Communist Party agreed to give up political power.

Gorbachev named himself Executive President and claimed additional power in an attempt to stem the growing unrest. The situation became ominous when insurgents made significant gains in local elections, and became worse when Lithuania declared itself a sovereign state and defied Moscow sanctions.

Nationalistic and independence movements started to erupt in other republic states and there were outbreaks of ethnic violence. To counter the growing problems Gorbachev assumed more power and attempted more political and economic reforms.

Malenkovich, Sergi and Ollie had been desperately trying to obtain US assistance to help correct the domestic problems. Outside investors were becoming disillusioned by the apparent government lack of capability to institute changes. The investors had sunk large amounts of capital into the privatization of industry and were being shut out of the operations of the businesses. Return on investment that should have paid to the investors was being held in Russia. The word was getting out and investors were pulling out of Russia. Malenkovich pleaded with Gorbachev to take action to allay the fears of private investors, but it was too late.

Russian civilians were starting to openly condemn Gorbachev. Food was still hard to get and if anything the standard of living had declined. Crime was beginning to grow and drug and alcohol abuse was openly prevalent in the young. With more openness, defections to neighboring countries were happening daily. The masses were unhappy again.

In August of 1991 hard-liners, including top officials, staged a coup. The military seized Gorbachev and placed him under house arrest. Malenkovich and his staff, including Sergi and Ollie were also arrested at the same time and placed in detention in the Kremlin.

They were kept in living quarters in the Kremlin and although confined to one area were relatively free to roam.

"In the old days," Sergi advised, trying to be cheerful, "by this time we would have been shot. I don't know where we will end up but I hope it's not Siberia. Gorbachev tried to pay people to settle there and it failed"

The detainees had no idea of what was happening outside the Kremlin. The coup was crushed by reformers led by Boris Yeltsin, the president of the Republic State of Russia. The world witnessed a semi-drunk man standing defiantly on a tank outside the Kremlin. The hard-liners and the military backed down and the Russians accepted Yeltsin as their new leader.

With the USSR on the verge of collapse Gorbachev and Yeltsin formed the Congress of People Deputies Transitional Government. A State Council headed by Gorbachev, including presidents of participating republics, assumed emergency power. The Council recognized full independence of Estonia, Latvia and Lithuania. It was soon apparent that Gorbachev did not have sufficient backing to continue governing and Boris Yeltsin's Russian State Government assumed the power of the Soviet government.

On December 21, 1991 the USSR ceased to exist and eleven of the twelve remaining republics formed the Commonwealth of Independent States.

Gorbachev resigned from government service on December 21, 1991.

While the free world was still in shock over the startling developments, the United States immediately deduced that a monstrous problem existed. Who was in charge of the remaining nuclear arsenal?

Malenkovich, Sergi, Ollie and the rest of Gorbachev's staff were released but none of Malenkovich's staff were retained in the new government. Sergi went back to teaching, Malekovich accepted a position in an independent state government, and Ollie returned to Air Marshall Gaidar's staff.

As soon as Ollie returned to the air marshal's staff he began to question the location and control of the nuclear arsenal. The air marshal immediately recognized the importance of accounting for and securing the nuclear weapons. He knew that it would be a disaster if any of the warheads fell into the hands of a fanatic dictator. With the help of military officers loyal to Yeltsin, they accounted for every nuclear warhead, moved them to secure locations and instituted controlled protection.

During the turmoil Tamara's father had suffered a heart attack. Because of the unrest Tamara had been unable to obtain help. She had tried to call Ollie and Sergi but they had already been taken into custody and she could not find them. Finally she did reach Helena, who was already frantic because she didn't know what had happened to Sergi. They managed to get her father to a hospital. Because of the unrest the hospital was poorly staffed. Her father survived the first attack but a second more serious attack caused his death on the second day of the coup. When Ollie returned to his apartment he found Tamara there. For the first time since he had known her, she was in tears and inconsolable.

He held her for hours until she quit sobbing and then contacted Sergi and Helena to help with the funeral.

A month after the coup Ollie walked into his office and immediately sensed extreme tension. Within minutes he learned that Air Marshal Gaidar has been relieved of his duties and that a major reorganization was imminent. Rumors were rapidly spreading that the entire military was going to be dis-banded and that everyone would be on his own to find a place in one of the independent states. Ollie was more concerned that the air marshall had not been heard from and had disappeared. Ollie called his home phone and got no response. Without taking anything from his office, Ollie left the base and returned to his apartment.

He parked two blocks from the apartment and started to walk. As he approached his apartment a military car stopped in front of his apartment. Several officers entered his foyer. Ollie stepped back into a doorway and waited. Four men had entered the apartment and only two came out. The two got into the car and drove away. It wasn't too difficult for Ollie to determine that the other two men were waiting for him.

He retreated to his car and drove through alleys until he reached the drop point that he and Sergi had established years ago. Ollie placed a signal to tell Sergi that they were in danger. Ollie walked to a public phone and made a call to the American Embassy to request pick up at a pre-designated pick up location, and then returned to his car. He removed the light that illuminated the car's license plate, and drove to another alley were he stayed until it became dark.

After dark he drove to near Gorkiy Park and parked his car in an inconspicuous place, and started walking toward the park. As he neared the designated pick up place an American Ford car pulled up along the curb. The interior light came on as the driver opened the door. Ollie recognized James Lang from the American Embassy. Lang opened the trunk and motioned for Ollie to get in. Lang then he closed the trunk, re-entered the car and started to drive.

Ollie could barely breathe. He was alone in total darkness, bouncing along in a car that might be stopped at any moment. After many turns and stops the car stopped for a few minutes. Ollie heard Lang talking to somebody in English. The car started to move, made a few turns and stopped again. Ollie heard and felt the car door slam and a minute later the trunk opened and Ollie could see that he was in a garage.

James Lang helped him out of the trunk and said, "Welcome to the United States Embassy."

Lang motioned for Ollie to follow and they made their way out of the garage and across the compound to the large, gray embassy building.

As Lang was leading Ollie through the large entrance foyer he said, "You will be here for a few days until we make arrangements to get you back to the States. There are some people here that you will be happy to see."

They entered a large room and Ollie was indeed happy to see Sergi and Helena. Helena was obviously confused and was further confused when Ollie came into the room.

Sergi took Ollie aside and said, "I have told her that because I worked so closely with Gorbachev I had evidently made some enemies in the new government that wanted me arrested. I told her that the US had volunteered to provide us with asylum. Just before you came in I told her that we are going to the US. She is really thoroughly confused."

"Are you going to stay in the States permanently?" Ollie asked.

"Yes, I have been thinking about this for years. I think I'm going to continue teaching. I could go to work for the CIA or some other agency but I think I'm ready to find a nice, quiet campus and enjoy life."

"Any idea of where you might go?" Ollie asked. "I'll want to keep in touch."

"Probably Georgetown," he replied. "I always liked the school and the area. What are you going to do?"

"I have a lot of unfinished business to take care of," Ollie replied. "After that, if the Air Force banked my pay like they promised, I think I will retire."

"What are you going to do about Tamara?"

"As soon as I am safely in the States I am going to contact her and ask her to join me." Ollie replied.

"Have you heard anything about Malenkovich?" Ollie asked.

"I asked Lang about him and he said he has been checking but so far hasn't received a pick up signal. He may have been picked up by the military already. If you hadn't alerted me I am not sure I would be here."

"I just missed being picked up myself," Ollie said. "If I hadn't used that procedure you schooled me in, to check my apartment from a distance when I suspected trouble, they would have picked me up. I keep saying "they". The people who came to my apartment were military. Who do you think sent them and why would they want me?"

"I suspect somebody in the military had suspicions about us and wanted us for questioning. I really don't care. I have been thinking about getting out since the first moments of the coup. I don't really know what is going to happen here so I'll be happy to go anywhere that is more stable."

It took several days to prepare Ollie's passport and documents. His papers identified him as a member of the US military and a diplomatic courier. The embassy provided him with the uniform of an Air Force major and routed him by commercial airlines to Washington, DC.

Sergi and Helena walked to the embassy car that was taking him to the airport. As they said goodbye they promised to keep in touch. James Lang provided Ollie and Sergi with a name and a phone number to call and advised them to contact the number in the States for help if needed.

Lang handed Ollie a key and said, "This is a key to a safe deposit box at the main branch of the Chase Bank in Washington DC. The box contains the document you requested and a savings passbook. Your back pay has been deposited in the bank. If you have any problems contact me through the CIA number I gave you, or call the State Department."

"I have one more favor to ask of you," Ollie said. "Try to find Air Marshall Gaidar and help him if you can. We probably got him in trouble by recruiting him to help us sell the military hard-liners on being patient. I feel responsible for him and he is a good man."

"I will see what we can do. I promise," Lang said, following him to the car.

Ollie got into the car with two Marine guards and a driver and waved goodbye.

The trip was nerve wracking. Ollie was paranoid, expecting to be swept up and seized at every airport between Moscow and Washington. When the plane took off from Paris for a non-stop flight to Washington he finally relaxed.

He started to think about returning to the US and wondered what he would find there. He had been away for forty years and was apprehensive about making a new life in what would now be a strange place. He knew he had some serious business to take care of before starting his new life. Promises made to his fellow prisoners in Irkutsk must be kept. Finding any living relatives was also on his list of things to do.

Not having Tamara with him would also be painful.

When he arrived at the Dulles airport international arrival terminal, he was pleased to see a man standing at the embarkation door, carrying a placard that identified him as his contact.

The man smiled broadly as Ollie approached and said, "Welcome back Lieutenant Miller. Let's pick up your bags. I have a car waiting."

"I have no luggage." Ollie said, "Only this small bag with toilet articles and this," holding up the leather courier bag that was handcuffed to his wrist.

They exited the terminal receiving area, bypassing the normal inspection by Immigration Service personnel. And walked to a pick up area outside the terminal where a car and driver were waiting, and drove to the CIA farm near Williamsburg, Virginia.

When they arrived, an elderly man with a pleasant, time-wrinkled face came into the foyer to meet him.

"I'm Paul Cannon," the man said. "I'll be debriefing you for the next week or two. You will be staying here until we are done and I promise to work as quickly as I can so you can get on with your life. We will get you some new clothes. My friend here will show you to your quarters and give you the scoop on the set up. I'm sure you are tired from your trip and want to get some sleep so I'll call you in the morning."

Ollie's guide directed him to a building where agents lived while in training or waiting for reassignment. Ollie's room was spotlessly clean and comfortable. In addition to the bed, the room had a desk and chair and an easy chair facing a television set and an adjoining bathroom.

The next morning the phone ringing awakened him. Paul Cannon was on the line to tell him that one of his assistants would soon be there to take him to breakfast and then to get him outfitted with civilian clothes. He would start the debriefing after lunch.

The next few weeks were extremely interesting to Ollie. In addition to his daily debriefing sessions he was brought up to date with what had happened in the US since he was captured in the 1950's. When Cannon could see that Ollie was getting bored with the debriefing he would excuse himself and one of his assistants would show Ollie a "Year in Review" tape that highlighted happenings for a complete year. Ollie enjoyed the tapes immensely and frequently interrupted the tapes to ask questions about people and places.

As promised, the de-briefings were efficiently concluded and recorded in two weeks.

When Cannon told him he was finished he asked Ollie about his plans.

Ollie had been thinking about what he would do first after his debriefing.

"I told you about the Americans I was with in Irkutsk. I am going to keep my promise and see if any of them returned to the US. If they haven't I am going to try to find out what has happened to their families and tell them what I know."

"I can help you with that," Cannon said. "I have a few good contacts in the Department of Defense and the Pentagon. Let me make a few phone calls to see what I can set up."

The next day the CIA provided Ollie with a Social Security card, identification papers, a passport and a driver's license. They also provided him with a car and driver who took him to the Chase Bank. Ollie introduced himself to the customer representative inside the front entrance to the bank. The pleasant young woman walked Ollie to the Safe Deposit area and after Ollie had secured and opened the box, helped Ollie to switch the savings account to a checking account.

Ollie was surprised by the value of the account. He had made calculations based on his monthly salary when he was shot down. The amount in the account was many times greater than he had calculated. Evidently the payments in were based on the increases in military pay over the many years. The account also included compounded interest. Ollie was a relatively wealthy man.

The Bank provided him with cash, an ATM card and a few blank checks.

The CIA had offered him the use of a furnished apartment in Bethesda and after moving in he took a cab to a nearby automobile agency and bought a blue Mercury Grand Marquis.

His first priority would be to complete his search for his fellow prisoners from Irkutsk and their families. When that task was completed, he could devote his time to investigating Mary's death and finding the remnants of his family.

CHAPTER *21*

Washington, D.C., USA, 1992

Paul Cannon's contact in the Pentagon was a bright young Air Force captain. Edward Thompson, a slight, blonde, open faced man sparkled with enthusiasm. He greeted Ollie warmly and after seeing Ollie through security and providing him with a temporary pass directed him to a conference room on the first floor of the huge five-sided building. Thompson had been briefed on Ollie's background and asked one question after another, shaking his head in disbelief as Ollie filled in the blanks between the outline the young captain had and his actual experiences. The fascination with Ollie's life continued for an hour. Finally Thompson realized that he was not addressing the reason for Ollie's presence.

"I'm really sorry," he said apologetically. "Your story is so interesting that I could talk to you for a month. I became so fascinated I forgot you were here for my help. How can I help you?"

Ollie opened his newly acquired brief case and removed a few sheets of paper with a handwritten list of names and cities.

"These men," Ollie said as he handed the papers to the Air Force captain, "were all American Air Force prisoners with me in Irkutsk in southeastern Siberia in the early 1950's. I am sorry I don't know the precise date. I had been in northern Siberia for a long time after I was shot down so I don't know exactly when I arrived at Irkutsk. All of these men were crewmembers of B29's that had been shot down over Russia. The

KGB officer at Irkutsk told me that they were crews of reconnaissance planes that had been sent into Russia from Japan on what he called ferret missions. I want to know if these men were ever released and returned. We all memorized each other's names and hometowns and promised that if any of us got out that we would do what I'm doing now. This is very important to me. It's so important that I want to do this first before I start trying to find out what happened to my family."

The young captain had been shaking his head in wonder as Ollie spoke.

"Why in heck would the US be flying B29's over Russia?", he exclaimed. "That could have started World War Three!"

"I don't know," Ollie replied. "They told me I would be testing the Soviet radar system and I did what I was ordered to do. I was just a dumb kid at the time and I never even thought about the political ramifications. The KGB officer told me that they had shot down at least ten B29's. If they were carrying full crews that would be over a hundred US airmen shot down over Russia. I don't know how many survived the crashes but that list proves that some did and were put in prison in Russia. I have got to know if they were sent home. If not, I want to know if their families were notified what happened to them."

"This is an amazing story," Edwards said as they started out the door. "I will have to tell my immediate superior what I am going to be doing." He stopped and wrote a telephone number and extension on a piece of paper and handed it to Ollie. "Call me in a few days and I'll let you know what I have found."

That evening he sat down at the desk in his apartment and dialed 412-555-1212 on his phone, and asked for Greenwood, Pennsylvania information. He first asked for the phone number of his brother Tim. The information operator informed him that there was no listing for that name. He then asked for the number for every relative he could remember. There were no listings. He explained to the operator that he had been away for many years and the operator patiently read the name of every Miller listed in Greenwood. He did not recognize a single name.

As soon as I find out what happened to Mary and get this Air Force matter completed, I will have to go Greenwood and see what has happened to my family, he said to himself.

Ollie spent the next two days touring the Capitol. He parked near the Lincoln memorial and walked through the park to the black marble Vietnam War memorial. At first he just walked up and down in front of the memorial, looking for Kevin's name. He finally gave up and asked the park ranger to look up the location of Kevin's name on the memorial.

The female park ranger paged back to the *M's* in the alphabetized list and looked up at Kevin and said, "I'm sorry sir, their is no Kevin O Miller listed. Are you sure you have the correct spelling?"

Ollie was mystified, "Yes I'm sure," he said, shaking his head. "He was my son."

The park ranger again looked through the list and then shook her head and said, "Sorry", and then looked at the next person in line.

The next morning he called Captain Thompson at the Pentagon.

"Thanks for calling," Thompson said, "I should have gotten your number. I don't have any information for you yet. A lot of the names you gave me are in the computer. Unfortunately there are multiple entries for every name. It's difficult since you don't have the serial numbers for the men. I have someone doing a check at the mines, that's where we have all the copies of records stored on microfiche. I have also contacted the Veterans Administration and The Social Security people. They are the most likely ones to have names and addresses. I called the IRS but they told me I would have to get some kind of special authorization to search their files. Give me a few more days and see what these people can come up with and give me your phone number in case I have to call you for more information."

Ollie could not mask his disappointment but thanked him for his diligence.

Two days later Ollie called Thompson and was disappointed to learn that all the searches were negative. The captain also reluctantly told Ollie that his superior had advised him not to expend any more effort on the search.

"Is there anyway I can talk to someone in Air Force who can tell me how I could obtain information on B29 flight crews flying out of Japan during the Korean war?" Ollie asked.

"Right off the top of my head I don't know. But I will check on that for you."

"Also, how can I get a list of the B29 top command officers during that same time period? I may be able to locate them and talk to them if they are still alive."

"I will check that out also but it will have to be unofficial. If there is any way you can get the serial numbers of the prisoners call me and I will ask my boss if I can try again." Thompson said, "Call me if you think I can help in any way."

Ollie called Paul Cannon at CIA headquarters. When he told him that he had been unsuccessful in his attempts to get information about the airman Cannon put Ollie on hold. In a few minutes came back and said, "I have set up a meeting for you tomorrow at ten am with Herb Montel of the Federal Bureau of Investigation at their main building down town. Do you know where that is?"

"I think I saw it the other day when I was at the Smithsonian," Ollie replied.

"It's in that area, at Pennsylvania and 10th," Paul replied. "Take your list with you. He may be able to help since they have offices in all the major cities."

The next morning Ollie found his way downtown and after finding a place to park entered the FBI building and advised the receptionist that he was there to see Herb Montel. A few minutes later a beautiful, well-dressed black woman came into the reception area and called his name. When Ollie stood up and put up his hand she said.

"Please follow me Mister Miller."

She led him to the elevator and made no attempt at small talk. When they got to the third floor she stepped out of the elevator and led him to an office and knocked on the door.

A middle age, dark complexioned man opened the door and motioned Ollie in and then shut the door.

"Paul gave me a brief rundown on your problem. How can I help?", Montel asked.

Ollie opened his brief case and handed him a copy of the list of Irkutsk prisoners and explained his problem and what he was doing.

Montel asked many questions to assure that the request was legitimate, and then ended the discussion by saying, "I'll talk this over with my superior and if he agrees to the allocation of resources we will do a search."

He rose and shook Ollie's hand and showed him to the door. The young black woman then escorted Ollie to the exit.

Ollie turned to thank the woman as he was leaving and asked, "Are you allowed to talk to visitors?"

She smiled and said, "No, and don't tell anyone I said no."

Ollie had provided Montel with his phone number. When a week had passed and Montel hadn't called, Ollie called Montel.

He recognized the voice that answered, "Mister Montel's office".

Ollie said "Good morning Miss No, this is Oliver Miller. May I please speak to Mister Montel?"

He thought he heard a slight chuckle just before she said, "One moment please."

Montel picked up his phone and said, "I have been meaning to call you. We made a cursory inquiry from every office near one of your addresses and came up empty. My boss has told me not to spend any more time on this but if I can be of any assistance give me a call and I will see what I can do."

"I guess I'll have to do the detail checking by going to the hometowns myself," Ollie said. "Do you have any suggestions?"

Montel thought for a moment and then said, "Start in the small towns. That will limit the number of duplicate names. Also go to the county seats and check their records. Almost all of them are open for public view. You can find things like birth certificates, wedding and death certificates and all kind of other information. It's tedious work but you may find what you are looking for."

Ollie thanked him for his advice and then went to the nearest bookstore and bought a Road Atlas for the United States. He also bought a huge roll up map of the United States and got marking pins and pens at an office supply store. When he got to his apartment he unrolled the map and taped it up on the wall. He then started down the list of names, marking the hometown of everyone on the list on the large map with a pin and a three by five card with each mans' name. If he couldn't find the town on the large map he would search the state maps in the Road Atlas until he found it and then would mark its location on the large map.

When he was finished he could see that they were a few clusters of pins and the rest were widely spread out. He decided to visit the small towns closest to Washington first, and then made up his travel list. He had purchased a spiral notebook for each of the men and had written their names on the cover with a felt tipped pen.

He sat for a minute, trying to decide if he would try to find the airmen families first or try to locate his own family. After some thought he decided to complete the airmen task first, thinking it would only take at most two weeks.

In the morning he would start his search.

Early the next morning Ollie packed his car and started south on I-95. When he reached Fredricksburg, Virginia he headed west on route 3 to Culpeper, a small town in the beautiful Shenendoah valley, just north of Charlottesville, Virginia. He found a motel on the outskirts of the small town and after checking in to his room opened the room phone book, opened a spiral notebook, and started writing down the first name, address and phone number of the people with the same last name as the name of the man on the prisoner's list who's hometown had been Culpeper. When he finished he dialed the first number. A woman answered the phone on the third ring.

Ollie said, "My name is Oliver Miller, I was in the Air Force with a man called James McCarthy from Culpeper. I am organizing a reunion and I am trying to track him down. Do you know him?"

There was a long pause and then the woman said, "He is not a relative of mine. I am sorry I can't help you." She hung up without further comment.

Ollie went down the list and got the same answer from everyone on the list. None of the people he contacted was even able to offer a suggestion.

This is going to be a lot harder than I imagined, Ollie thought to himself.

The next morning he drove to the county court house and started checking records. The records were stored by year. Since Ollie had no idea of when James McCarthy was born he had to estimate his age and then go back to the probable year of his birth and then work both ways. Herb Montel was right, it was tedious work. It took almost three hours to find the birth certificate. Now he had a date and the name of McCarthy's mother and father and the physician. It took another four hours to find the wedding license for the parents. That gave him the maiden name of the mother and allowed him to make another list of names to call. There was no marriage license on file for James McCarthy.

Ollie rubbed his weary eyes. He quit searching records for the day and went back to the motel and started calling. The results were the same; nobody had any knowledge of James McCarthy.

Next he started to visit the cemeteries in Culpeper. He would look up the caretaker and go through the list of lot owners. That proved to be a dead end. All he found were names he had already checked and names that were not in the phone book.

He found a memorial in the town with the names of the men from Culpeper who had been killed in World War II. There was no Korean War monument.

Ollie went back to the courthouse and started asking clerks in the different offices if they had ever heard of James McCarthy who enlisted in the Air Force during the Korean War. Most of them directed him to the woman in the Register of Wills office who was sixty-five and was reported to know every one in Culpeper. Ollie went to her office and after a pleasant conversation left without additional information.

He next visited the library, hoping to find old newspapers on file. Unfortunately the library hadn't started putting newspapers on microfiche until 1969. The few papers Ollie looked at gave little hope of finding any new information.

The clerks at the elementary and high schools allowed him to check their old records and he did find an address. He drove to the address and knocked on every door in the neighborhood and found no one who knew the McCarthys.

His next stop was the police station. At first the clerk at the police station refused to cooperate. When Ollie explained his mission she finally relented and allowed him to look through the musty old files in the basement. Nothing turned up.

The parish priest at the local Catholic Church also allowed him to look through old files but he could not come up with any new information. He had been working diligently for a week and was at a dead end.

Discouraged, Ollie packed up his clothes, loaded them in the trunk of his car and headed back to I-95 and then south to Smithfield, North Carolina, just off I-95.

The results in Smithfield just about duplicated the results in Culpeper. Ollie met some very nice people who tried to help him but once again was frustrated.

Ollie had to face the reality that it had been forty years since the men had been in the military and it could have been sixty years since the men had left the town.

Undaunted and still hopeful, Ollie continued south on I-95 to Lumberton, North Carolina and took Route 74 west and then some back roads to Rock Hill, South Carolina, just South of Charlotte. He checked into a motel and started assembling his calling list. Rock Hills population was five times more than the first two towns he had visited and so were the listings for Paines, the last name of the man on his list from Rock Hills.

He was well into the list, perhaps to the tenth name when a woman who has answered the phone said, "Yes, I knew Bob Paine. He was my husband. He didn't come back from Korea."

Ollie asked, "Was he in the Air Force?"

"Yes he was", she answered. "He flew in a big plane like the one that dropped the Atomic bomb."

A chill went down Ollie's spine. "Miss's Paine, I have traveled a long way looking for you. I'm in Rock Hill and I would like very much to talk to you."

"What do you want to talk about?" She asked.

"It's really to complicated to talk about over the phone. Can I come to your house?"

The woman hesitated and Ollie realized that she was both confused and wary.

"If you have any concerns, have some of your relatives or friends there. This is very important to me and may be of more importance to you."

The woman thought for a minute and then agreed to his visit and gave him directions to her home.

Ollie found the house, weather-beaten and badly in need of repair and paint, on the outskirts of the town. There were two old cars parked in the dirt driveway when he pulled in.

A middle aged, life worn man in old, faded work clothes answered his knock and let him into the living room where a gray haired, stooped older woman, dressed in a shabby house dress, and a younger man were waiting. They rose from the old faded stuffed chairs when Ollie entered.

Oliver introduced himself and the woman said, "I'm Sybil Paine. These are my two sons Roy and Al."

As Ollie shook hands with the two men, the man who met him at the door said, "What's this all about and what do you want?"

Ollie sat down and started to tell them his story.

When he got the part about meeting the airmen in Irkutsk and their promises to each other that the first man out would contact the families, the woman began to cry. "Oh God, oh God, he might still be alive. He could have been in prison for all these years."

One of her sons tried to comfort her and the other said with emotion, "I knew those government bastards weren't telling us the truth. I knew there was something fishy."

Ollie looked at the three and asked, "What did they tell you?"

"All they would tell us was that he was missing in action, nothing else. Mom tried for years to find out more but they wouldn't tell us anything. We got our old congressman in Washington to try to help but they still didn't tell us anything. Our congressman once said that it was a confidential thing, whatever that means."

The other younger brother who had been trying to straighten out his thoughts finally said, "What would my father and his crew be doing over Russia. We weren't fighting them were we?"

"No we weren't," Ollie replied. "I think they were on some kind of secret mission."

"And they were shot down in Russia and put in prison and our government didn't get them out? This is unbelievable."

Ollie looked at the woman and asked, "Did you save any letters or anything else that might help me find out what the government knew and didn't know.

"I have a box up in the attic with some letters I got from Bob and the letters I got from the government. You can get them Roy, bring down the tin box that's in the cedar chest."

Roy came back in a few minutes with the box. Mrs. Paine opened the box and handed the papers to Ollie.

He sorted through the papers until he found the letters. In the return address, on the upper left side of the envelopes, were Bob's name, rank, serial number and mailing address. Ollie copied all the information into the spiral notebook with Bob's name and then started to read the letters from the military and her congressman. When he finished he looked at the group and said, "I would like to make copies of these. I will have to go into town. One of your sons can come with me if you want."

"I'll go with him Mom," Roy said. "We won't be long."

On the way back to town Roy tried to get more information from Ollie and wanted to know all about the conditions in the prison. He was relieved when Ollie told him that it wasn't really that bad.

He asked how Ollie had got out. Ollie thought it better to just say that when the communist government collapsed he had the opportunity to escape.

Roy asked Ollie if his mother might get back pay if his father was held in prison after a government mission.

"Somebody will have to pay and I pledge to you that I will not let the government off the hook until they acknowledge what happened and make restitution."

"That would be good," Roy replied. "Mom didn't give up hope for a long time that dad would come back. She really has had a hard time."

While they were driving to town Roy told Ollie that his father had been a career Air Force man who had stayed in the military after World War II. His father had inherited the house Sybil was living in from his father. The family lived there when their father was stationed outside the country. When their father left for Korea the family had moved back into the house and had been there ever since.

They found a place to copy the documents in a strip mall a short distance from the Paine home. Ollie carefully removed the documents from their envelopes, one at a time, made a copy of the document and the envelope, and then reinserted the document.

It took less than an hour to make the copies and return to the house.

"I'll tell you what I plan to do," Ollie said. "I'm going to every town on my list. Hopefully I'll find other family members. I have already contacted an Air Force officer in the Pentagon who is trying to help me. I'll give you his name and phone number and my address and phone number. I'll be traveling for several weeks. When I get back to my home base I'll write you and tell you everything I know and we will figure out what we should do next. You can write to me at my home address if you think of anything that might help."

The three Paines followed him out to his car and thanked him profusely for calling and encouraged his efforts. They stood in the dirt driveway waving until he was out of sight.

Ollie drove back to I-77 and headed north and then took I-85 to Greensboro, North Carolina. The trip was a waste of time. The people he met and talked to wanted to help but in the end Ollie did not collect any new information. After seven days of frustration he headed back to I-95 at Petersburg, Virginia and back to Bethesda, Maryland. He arrived at his apartment after two in the morning and fell into bed, exhausted and discouraged. Hundreds of miles and over four weeks on the road and he had one serial number and copies of a few documents.

The next morning he called Ed Thompson at the Pentagon and briefly outlined the results of his trip. Ed promised to run Bob Paine's serial number through the computers and review the documents Ollie said he would mail.

Ollie spent the rest of the day taking care of his laundry and preparing for the next leg of his investigation. He had come to the realization that knowing only the hometowns for the people on his list was probably not going to be much help. His record searches had already proven that. Just because someone grew up in a town didn't necessarily mean that there would be any records.

CHAPTER *22*

Once back in his apartment in Bethesda, Ollie called Ed Thompson at the Pentagon and once again filled him in on his trip. He was totally surprised when Ed told him that he had run Bob Paine's serial number through the computer and come up with no match. Ed was totally confused by the results.

"I don't know why I didn't think of this before," Ollie said. "How about running my serial number through the computer. I know I exist."

Ed agreed and Ollie told him he would check in when he returned from a trip that would take him to six cities scattered about the US.

The next part of his investigation consumed nearly a month. Traveling by air he visited the historic Alamo city of San Antonio, Texas, with its scenic river walk shopping district and quaint missions; Tucson, Arizona; dusty, dry and hot Yuma, Arizona; picturesque and delightful San Diego, California. He flew from there into the airport on a plateau overlooking Great Falls Montana, and then to the self proclaimed middle of nowhere, Cedar Rapids, Iowa. He was successful in three of his last five stops. Cedar Rapids was purposely last on his list. It had been Bill Snelling's hometown. He knew that Bill, at least when he was flying with him in MATs, and later in Irkutsk, had a sister living in Cedar Rapids. It took five days of digging but he was finally successful. Through Bill's parents marriage license he found a cousin on the mothers side who knew Bill's sisters married name and where she was living. Bill found her in Sioux City, Iowa and spent three days with her.

Her tale was the same as all the others. Her parents had been notified that Bill was missing in action. After many inquiries they had been notified that he was presumed dead. Like the others left at home, they had watched TV and seen prisoners being returned at the end of the Korean War. When Bill didn't return her parents had started pestering the Air Force, the Department of Defense and their congressman and senator. The results were the same; no information and cryptic replies and then nothing. Bill's parents had both died and most of their personal papers had been discarded. Fortunately Bill's sister had kept some letters from Bill and he found his serial number.

"The Russians lied to us," Ollie exclaimed, his face red with anger. "They told us Bill had signed a confession and had been returned to the States. They used him to break us. They knew how much we all respected Bill and they used that to their advantage. I always had doubts. I didn't think that Bill would confess but I wasn't sure."

Bill's sister was grateful that at last somebody was able to provide her with information about her brother and told Ollie that she would be willing to do anything to help, even if it meant moving to Washington temporarily.

With the investigation on his list of names complete, Ollie had one last stop to make before heading back to Bethesda. He was going to stop in Chicago and visit with his old friend and RO from his flying days in Korea.

One of the first people Ollie had called after returning to the US was Bill Thomas. It had taken him only a few minutes to locate and talk to him on the phone. They had talked for an hour, filling each other in on the happenings in their lives since Ollie had disappeared. Bill's information on Mary was very limited.

Ollie had promised to spend several days with Bill to renew their friendship and now that he was in Chicago, that time had arrived. Ollie called Bill from Iowa and told him when he would be arriving at O'Hare airport. Bill insisted on picking him up. As Ollie entered the passenger area at O'Hare he searched the people waiting on passengers and didn't spot Bill. A florid faced man with a protruding stomach started waving and shouting, "Ollie, over here."

Ollie could not believe the change in Bill, from a young, slim, athletic man to the present overweight man that looked twenty years older than he really was.

Over the next several days Ollie gradually learned the story of Bill's life since leaving the Air Force. He had not been assigned to another pilot after Ollie mysteriously disappeared. He had kept in touch with Mary and related the Air Forces mistreatment of both he and Mary when they started making inquiries about Ollie. He lost track of Mary when he was shipped back to the States to a do nothing job. He was discharged and returned to Chicago and had attended college for a few years and then had dropped out and had gone to work as a car salesman. He married the car agency owner's daughter and things went very well for about four years. His marriage started to disintegrate and he was fired and his wife divorced him and retained custody of the daughter. He had been bouncing aimlessly from car dealer to car dealer and was evidently a successful salesman.

Although Bill did not disclose the reason for the breakup, it was easy for Ollie to read between the lines. Bill was an alcoholic.

Bill related as many of the details as he could remember following Ollie's disappearance and Ollie took notes for future reference. He left Chicago saddened and concerned for the life of his friend.

Ollie returned to Bethesda and immediately called Ed Thompson at the Pentagon.

"I have information on seven of the fourteen names on my list." Ollie advised. "Surely something will show up on the computer".

"I will get our people on it today," Thompson replied. "Are you going to be in your apartment for awhile?"

"That depends," Ollie replied. "If you have any information about the Fifth Air Force command officers during the Korean War I will check them out while you are running the latest names through the computer."

"Oh yes, we did round up that information for you. I have a list of the first and second levels of command and I also had my people dig out the information on Air Force Intelligence personnel who were operating in Japan. You have to realize that the list is not very long. Since we are looking for people who were in there forties during Korea, most of them are either dead or very old. Just a minute and I will have my secretary give you the information."

Ollie waited patiently until a pleasant female voice said, "Hello Mister Miller. If you have paper and pen ready I'll read the information to you."

Ollie copied the names, addresses and phone numbers of three people. Two were retired generals who had been in top command positions. The third was a retired colonel who had been in Special Operations. When Ollie called them on the phone they all, at first, refused to talk to him. After some persuasion they all agreed to talk to him face to face. Ollie hung up from the last call and called his travel agent and arranged a one-week trip to visit all three men.

His first stop was Naples, Florida. Ollie flew nonstop from Baltimore to Fort Myers Florida, called the man he wanted to talk to tell him he was at the airport and then rented a car. He drove south on I-75 to Naples and then west to Gulf Shore Boulevard.

Retired General Richard Meoli lived in a condo overlooking the Gulf of Mexico. Ollie parked in visitors parking at the upscale hi-rise and entered the foyer of the eight-story building. He found the general's condo and rang the doorbell. A slight, dark Hispanic woman answered the door.

"The General is playing tennis," the woman said in answer to Ollie's question. "He should be home soon. He said for you to wait here."

Ollie relaxed on the lanai that faced the Gulf, watching the sea gulls and the people walking on the beach below. He heard the general when he came in the front door and walked out toward the foyer. The general, still looking slim and athletic despite his age, extended his hand and said, "Welcome to southwest Florida Mister Miller. Why have you come all this way to talk to me?"

Ollie and the general sat on the Lanai and the housekeeper served them iced tea. Ollie told the General his story up to the time that he met the American airmen in Irkutsk.

When Ollie finished the general said, "How do you think I will be able to help you?"

"You were in a command post in Korea during this time. I want to know if you had anything to do with a ferret reconnaissance program?"

"Yes I did," the General replied. "It was a classified, confidential program."

"That much I know," Ollie replied. "I was hoping you could help me with the Air Force. They are telling me that there is no information on the prisoners that I met and they have denied that they ever existed. I made a promise to the men in Irkutsk that I would talk to the Air Force and their loved ones to allow the families to know what happened. Also, since these men were on active duty and lived for long years as prisoners, their families are owed the pay the men would have received."

"Why isn't the Air Force helping you?"

"They are trying but they are running into stone walls. Do you know what happened to the records on these men?"

"No I don't," the General replied. "I don't know what else I can tell you. I don't know if this information is still classified. I will have to call the Brass in Washington on this. Call me back in a few days and I will tell you what I have found."

G. B. Mooney

Ollie's next stop was Dallas, Texas. This trip was a waste of time and money. The retired general would not answer a single question and politely told Ollie to leave.

The last man on the list provided by Thompson was for the retired special ops colonel who was living on South Padre Island in the southeastern tip of Texas. Ollie flew into Brownsville Texas and rented a car and drove north to South Padre.

"You are talking about a project that was top secret and as far as I know has never been declassified. Since you are running around the country broadcasting information I think I'll hold you here until I get instructions from Washington." The retired colonel advised with hostility.

"Try it and I'll bury your stupid ass in the sand outside," Ollie said, rising to face the colonel. "It was probably a jerk like you who made the decision to lie and cover up the fate of over a hundred Americans. I hope that someday somebody screws you or somebody you love."

"If you leave I'll call the police and have you arrested before you leave Texas," the colonel shouted, moving toward the phone.

Ollie cut him off and tore the phone out of the wall and turned to the colonel. "I hope you realize that someone like you cost me my life and since you are here, nice and handy, I'll be more than happy to have you be the one who pays," Ollie said in a voice that would cut steel. "Make one more stupid statement and I'll stick this phone down your throat."

"Okay, okay, just leave," the colonel said. "But I am warning you, this is not over between you and me. I still have contacts in Intel and I intend to use them."

"You and all your buddies can kiss my ass," Ollie said as he left. "Before I get to the airport I am going to call my contacts in the CIA and tell them about your threat. They hate people like you. If I were you I would keep a low profile or your friends, if you have any, might find your body floating in the Gulf."

"Are you threatening me?" The colonel bellowed.

"Yes." Ollie said as he headed for the door.

Ollie left South Padre Island and decided to drive back to Houston instead of Brownsville, just in case the colonel kept his threat to call the police. When he was well on his way he stopped at a public phone and called Paul Cannon and told him about his experience with the colonel.

"If you don't hear from me in a couple days, do me a favor and call the police departments in this area to see if they have me in jail."

"I don't think you will have any problems but check in with me when you get back."

Ollie flew into the Baltimore airport and arrived back in his apartment late that night. He fell into bed and was asleep in minutes. The next morning he called Paul Cannon and reported in and then called Captain Thompson at the Pentagon.

He immediately sensed the coolness in Thompson's voice.

"Did you find anything in the computers with the information I gave you?" Ollie asked.

"No we didn't," he answered laconically.

"How about with my serial number," Ollie asked. "I am sure I exist."

"Don't be too sure of that," Thompson replied. "According to the computer, you never were in the Air Force. Also, my immediate superior's boss called me in and when he found out you weren't on the computer he launched an investigation of you. He is not sure just who you are and doesn't trust the CIA. I have orders to report to him immediately if you call me and to tell you I'm not to talk to you again. Sorry."

The sound of the phone hanging up caused Ollie to look at the phone in confusion. *What was happening?*

He dialed General Meoli's phone number in Naples, Florida. When the housekeeper answered the phone he asked to talk to the general.

"Who is calling?" The housekeeper asked.

"This is Oliver Miller," Ollie replied. "I talked to the general a few days ago.

"The general told me to tell you that he has no information for you, and that you are not to call him again."

I wonder what caused that? He asked himself.

Where do I go from here? He wondered, *I can't stop now. I know that these people exist. I have worked too hard to give up and I can't let down the people on my list. I sure can't let down the families. But, what do I do next? None of the Federal Agencies have been helpful.*

CHAPTER 23

Washington, D.C., USA

Lt. Colonel Richard Shields was the picture that Air Force public relations wanted you to see in your mind when you thought about an American pilot. Tall, square shouldered, slightly sun bleached short brown hair, suntanned, intelligent piercing brown eyes, dressed in his blue uniform with a chest full of ribbons beneath his silver pilots wings, he was imposing man.

His squadron was the first to arrive in Saudi Arabia after Iraq invaded Kuwait. They flew nonstop to Riyadh, with in flight refueling. After a short rest they flew the first combat mission against Iraq. Richard Shields shot down two Iraqi MIGs on his first flight. The Iraqi Air Force hid and Shields spent the rest of the Persian Gulf War flying seek and destroy combat missions. Now he was flying a desk in the Pentagon and hated his job.

Over his strong objection he had been selected for fast track command training. Now he was spending the mandatory year at the Pentagon, learning and hating the intricacies of Defense Department politics and intrigue. He considered the assignment a waste of time and most offensively, the assignment limited his flying time. He was allowed a few hours flight time a month to maintain proficiency but it wasn't enough to satisfy his need to fly.

Just like a kid counting down the days to the start of summer vacation, Shields kept a calendar on his desk and at the end of each day put an X through the date with a magic marker. To make matters worse he was in Public Relations, responsible for routine inquires from non-military types.

The request to provide help to Oliver Miller came down through channels. It seemed like a routine request; an ex-Air Force person trying to track down his Korean War buddies. He had assigned the request to Captain Thompson and then gone on to less important items.

A month latter Thompson had brought him up to date on his assignment and he had told him to close the search.

Now two investigators from Military Intelligence were sitting in his office looking very unhappy.

When they started to ask questions he had Thompson come to his office to provide details.

Thompson gave a thumb nail sketch of his meeting with Ollie and his attempts to find the airmen he had been imprisoned with in Irkutsk. Colonel Shields became interested when Thompson related Ollie's activities after being shot down. He had only briefly glanced at the request before assigning it to Thompson. Ollie's life and escape and his attempts to fulfill his promise made to the US airmen prisoners in Russia peaked his interest. *What had these men been doing and what had happened to them?*

He started to ask questions and the Intelligence men asked Thompson to leave. After he left the senior intelligence officer shut the door and turned back to Colonel Shields.

"When your man entered the serial numbers for Paine and Miller in the computer it triggered a notification to Intelligence. All I can tell you right now is that this matter is classified as Top Secret. I don't want you to provide any more information to Miller or to anybody, and I mean anybody, without contacting us."

"What the hell is this all about?" Shields asked. "It sounds like some airmen were let hung out to dry by our own government. That sure as hell interests me. I have flown over enemy territory and always assumed that my government would do everything possible to get me back if I was forced down. Have I been wrong?"

"I am going to tell you this just once," the top intelligence officer said. "This is Top Secret and none of your business. Just let us take care of this. Also I will tell you that we are going to investigate Miller and his path into the CIA and the Pentagon. We don't even know if this guy is legitimate. He was someplace for a lot of years, doing we don't know what. We want to check him out. If he calls again, brush him off and call me immediately."

After Ollie quit staring at the phone when General Meoli's housekeeper hung up, he called Paul Cannon at his CIA office.

When Cannon answered the phone Ollie related the results of his investigations and then told him how surprised he was by the statements of Captain Thompson from the Pentagon and General Meoli's decision not to talk to him.

"Why don't you send me copies of all the documents you have and I'll see what we can do with them," Cannon said. "While I'm waiting for the mail I'll call the Pentagon and see if I can get any information."

Ollie hung up and sat down and tried to think about what he could next do to solve the questions about the men from Irkutsk. He decided to wait a few days to see if Cannon would be able to help.

After making that decision he started on the next item on his agenda, trying to locate Helena and Sergi. It proved to be very simple. He called Georgetown University and after asking if Sergi was teaching there was immediately transferred to Sergi's office. When Sergi answered, he couldn't believe it had been so easy to locate him.

"Hello Sergi," this is Ollie. "I can't believe that I made one phone call and found you!"

"I can't believe it's you," Sergi answered excitedly. "Where are you?"

"I'm in Bethesda. When can we get together?" Ollie asked.

"I'll be through for the day in an hour. Do you have a car? If you do we can meet at the University?"

"Sounds good to me. I'll leave here as soon as I hang up."

"Park in front of the main administration building and I'll find you. You can follow me to our apartment. I can't wait to tell Helena that you are coming for dinner."

Ollie found the Georgetown University administration building and had been standing outside his car for only a few minutes when Sergi pulled up in a white BMW.

Sergi got out of the car and almost knocked Ollie down when he hugged him.

"Let's get back to my apartment. I have a million questions to ask."

Ollie followed Sergi through the quaint streets of Georgetown and parked behind him when he stopped in front of an old, but fashionable brownstone walk up.

"There are three apartments in the building," Sergi said as they walked up the front steps. "Our apartment is on the second floor."

Helena met them just inside the front entrance door and she too almost knocked Ollie down when she hugged him.

"Come in," She said. "We have lots to talk about."

Their apartment was comfortable and tastefully decorated. Sergi and Helena took him on a tour of the apartments two bedrooms, two baths, living room and kitchen/dining room.

"Just a little nicer than our flat in Moscow." Helena said with a laugh.

Sergi and Helena had also left Russia and arrived in the US without problems. Immediately after arriving Sergi had applied to Georgetown and they had offered him a full professorship teaching Russian History.

The CIA had special processed their request for citizenship and he and Helena were already American citizens. A change to living in the US was not a problem for Sergi since he had spent so much of his youth in the Washington area.

. "Have you heard from Tamara?" Ollie asked. "I have tried to call her twice a week since I got here and have written her a dozen letters and haven't heard a thing."

"We haven't heard from her either," Sergi replied. "Write her another letter and I'll see if I can get it to her through diplomatic channels."

When the clock showed two am Ollie made the move to leave. They both wanted him to stay but he left saying, "You have to work tomorrow. I don't. I will keep in touch and I'll bring you a letter for Tamara in few days."

Following Ollie Miller's phone call Paul Cannon had called Bob Palmer, his immediate supervisor in the CIA and advised him of the Pentagons actions. His boss had advised him to continue his effort and offered him the help of a paper trail specialist.

"Thanks, I can use the help. I'll call as soon as the documents arrive. While I'm waiting I'm going to call the Pentagon and get their read on what happened."

He called Ed Thompson at the Pentagon and was immediately transferred to his boss, Lt. Colonel Richard Shields. When he questioned Shields all he said was, "I have been advised by my superiors that we are not to spend any more time on this item. That's all I can tell you."

The next day Cannon was called in to the office of his boss.

"What is happening with this Miller project?" Palmer asked. "I'm getting information that Military Intelligence has started an investigation into this area. Why would they be interested?"

"I don't know," Cannon replied. "Miller isn't a threat to them as far as I can tell. They might want to put a lid on this because what the Air Force did was illegal. But it was so long ago that I don't know why they would be worried. Let me do some back checking in our records to see if I can come up with anything. I could use that clerk immediately if one is available."

The next morning he started the clerk on a search of records, looking for any reference to Oliver Miller or Air Force secret activities during the Korean War.

The next day Ollie's documents arrived and after reading them he assigned another clerk the task of looking for records pertaining to the airmen.

An hour after the clerk left to check for records of the airmen she was back in Paul Cannon's office.

"I entered all the names and serial numbers into the computer and got an "Accesses Denied" message. Ten minute later I got a telephone call from Military Intelligence telling me not to leave my work station and that they were on their way over to talk to me. What the hell is going on?"

"I don't know," Cannon answered. "Have a seat and we will wait for them here."

He was on the phone with his boss, telling him about the phone call, when two Military Intelligence officers walked into his office.

"Are you the person we spoke to on the phone?", the senior officer asked, looking at the clerk.

When she answered yes, the officer, clearly agitated, said, "I told you to stay at your workstation until we got here."

"Just a minute," Cannon interjected. "This lady works for me and had no idea who you are or what you wanted. She came directly in here to report. That is exactly what I would want her to do. Calm down and tell me what's going on. My boss will be here in a minute."

The Intelligence officer sighed and turned to the clerk and said, "You can go. Leave all your papers here."

"We want a copy of Miller's debriefing," the Military Intelligence officer demanded.

"It's not CIA policy to release debriefing tapes," Cannon replied. "I can give you a synopsis that we have available for release."

He opened a desk drawer and after searching for a few minutes slid a document across the desk.

The Mil Intel officer glanced at the document and said, "I want a complete transcript."

Paul was about to tell him what he could do with his request when his boss, Bob Palmer, walked into the office and closed the door behind him.

"Who the hell are you people and what the hell do you mean by stomping in here past reception without calling?" Palmer demanded angrily.

The two Military Intelligence officers didn't flinch. The senior officer looked back and forth between Cannon and his boss and said, "I'm following orders that came from the top of the Armed Services Command. If you have a problem why don't you take it up with them. I'll give you names and phone numbers to call."

"Why don't you do that now and let me talk to them," Palmer said. "But first I want to know why a simple request for information triggered this overkill response?"

"All I can tell you is that this is a top-secret issue," the Intelligence officer replied.

Cannons boss left to make a phone call. He was back in fifteen minutes.

"Bring your documents," he said. "We are meeting the Deputy Director at the Pentagon in an hour to get some answers."

Colonel Shield's boss walked into Shield's office and grumbled, "Pick up your file on the Miller thing and come with me. We have been called to a meeting upstairs."

Shields gathered the file while the colonel waited impatiently and then followed him to the elevator. When they got to the top floor they walked down the hall and into a conference room. An aide motioned for them to sit down and a few minutes later a three star general, Shields recognized as the top Air Force officer in the Pentagon, walked into the room with three civilians.

The General asked Shields and his boss to identify themselves and their position and then introduced Paul Cannon, his boss Bob Palmer, and Tony Maranacio, Deputy Director of the CIA.

Why is the top brass of the Air Force and the CIA so interested in Oliver Miller? Shields wondered as he scratched his head.

The General answered the question with his opening statement.

In his most authoritarian voice the General said, "Nothing discussed here is to leave this room." After making this statement he looked directly into the eyes of each participant and said, "is that understood?"

The Deputy Director looked at the General and said, "I don't want to get into a pissing contest with you but I will not agree to that until I hear what you have to say."

The general glared at the Deputy Director and continued, "During the Korean war the US Air Force ran some secret missions out of Japan, testing the Russian Air Defense system and obtaining reconnaissance information about facilities in Russia. We first sent a single F94 with special radar sensing equipment and it was shot down. Oliver Miller was the pilot of that plane. As you all know, Miller is now back in this country and is running around saying he met some American airmen in a prison camp in Russia. He is trying to find out what happened to those men. The men he is looking for are just a small number of the men we lost on secret reconnaissance missions over Russia. We lost over ten planes and crews in southeast Russia alone and did not recover any of them. The airmen were listed as MIA and their families were subsequently advised that they were presumed dead.

The highest levels of the government made the decision not to pursue recovery of these crews. We were at the very beginning of the Cold War with Russia and by acknowledging the illegal activity could have triggered a major escalation of hostilities and perhaps brought Russia into the Korean war, or worse. As of this moment this is still classified as Top Secret even though it happened forty years ago."

The Deputy Director spoke up when the General hesitated, "The Cold War is over. The Russia we were worried about when this happened doesn't even exist. Let's just declassify this and let the people know what happened to their sons and husbands."

"That would be a public relations nightmare," the general said, his voice making it clear that the director was an idiot. "Can you imagine what the press would do with this and what the rest of the world would think?"

"As a matter of fact I can," the director said patiently. "They would question the intelligence of the people who planned and executed the program, feel compassion for the men who were sacrificed, and thank the people who brought it to light and resolved the problems. Why don't you take that to your boss? That's the suggestion I'm taking to mine."

The director rose and said, "This meeting is over." Looking at the general he said, "If you can't resolve this with your boss, have your boss call my boss. This doesn't warrant any more of our time."

As they were leaving the general, who by this time was fuming, said, "Remember what I said. Keep the lid on this or the shit will hit the fan. I guarantee it."

After the CIA contingent left the general looked at Shields and his boss and said, "I'm holding you responsible for keeping this matter under control. Those damn spooks don't know crap about politics or public relations. Also, I'm continuing our Investigation of Oliver Miller and his association with the CIA. Who knows what they have been up to or what deals they have made. For all I know they may have a political agenda. They may be trying to embarrass the president who I know they hate, or they may be gunning for me. Since we don't know the answer to these questions I want to take the initiative on this. I'll call

Intel and get them moving on this. Remember, this is classified so I'm holding you responsible for security."

The general collected his papers and exited the conference room. Shields and his superior returned to their offices.

What a pompous, paranoid ass the general is, Shields thought. *He is so busy worrying about politics and covering his ass and the ass of the president that he hasn't even considered or thought about what might be the correct course of action. No wonder I hate this job.*

CHAPTER *24*

Paul Cannon waited impatiently for the deputy director to advise what action he should be taking. When Oliver Miller called Cannon had told him that his people were working on the project and that he would call when he had any information. He was just starting to collect data on another project and was busily making notes when his paper trail specialist who had been working on the Miller project knocked on his door and asked for a few moments of his time.

"I'm not through with my search yet and but I have found some interesting documents that I'll tell you about later. First though, I did find something about Miller that will be of interest to you. When I listened to Millers debriefing tapes he said that he was told by his contact in Hanoi that his son had died. That information could only come from our bureau chief in Saigon. I ran a crosscheck on Kevin O Miller and his name shows up in our files. He is not dead. We did a background check on him in 1985! One of the companies he owns is International Information Service. You know them; we contract with them for human Intel in a lot of countries. A friend of Kevin Millers runs the IIS operation. I'm sure you know him, it's Tom Montgomery. I'm also sure you know what the implications are and what I'm thinking."

Paul had been listening intently. He was intimately familiar with IIS and Tom Montgomery. Paul had used IIS many times and had worked with Tom Montgomery on several hairy operations. More importantly, he realized the importance of what had just been disclosed. The CIA had lied to Ollie, telling him his son was dead. The CIA had lied to keep

Ollie in Hanoi and by lying had deprived Oliver of twenty years of his sons life.

The clerk looked at him and said, "From the expression on your face I know you know the implications of what I just said."

"All too well", he replied sadly. "This is one of those classic bad news, good news things. Unfortunately we will have to deal with this. Now the questions is what do we do next?"

"After you figure that one out I have another problem that needs addressing," the clerk said. "I found that the CIA was also involved in the ferret missions in Korea. I knew we were in the later flights over the western Russia but didn't know we were in Korea. At any rate, because we were involved, I became aware that there are records on planes and personnel that were shot down during the cold war by the Russians. A State Department lawyer collected thirty-five cardboard boxes of information that is stored in the National Archives Records Administration over at Suitland, Maryland. I have been advised that the Defense Department suppressed the information because they would have been embarrassed to have to admit that we were using aircraft to spy on the Russians. Ollie's friends from Irkutsk weren't the only people held by the Russians. Lots of other families don't know what happened to their relatives. I understand that other families of missing airmen have been badgering the government for forty years and have been stonewalled just like Ollie. We will have to figure out what we want to do about that information.

God! There may still be Korean War airmen alive in Russia! Imagine what that would be like. Spending forty years waiting for your country to free you. I am really disturbed by this and none of my family is involved. I know that we have done some heartless things in the name of protecting the US, but this one is the worst I have come across. When I realized the implications I felt like a cold spike had been driven into my heart. Imagine what the families of those poor men must have been feeling for all these years."

Cannon rubbed scratched his head, his sadness apparent, and said, "I agree. Thanks for doing such a thorough job. I will have to discuss that with my boss. Right now I am going to finish Oliver Miller's project first."

Ollie was just returning to his apartment. It was turning dusk when he got out of his car and started up the stairs to his apartment. When he opened his front door and turned on the lights he was confronted by three men, facing him with drawn weapons.

He was startled and started to back out the door, "Who are you and what do you want?" He asked with a tremor in his voice.

The man closest to the door restrained him and closed the door.

A second man, dressed in civilian clothes, said, "We are with Military Intelligence. We are here to place you under arrest for treason."

"Treason?" Ollie exclaimed. "You have made an error. I'm not in the Military so how can a Military organization arrest me. Show me identification and while you are doing that I want to make some phone calls to get this straightened out."

The third man grabbed Ollie, roughly turned him around and placed handcuffs on his wrists and said, "Shut up traitor and you'll be better off. Just do what you are told."

One of the other men grabbed his arm and started pushing him toward the door. As they were leaving one of the men said, "Do we have all the papers and notebooks we found?"

The third man held up a briefcase and said, "It's all here, lets' go."

They steered Ollie down the steps and to an unmarked car and put him in the rear seat. None of Ollie's neighbors witnessed his departure.

Ollie was still not familiar with the roads around Washington so he was not sure were they where taking him. He did see a sign for I-495 and then another sign for the Route 50 East turn off for Annapolis, so he knew he was on the eastern loop around Washington.

After what seemed an eternity they approached the gates to a military complex. The car stopped at a guarded gate and after a brief discussion a military policeman, dressed in Air Force Blue, waved them through the gate. They drove through the base and stopped in front of a large brick building. The men dragged Ollie out of the car and into a building and placed Ollie in a cell and left. Once again Ollie was imprisoned without knowing where he was or knowing how to get help.

When Ollie didn't show up for a planned dinner Sergi began to worry. It wasn't like Ollie not to call if he was having a problem and couldn't make an appointment. The next day, after his last class, Sergi drove to Ollie's apartment. He noticed that Ollie's car was in the parking lot in front of the apartment. When Ollie didn't answer his door, Sergi checked with several of his neighbors and could learn nothing. One of the neighbors told him that a couple on the first floor had keys for all the apartments for emergencies. Sergi got the lady to open Ollie's apartment. Ollie was not in the apartment and it was obvious that it had been searched. The lady wanted to call the police but Sergi talked her out of phoning, explaining that it was a domestic dispute and that he would take care of the problem.

Sergi drove back to his apartment and looked up the phone number the CIA had provided when he was set free in the States. He dialed the number and when the phone was answered identified himself. There was a slight pause and then a voice he did not recognize said, "What can I do for you?"

Sergi explained who he was and why he was calling. The voice at the other end asked if he knew Ollie's contact. When Sergi said no, the voice said, "Give me your name and phone number and I will look into this. Sergi provided the information and the voice on the phone made no comment and said "Goodbye."

Sergi looked blankly at the dead phone, not knowing what to do next.

Paul Cannon was sitting in his office looking at the man who had just relayed a message from Sergi. Cannon picked up his phone and dialed his boss.

When Palmer answered, Cannon said, "Oliver Miller hasn't been in his apartment for at least three days. When his friend went to his apartment to find out why he hadn't shown up for a dinner engagement he found Miller's apartment had been turned."

His boss responded, "Give me his address and I will get a team on it today."

The team made a detailed search of Ollie's apartment and reported to Paul's boss.

"They didn't find much;" his boss said when he called Cannon. "But somebody did have his phone bugged and the idiots forgot to remove the bug. Guess who uses the type of bug they found?"

"Probably half the intelligence community but I would guess that you are thinking what I am thinking; our own Mil Intel."

"You have read my mind," his boss said. "I think I will call the Deputy Director. Maybe he can rattle their cage and find out why they would pull such a dumb stunt."

General William Wentling barely acknowledged the presence of the pugnacious looking captain who had entered his office. He continued working, allowing the Captain to stew. After a few minutes he looked up at the captain and motioned for him to be seated.

Someday I am going to get that chair fixed like the one Admiral Rickover had in his office, with the front legs shorter than the back legs so whoever sat in the chair felt like he was sliding off. What a way to make people uncomfortable and intimidated, the General thought to himself.

"Have you read Miller's debriefing documents and all the information that Intel gave you?" The General asked.

"Yes sir, I have." The undaunted captain replied. Dealing with prima donnas was not new to him.

"I am arraigning for the court martial to take place next week and have selected some good men for the board. You should not have any problems. Will you be ready?"

"I haven't found any precedents or similar cases to base our prosecution on. "The captain replied.

"That's not what I asked you," the general said haughtily. "I asked if you would be ready by next week."

"I can be ready tomorrow if you want me to be." The captain replied. "It depends on how bad you want him to be convicted."

"Maybe I had better find another prosecutor." The general said, shaking his head in disgust.

"That will be your choice," the captain replied. "I am not pleased that I am involved in this case. I think you should be giving this guy a medal. If you want me to continue I will, but I think any defense will win this unless you have the review board totally stacked. If you do I am even less interested in this case."

"You are bordering on insubordination." The general said ominously.

"Why are you pursuing this at all?" The captain asked. "I can't see what you will gain other than bad will. If this gets into the press you will make the armed forces look ridiculous."

"I have my reasons," the general barked, "I don't want a subordinate who questions my motives on this case. You are relieved and you can be assured that I will talk to your commanding officer about your attitude. If he can't find a duty that you won't like maybe I will arrange one for you. How would you like to spend the rest of your career in Diego

Garcia? Perhaps a tour on that God forsaken island would improve your attitude. You are dismissed."

With so many good men in the military, the captain thought as he left the general's office, *how did a complete asshole like this make it to the top?* The thought made him smile, remembering the old joke about the Pentagon that went, *If assholes could fly, this place would be an airport!"*

As soon as the captain left the office the general was on the phone seeking a new prosecutor. *I am going to shut Miller down even if I have to prosecute him myself.*

CHAPTER *25*

Washington, D.C. USA

Lt. Col. Richard Shields was about to take action that was completely out-of-line; something that could possibly jeopardize his military career.

When he had sat in the meeting with the general and the deputy director he had been totally disgusted with the Air Force approach and had agreed with the CIA.

Paul Cannon had called him at his office the next day to thank him for his assistance. Shields suspected that Cannon had been watching him and that his disgust with the general's approach was apparent. Before he hung up Cannon had given him his home phone number and said, "If you ever want to talk about anything give me a call."

Shields parked his car in the parking lot at a mall near his residence and found a public phone and was about to take a tremendous risk.

When Paul Cannon answered the phone Shields did not identify himself. All he said was, "Miller was arrested and taken to Andrews Air Force Base. He is being held there for a court martial."

He hung up the phone without saying anything else and left the mall.

Paul Cannon hung up the phone, shaking his head in disbelief. *How stupid can they be?* He asked himself.

He debated with himself for a few minutes and then decided to call his boss at home.

His boss was clearly agitated and agreed with Cannon that perhaps they should have the deputy director talk to their favorite senator.

The next morning the deputy director called Senator Jerome Mahoney. When the senator came on the line the director said, "Good morning Jerry. I know how busy you are but would it be possible for me to have a few minutes of your time this morning?"

"Good morning to you Tony. What's my favorite spook up to this time?" The senator replied.

"I have a situation where Mil Intel has arrested one of my operatives who we just extracted from Russia. My man was shot down on a secret mission over Russia during the Korean War and became one of our operatives in Russia. You may have even met him when you were in that prison in Hanoi. He was there when you were and used to visit American prisoners sometimes in civilian clothes and sometimes dressed as a Russian officer. Does that ring any bells?"

Jerome Mahoney's thoughts flashed back twenty years. He had been a Navy A6 pilot, and had been shot down over North Vietnam. He had been treated brutally while a prisoner of the North Vietnamese. Because of his experience he was an outspoken critic of military bureaucracy that had done little to dissuade the North Vietnamese in their brutality. He had led the American delegation that had visited Hanoi after the end of the war in Vietnam and had continued to support investigations into determining the fate of MIAs. He did faintly remember being questioned by a Russian officer who spoke English without a trace of accent. Their was also some-thing else trying to escape from a deep spot in his brain into his memory. It was just indiscernible, below the surface of his thinking.

"Sounds like something I would be interested in. Why don't you join me for lunch in my office and fill me in with the details." The Senator said while motioning his secretary into his office. She would have to rearrange his schedule; something she had to do several times every day.

When the deputy director arrived, a senator's aide had already set out a light lunch.

The senator said, "All right, tell me the details."

He listened intently while Maranacio told Ollie's story even down to the disclosure that the CIA had lied to Ollie to keep him in Vietnam. Occasionally the senator would put down his sandwich and make a few notes.

When he finished the senator said, "I totally agree with your position just to expose and dispose. Although I understand the Air Force sensitivity, nobody in the chain of command would be hurt."

"Now that you understand the background," Maranacio said. "What can we do to get Miller free?"

"I will take care of that," the senator replied. "One of my aides was on the Judge Advocate General's staff when he was in the military. He is a lawyer and my expert on military law."

The senator picked up his phone and asked said, "Helen, get Jimmy in here as soon as you can."

He listened for a moment and said, "That will be fine, send him in as soon as he gets here."

They continued with lunch while waiting. Maranacio, the deputy director gave the senator a condensed copy of Ollie's debriefing tape.

"I know you will be interested in the section about Vietnam. This man saved a lot of our airmen by getting out information on SAM sites. He also kept us advised on the names and serial numbers of the prisoners he came in contact with in Hanoi. A lot of those names you checked out in Hanoi after the war came from Miller. He also was giving our kids antibiotic shots. The VC thought he was using truth serum. He was also giving morphine shots to people who were in real pain. He was supposed to be pumping the American prisoners for information. I don't know how he pulled it off but we really missed him when the Russians pulled him out."

The senator's aide knocked on the door and entered. The senator introduced the young man to the deputy director and asked him to be seated.

The senator gave a ten-minute recap of the information that the Maranacio had provided and then looked at the director and said, "Does that cover the highlights?"

"Very well," Maranacio smiled. "You may have a future in politics."

"I haven't listened to this yet," the senator said, looking at his aide, holding up the copy of Ollie's de-briefing tape, "You can do that later. Based on what you have heard so far, does the Military have a legitimate charge of treason?"

"I would think that their charge is based on the time between Miller agreeing to work for the Russian Air Force and what would have been his discharge date if he hadn't been shot down. They are assuming that technically, during that time period, he wasn't working for the CIA and was working for the Russians while he was still in the American Air Force. That's the only basis for treason that I can foresee."

"The big question for me is why in the world is the Air Force pushing this when the guy ended up deserving a medal?" The senator said while shaking his head.

"Jimmy, I want you to call one of your old buddies in JAG and find out if they know when the court martial is scheduled and where it will be held. I want to know how long we will have to get ready to defend Miller."

The young aide picked up the tape and left the office. As the Deputy Director was leaving the aide returned and advised that the court martial was being at Andrews Air Force Base a week from the present date.

"That gives us a week to get ready," the senator said.

The day before the court martial the senator called the JAG and informed him that the he and his aide would be at Andrews and wanted to sit in on the trial and asked him to make sure that their credentials would be at the gate.

The next morning the Senator's driver drove them to Andrews.

The senator and his aide entered the trial room just as the prosecutor was starting his opening remarks. There were no other spectators in the room. The senator waved to the few people on the panel that he recognized and then sat down behind Ollie.

When the prosecutor finished his statement the senator raised his hand. The presiding officer looked at him in surprise and asked why he had raised his hand.

The Senator stood up, introduced himself and said, "I just want to ask Mister Miller's attorney a question."

He walked around the table where a rumpled, disheveled Ollie and his defense attorney were seated, and addressed the young attorney, who, by his youthful appearance, must have just graduated from law school.

"How long have you had to prepare Mister Miller's defense?" He asked.

"I got the files yesterday morning, sir," he said, his uncertainty and discomfort registered in his hesitant response.

The senator then turned to the panel of judges and said, "My senate aide, James Mankewicz is a lawyer and during his military career worked for JAG. Mister Mankewicz and myself will be joining Mister Miller's defense team. We have had a week to prepare."

He then turned to the young defense attorney and said, "I assume that will be acceptable to you?"

The relieved attorney said, "Yes sir, I would be proud to be a member of your team."

The Air Force officer on the panel of judges had been trying to interrupt from the moment the Senator started to speak. Finally he got the opportunity to speak and forcefully said, "I object."

Before he could say anything else an Army officer of the same rank said, "Why in the world would you object? You have brought serious charges of treason and this man is entitled to a proper defense."

The chief trial judge thought for a moment and said, "I agree, you two men can be seated. Do you want some time to talk to Mister Miller's appointed lawyer?"

The senator said, "No sir, Mister Mankewicz is ready to make an opening statement."

Mankewicz rose and faced the panel and for one half hour presented the story of Ollie's life in the Service of his country in detail. He described the early years of Ollie's incarceration in Siberia and his subsequent brainwashing in Irkutsk. He recounted the lies told him by the KGB and the false documents that they had shown him to convince him that his country didn't acknowledge his existence and didn't want him back. He explained in detail how the CIA had recruited Ollie and then recounted the dangerous service that Ollie had provided to a country that he thought didn't want him. He ended by describing Ollie's efforts to find the families of his fellow prisoners at Irkutsk and then turned to the senator to conclude the opening statement.

The Senator rose and faced the panel.

"You all probably know that I was prisoner in Vietnam after being shot down. The man you are trying for treason saved my life."

He pulled up the pant leg covering his right leg and showed them a prosthesis that was attached to his knee. "My right leg was severly damaged when we were hit by ground fire. The Vietnamese didn't even bandage it. By the time I got to Hanoi the infection was so bad that I was going to die soon. This man, at great risk to his life, gave me antibiotic shots that saved my life.

We admit that for a short time he did, after years of brainwashing and lies, choose to do something with what was left of his life.

More importantly, when asked he served the country that he thought had disowned him and saved many American lives at great risk to his own.

Why is the Air Force pursuing this? If it's to suppress the fate of the American airmen that gave their lives in an ill advised spy activity, we should just openly present what happened and tell the families of the airmen what happened to their loved ones.

Do any of you remember Gary Powers and his U2 spy plane that got Eisenhower in trouble with Khrushchev? We have gotten over that haven't we?

So what is the Air Force worried about? Mister Miller should be getting a medal instead of being on trial.

I move that the charges against him be dropped. He has been incarcerated unjustly and been deprived of fulfilling his pledge to his fellow airmen.

Please note that he placed this duty before trying to determine what has happened to his family.

Please drop the charges and for Gods sake give the man a medal!"

There was complete silence when the Senator completed his statement.

The presiding judge asked all but the court martial panel to leave the room.

Ollie and his young appointed defense attorney waited outside the room with the senator and his aide. It gave them the opportunity to thank the senator and his aide for their help.

The senator brushed off their thanks, "Mister Miller, you saved my life and I am going to stay with this until it is resolved. After that we will take care of the missing airmen's families."

The argument inside the trial room raged for at least a half an hour. Finally the lowest ranking officer on the panel came to the door and said, "You can come back in now."

When they were all seated the presiding chief judge said, "Thank you senator and Mister Mankewicz. You have prevented a gross injustice. The charges against Mister Miller are dropped. I will do everything in my power to see that he gets proper military recognition. Senator, I hope you will continue to help Mister Miller in his quest to relieve the minds of the families of the missing airmen."

Ollie shook the hand of the jubilant defense attorney and then turned to the senator and his aide.

"I couldn't believe this was happening to me," Ollie exclaimed, "I am so happy that you took the time to help. I want to thank all the people who helped if you can tell me who they are."

"We will talk about that on the way back to Washington," the Senator said. "I also want to work with you on the lost airmen project. I have some ideas I want to bounce off you."

They talked the entire time they were in route to Washington. They dropped the senator off at the Senate Building and Mankewicz rode with Ollie back to his apartment, finalizing plans for the airmen project.

Ollie thanked the young aide for rescuing him and then ran up the steps to his apartment and called Sergi.

"Where have you been?" Sergi asked with obvious concern.

"It's a long story," Ollie said. "How about I treat you and Helena to dinner tonight and I'll tell you all the details and tell you about my new friends."

Senator Mahoney and the deputy director were correct. When the details of the ferret reconnaissance missions hit the news there were a flurry of recriminations from the doves of the world and then complete sympathy for the remaining families of the lost airmen. The files of the men Ollie had known at Irkutsk were declassified and the list of missing airmen that had been at Irkutsk was sent to Russia. After a month of diplomatic haggling, the Russians agreed to allow an American team into the records stored at Podluk. They accounted for every airman on the list. All had lived varying lengths of time but none were still alive.

With the fate of every Irkutsk prisoner now known, Senator Mahoney held hearings. After hearing testimony the committee recommended financial remuneration to the heirs of the airmen, settling on back pay based on the average life span of the prisoners.

The Air Force, after early embarrassment, at a special ceremony, awarded Air Medals and Purple hearts posthumously, and a generous financial settlement to the families of the airmen. Ollie, apparently the only known prisoner who survived the secret missions, was promoted to Lt. Colonel and officially retired from the Air Force with a thirty-year pension.

Ollie was asked to address the families of the lost airmen. His speech was short and moving. He talked about the men he had met in Irkutsk and tried to offer some condolence to the families. He broke down and sobbed when reminiscing about Bill Snelling, his old friend from MATS, who was removed from Irkutsk and died after six months in a Siberian Work camp. He tried to convey the feeling of desperation and loneliness that he had experienced while futilely waiting for his country to save him. He ended with a plea for the military to obtain release of all prisoners of war and for the US government to support Senator Mahoney in his continuing search for MIAs.

Bill Snelling's sister was selected as the spokesperson for the families. Her comments were brief and poignant, recalling the grief suffered by her family when Bill was listed as MIA. She then thanked Ollie and the senator for their efforts that would at last bring closure to the lost airmen's families.

There was a party for the Irkutsk prisoner's families after the ceremony. Ollie was wandering through the guests, when he came across Paul Cannon. Paul took him aside and said, "There is somebody here I want you to meet. Without his help you might be in Leavenworth today instead of becoming a celebrity. Paul steered him toward a tall Air Force colonel. When they approached the colonel turned and Paul introduced the men.

"Ollie, I'm sure you remember Captain Thompson from the Pentagon. This is Colonel Richard Shields; he was Thompson's boss at the time."

As they made their way to a secluded spot Cannon turned to Shields and said, "I never did get a chance to thank you for the phone call."

"What phone call?" The colonel said innocently.

Cannon left saying, "You two should talk a little. You share a love of flying."

"Paul tells me that your lady friend in Russia was a MIG pilot. What was her name?"

"Tamara Krasnov," Ollie said as the vision of her bright blue eyes and blonde hair came flooding back, causing a twinge in his heart.

"Not Lieutenant Colonel Tamara Krasnov!" He exclaimed. "I saw her do impossible things with a MIG at the Paris air show. We studied films of some of her maneuvers one frame at a time. We couldn't figure out the control movements she used for the maneuver."

"That's my girl," Ollie said with a smile. "I asked the same questions and all she ever said was "I think about it and my plane knows what I'm thinking and does it."

The two men spent the rest of the evening talking about flying. Ollie was happy that the colonel was back to his first love of flying. He knew the feeling exactly and was envious.

When they parted Ollie thanked him for jeopardizing his career to help him.

"I put myself in your position. What you did was more than most men would have done. I knew that you didn't deserve what was happening so what I did was a no brainer. I think anyone who has flown combat would have done the same thing. I hope that without the senators help the outcome would have been the same. There are a lot of solid men still in the military."

When they were saying goodbye the colonel said, "How would you like to strap on a hot jet and go flying with me?"

"I would go with you right this minute if you would take me," Ollie smiled

"Your on," Shields laughed. He wrote a phone number on a slip of paper and handed it to Ollie, "Call me anytime and we will set up a date."

A sleek supersonic T38, under the direction of a ground controller, taxied into position and came to a stop. The engine wound down to silence when power to the engines was cut. The canopy came open and a ground crewman slid ladders into place alongside the cockpit. Both occupants unhooked from the plane and climbed down the ladders to the tarmac. A beaming Ollie took off his helmet and grasped the hand of Colonel Shields. "That was one of the biggest thrills of my life." He exclaimed. "How can I ever thank you?"

"I am so happy that you called me. I can't imagine how I would feel if I had been denied the thrill of flying a jet for as long as you have. I mean it when I say that anytime you call I will try my best to get you a ride."

The two pilots changed from flight suits into jump suits and then headed to the officers club for lunch.

"You sure haven't lost your touch," the Colonel said. "I have some men in my wing that could learn a few things from you."

"My only regret is that I am too old for military flying," Ollie said. "I guess I will have to be satisfied with buying a light plane and once in a while bumming a ride with you when I want to go fast."

"I have wanted to ask you a question for some time now," the Colonel said. "What happened to Tamara?"

"I don't know," Ollie replied. "I had to leave Moscow in a hurry and didn't have the opportunity to talk to her. Since I have been in the States

I have been trying to contact her but haven't been successful. I have a friend who is trying to reach her through diplomatic channels."

"You asked what you could do to repay me. I just thought of something," the Colonel said with a smile. "You find her and bring her to the States so I can use her to teach advanced aerobatics to my men."

"You know, if I can contact her that may be the thing that convinces her to come here to live. Now if you tell me that I can tell her that you will let her fly one of your birds occasionally I am sure I can talk her into joining me."

"You have my word," Colonel Shields said, sealing the deal with a firm handshake.

Paul Cannon was sitting with his boss in the office of the deputy director, for their weekly update review. When their discussion was over the DD put his hands behind his head and rocked back in his chair.

"Have you told Ollie that his son is alive?"

"Not yet," Paul replied. "I've been letting things settle out for awhile. I didn't want to agitate him so soon. I'm sure he will be very unhappy when I tell him. Twenty years of his only son's life denied him. What a terrible waste."

"How are you going to handle telling him?"

"He told me his next task was to go back to his hometown to see if he can track down any relatives that may be alive. He tried by phone but could not locate anybody. I've told him that we would check it out for him to save him time. I have a man in his hometown now doing a complete investigation. He should be finished by the end of the week. When he submits his report I'll go over it and then sit down and talk to Ollie. I'm still working on some plans to help the process."

The DD nodded his head and remarked, "OK, if there is anything I can do just ask."

"There is something you can do that may help," Paul replied. "Ollie has been trying to contact Tamara Krasnov through State Department channels and has been unsuccessful. We have resources in Russia that we can use to contact her. That would help."

"I will check that out and get back to you," the DD said, standing to signal that the meeting was over.

Tamara opened the door to her quarters, removed her parka and sat down wearily and sighed. Her world had been in turmoil for months. After the failed coup and formation of the new government the Military had been in complete disarray. The air marshal and several of his top generals has disappeared and leadership was being seized and released by different officers almost on a monthly basis. He duties had been severely curtailed and she wasn't flying at all. She was concerned about the security of her country as were the rest of her fellow career officers.

The disappearance of Ollie, Sergi and Helena was a total mystery. Nobody could tell her what had happened to them. When she started asking questions several of the new security force had showed up at the base and questioned her for hours. She didn't understand their questions and did not obtain any information that helped her to determine what had happened to her closest friends. She was lonely and confused. More puzzling was her feeling that she was being watched.

After resting she forced herself to get up and get cleaned up for dinner at the mess hall. She picked up her parka to hang it up and removed her gloves from the parkas' pocket. A small piece of paper fluttered to the floor. She picked up the paper and unfolded it. There was a short message.

"OSH wants to talk to you. Call this number."

She studied the note for a minute and then realized the significance of the OSH. It must mean Ollie, Sergi and Helena.

"And I want to talk to them," she muttered.

The next day was her day off and as usual she packed up and headed for her father's apartment. After her father's death she had retained his apartment for herself. She stopped at a public phone and dialed the number on the note. An operator said, "United States Embassy."

Tamara asked for the extension that had been identified. The phone rang once and a male voice answered.

"This is Tamara, what do you want?"

"Hello Tamara, I have a letter for you from Ollie."

He quickly gave her instructions for picking up the letter and they both hung up.

Tamara found the pickup point without difficulty and retrieved a letter and stuffed it in her pocket and walked back to her car. A short time later she was back in her apartment. She opened the letter before she had the front door fully closed.

Chapter 26

Months of fear and wonder faded away as Tamara read Ollie's letter. She had been imagining the worst and was relieved that Ollie, Sergi and Helena were alive and safe. Tamara did not completely understand or accept some of the statements in Ollie's letter describing the reasons they had to leave without contacting her. She knew that something was amiss when the security police questioned her and when she could not obtain any information from the new government. The security police had told her at least ten times to notify them if Ollie contacted her. Their interest caused some confusion in Tamara's mind. It seemed to her that the early days of paranoia after the coup had dissipated, yet the police were still seeking Ollie and Sergi.

The new Confederation of Independent States was running the country and was moving toward stabilization and more freedom for the people. She suspected that Ollie and Sergi had been involved in more than helping Gorbachev. Gorbachev was being openly castigated by the people for his failures but he hadn't been dealt the fate of passed deposed leaders. He was a free man and was often seen on the streets of Moscow and seemed to be trying to help the new government establish trade and relations with its former enemies. *If Gorbachev was not being harassed, why were Ollie and Sergi still on the Security Police wanted list?*

In the letter Ollie had begged her to come to the United States. He said that he had made all the arrangements with the State Department and that all she had to do was present herself at the United States embassy and they would take care of getting her to the States.

Leaving her Russia to become a citizen of another country had never occurred to her. She knew that life in the new Russia would be unstable but she had lived through turmoil and disasters before and was confident that she would survive.

On the other hand, because of her travels, she knew that there were much better places to live. She had read and believed all the adverse propaganda about the imperialistic, decadent Americans. She was intelligent and realized that her government had sometimes overstated the bad features of enemy countries. *If they were so bad, why was the new government trying so hard to emulate the bad capitalists?*

She read and re-read the letters and thought of nothing else for several days. When she returned to her base her new air marshal superior called her into his office. He gave her the bad news that she was being removed from flight status. Her squadron had been assigned to her executive officer. She protested vehemently when the air marshal said that they wanted a younger person to take over her position.

The air marshal had known this would be difficult for Tamara. He had experienced the same frustration when he was removed from flight status. He tried to empathize with her, telling her about his feelings when he came to the end of his flying career. She was not mollified and said, "How old were you when they told you couldn't fly anymore?"

When he hesitated Tamara said, "I knew it, you were a lot older than I am now weren't you."

He continued trying to console her, telling her about her new assignment and how important it would be to pass her experience on as a classroom instructor in the flight training program.

Tamara reluctantly gave up. She knew the decision was not reversible and that the air marshal had only put up with her outburst because of her past record and her father's reputation. She left the marshal's office and went back to her squadron office. When the squadron pilots were assembled she told them what they obviously already knew. The new squadron leader was sincere when he said that he knew that someday he would reach the same fate and knew how he would feel. The rest of the squadron tried to console her and finally they disbanded. Tamara packed up her few personal belongings and retreated to her quarters.

In his letter Ollie had assured her that she could continue flying if she joined him in the States. He had told her about his new Air Force friend and the pleasure that he was experiencing flying the new fighters. He relayed his friends promise to allow her the same opportunity if she joined him. Ollie had also written that the US Air Force had kept all his pay in escrow and that they could live comfortably and would only do what they wanted to do. He said he was going to buy a plane that they could both fly but that he would wait till she joined him so she could help pick the plane.

Ollie painted a nice picture but she was not convinced that it would be a good move.

Washington, D.C.

Paul Cannon's secretary buzzed him on the inter-com and said, "Oliver Miller is in the lobby. Do you want me to go down and escort him to your office?"

"No," he replied, "I'll pick him up."

He took the elevator down to the entrance foyer and found Ollie waiting patiently at the security desk.

They greeted each other warmly and as Ollie attached his visitors badge they made their way to the elevators.

Cannon had been dreading this moment for months. He was going to have to tell Ollie that his government had deceived him for its own gain without regard for his best interest. He wasn't sure just how Ollie would receive the disclosure. He also had another unpleasant task to perform. He would save the good news till last and hope for the best.

When they were seated in Paul's office Ollie said, "OK, what have you found out about my family?"

"Not very good news, I am afraid," Paul said, opening a manila folder and removing a typed report. "I am going to give it to you straight but I have to warn you that it isn't good."

Ollie looked dejected and said, "All right, tell me and get it over with."

Paul picked up the folder and said, "Your mother and father both died in the seventies of natural causes; your mother from cancer and your father from emphysema

Your uncle George and Aunt Cil and Uncle Mike and Aunt Mary also passed away in the late seventies, all of natural causes.

Your cousin Bobby was killed in an automobile accident, evidently after he had been drinking.

Your cousin Rose had a stroke and is in a nursing home. She has a surviving daughter and son that still live in western Pennsylvania.

Your cousin Mary Jo died at age forty-six. She had heart problems."

Paul paused and looked up from his report. Ollie had not said a word since he started. Ollie was sitting with a stoic expression on his face, but was betrayed by the tears silently streaming from his eyes.

Ollie looked at Paul and said, "How about my brother Tim?"

"I am sorry Ollie, he was injured in an industrial accident and never did recover. He died about three years ago. He was married and had some children. His widow and your niece and nephew have moved to South Carolina."

"You were right, that wasn't a good report but I really want to thank you for all the effort I know it took to dig that all up. I am still going to Greenwood. I want to see the town and I will look up Rose's kids. If you can tell me where Tim's widow is living I will also go see her."

Paul hesitated and then said, "I do have some news that should help you recover from all the bad news."

"I can really use some good news," Ollie said, "What is it?"

"First, Air Marshall Gaidar is okay. He is in the Air Force in a high position in one of the independent Russian states."

"That is good news," Ollie said, "What is the other good news?"

Paul hesitated and then looked Ollie in the eyes and said, "The best news is that your son Kevin is alive and well."

Paul observed the look of lack of understanding, confusion, gradual realization and then happiness that flooded Ollie's face. Ollie was speechless for a full minute.

"I can't believe this. Are you positive? How? What happened? Where is he?"

Then his face darkened and he asked angrily, "Did somebody lie to me? What do you know about it? Tell me, did somebody in the CIA lie?"

"I am afraid somebody did lie to you," Paul replied. "It's too late to do anything about it now. You can move on."

"I know why the CIA lied," Ollie declared angrily. "I wanted out and whoever wanted me to stay in did it for his own selfish reasons. Do you know who lied?"

"Yes," Paul replied. "It was our bureau chief in Saigon. You are right, he thought you were too valuable an asset to let you out. I will tell you this. He went to the mat with the top brass to get Kevin out. He was clear up to the Joint Chiefs to get approval. It was a very hairy and expensive operation that involved a lot of people who risked a lot."

"He still deprived me of twenty years with my son," Ollie said, his anger unabated. "Is he still alive? I would like to meet him. Just long enough to let him know what I think about his decision."

"He is alive and still working for the company. I talked to him the other day. He is on assignment at the farm in Williamsburg as an instructor for the next month," Paul said. "But I don't know what you can gain by talking to him."

"I just want to meet him face to face," Ollie replied. "I'm not going to injure him."

"OK, let me call him and see if he can see you tomorrow."

Paul placed a call to Williamsburg and after asking for James Wilson, waited a few minutes and then spoke to the person on the other end. After a few minutes Paul turned to Ollie and said, "It's all set. He will see you tomorrow at fourteen hundred. He will leave word at security that you are expected and will pick you up at security. Just ask for James Wilson."

"I have another question," Ollie asked. "Does Kevin know about me?"

"No he doesn't," Paul said. "Why don't you go down to the farm and see Wilson and then go to Greenwood? While you are doing that I will try to arrange something special for your reunion."

Ollie left that afternoon and drove down I-95 to Richmond, Virginia and then headed southeast to Williamsburg. After lunch he drove to the entrance to the CIA complex and checked in with security. The guard made a phone call, opened the gate and directed him to the foyer of the main building. The guard at the entrance desk made a phone call. A few minutes later a mature woman, dressed in a conservative, blue skirt and jacket, arrived and escorted him to a conference room just around the corner from the entrance. When Ollie entered the room a short, muscular man, dressed in a worn tweed jacket and tan slacks rose and extended his hand.

"I am James Wilson," he said. "I'm very happy to meet you. I'm so pleased that you are back in the States. You helped save a lot of American kids and I want you to know that I'm grateful."

Ollie shook the extended hand. Although Wilson looked muscular, Ollie could see that the man was in his mid-sixties. Years of stress showed in his eyes.

"I wanted to talk to you face to face," Ollie said. "No, that's not true, I wanted to meet you so I could beat the crap out of you. I'm sure you know why."

"I do," Wilson replied. "In your position I would feel the same way. So if it will make you feel better, take your shot."

Ollie thought about it seriously for a few minutes and then sighed, "What good would it do? It wouldn't bring back the twenty years."

"If it's of any help," Wilson said. "I was making decisions like the one about telling you that your son was dead, everyday. In fact, my decision about you was one of the easier ones I had to make in Nam. I traded your life for the sake of the many others you could possibly save. I was very sorry when Ti messaged us that you had been recalled to Moscow, but I understand that you continued your valuable service there."

"I am trying very hard to accept your position," Ollie said in a normal tone of voice. "Perhaps someday I will be able to forgive you and the rest of the people in government who manipulated my life. But don't bet on it. I am sorry I wasted your time."

"It is the least I could do," Wilson said with sincerity.

"What happened to Ti?" Ollie asked.

"After we pulled out I lost track of him," Wilson replied. "I made two visits to Hanoi later but was never able to find him. He was one of our best assets in North Vietnam and I sure could have used him there after we pulled out."

Ollie left the farm and drove back to his apartment in Bethesda and called Paul Cannon.

"You will be happy to know that Wilson is still in one piece," Ollie said laconically. "I thought about punching him out but it would have only felt good for a few minutes and then I would feel bad for having made a fool of myself."

"I hate to destroy your ego Ollie, but I don't think your best shot would not have made Wilson blink. He is one of the toughest, physical men I know. Just because he looks old doesn't make him feeble. Oh, I forgot to tell you, he is at the farm as an instructor in Karate. I have seen him destroy black belts in less than a minute I am glad you didn't take a poke at him. You may have embarrassed yourself. When are you going to Greenwood?"

"I have a flight out of Dulles to Pittsburgh at eight thirty tomorrow morning," Ollie replied.

"If you bought a round trip ticket cash it in for one way," Cannon said. "I'm having a plane pick you up at the Executive terminal in Pittsburgh. Call me the day before you want to leave and tell me when you will be at the airport."

"Why the special plane?" Ollie asked.

"Your son lives on Hilton Head Island in South Carolina and they don't have commercial service into their small field. I have made arrangements for a private plane to fly you there."

"All right, I will call you the day before I want to be picked up. How do you know that he will be home?"

"That's all been taken care off," Paul replied. "Finish up your activities in Greenwood and give me a call."

CHAPTER *27*

The flight from Dulles to Pittsburgh was smooth and uneventful. Ollie sat on the right side of the plane, hoping to catch a glimpse of Greenwood while flying to the Pittsburgh airport.

Ollie didn't pick up any landmarks and before he could get his bearings they were descending into the airport and the fasten seat belt sign came on. He picked up his carry on, fold up luggage from the coat storage closet and left the plane and headed for the car rental area.

The clerk at Avis gave him a marked map, showing him how to get out of the rental car pick up area and on to Route 30 east to Greenwood. A shuttle van took him to the Avis car pick up area and the clerk at the desk gave him the keys for a Ford Taurus. He loaded his carry on luggage in to the trunk of the small car and started out the gate and found his way to the Parkway, following the direction signs.

He had trouble keeping his eyes on the road as he crossed over the Mononghehala River multi-level bridge into the city. Just in time he spotted the ramp turnoff and maneuvered through traffic to the right lane and turned off the ramp onto the east bound Parkway that runs along the Mononghela River. The steel mills that had been the heart of the city were gone, replaced by black, vacant lots.

At Forest Hills he got off the Parkway and on to Route 30. The old road was familiar and he began to recognize landmarks from his youth. Twenty miles later he was approaching Greenwood. What had once been a huge field west of town was now a giant mall. At the eastern end of the by-pass around the town there was another huge mall with a tangle of traffic. As he left the mall area he began to recognize the terrain and in a few minutes reached the turn off to the Mountain View Inn. It was the only place to stay he could remember and he had phoned ahead for reservations. Even the old Inn had changed. The old single building with a bar, small dining room and a few rooms upstairs, had spread out to five times its original size. The only thing that remained unchanged was the huge foyer with its antique furniture and wood burning fireplaces.

The next morning Ollie had breakfast in the Inn dining room, sitting at a window table that faced east. He recognized the gradual rolling hills that formed up in to the Allegheny Mountains to the east. He had flown over these hills and mountains many times when he was a young boy.

After breakfast he drove into town and slowly covered each of the hilly streets. His home on Maple Street was gone, replaced by a parking garage. The row houses and small bar across the street were still there. The courthouse main building was unchanged but the jail had been torn down, as had all the other buildings on the courthouse block. The space had been filled by additions to the courthouse and new government buildings.

The factory where his father and uncle had worked was gone and the old sprawling factory that had manufactured valves had been torn down and replaced by fast food restaurants and office buildings.

.He continued to drive around town, stopping to walk around the parks and streets were he had played as a child. Several times he was overcome with melancholy when he remembered a specific event. The worst memory came back when he walked out of the park were he had been playing the day he saw the Western Union messenger stop at his home, delivering the message about his brother.

He had lunch in one of the noisy downtown restaurants and then headed southeast toward the place he had liked most when he was growing up. He found the old, narrow side road and drove up the steep hill that he had walked so many times. At the top of the hill the road curved to the left and instead of the old airport hangar, there was a modern brick home. The airport had changed into a housing development. Of all the changes in his hometown, the demise of the airport was the saddest.

Ollie spent the rest of the afternoon in the catholic cemetery looking for his parents and relatives grave sites and then started driving around the back roads, getting lost several times, before returning to the Inn. Once in his room he called the phone numbers that Paul Cannon had given him. The woman who answered the second ring had a difficult time trying to understand who Ollie was and why he was calling. After a few minutes or so she grasped what he was saying and then said, "You must be Kevin's father. You are supposed to be dead!"

Ollie again explained what had happened and then asked, "Have you ever meet Kevin?"

"Oh sure," the woman answered. "He's paying my mothers nursing home bills. He comes here about twice a year to see her."

"Will you call your brother and explain that I'm here? I have been calling him for hours and nobody answers. I would like to meet you tomorrow and visit your mother and then maybe we can have dinner."

He gave her his number at the Inn and then walked through the Inn foyer to the dinning room for dinner. After dinner he sat in the foyer, reading the local paper. The desk clerk answered the phone and then walked out into the foyer and said, "Mister Miller; you have a phone call. You can take it at the desk if you want."

It was Rose's daughter, "I have reached my brother Gene," she said. "Can I meet you at the Inn tomorrow morning and then visit my mother. The nursing home is just a short distance from the Inn. Gene works during the day but he can meet us at the Inn for dinner if that is okay."

"That will be fine," Ollie said. "If you can be here at noon we can have lunch."

Rose's daughter, Cynthia, was a delight. She was effervescent and graceful and was enchanted by the tales Ollie told her about her mother's youth.

"She was always a bit of a tomboy," Ollie related. "She could really handle herself in a fight. Many a young man found that out the hard way."

"That is so hard for me to believe," Cynthia said, her intelligent eyes sparkling. "She was always so gentle. We had a dozen animals in the house. Everybody in the neighborhood dropped off his or her stray or unwanted animals there. They knew mom was so soft hearted she would take them in."

The visit to the nursing home was disheartening to Ollie. Rose's stroke had been severe, leaving her totally physically and mentally handicapped. She could not move without assistance and, although her eyes were open, she could not communicate.

Ollie spent the afternoon talking to her, telling her about what had happened in his life, hoping that she could understand. When he was leaving he kissed her on the cheek and said, as his eyes misted, "Thanks for teaching me to dance. I will be back to see you soon."

As they were saying their good-byes after dinner, Ollie gave Rose's children his address and telephone numbers and promised to keep in touch. They both were happy that he would soon be reunited with Kevin. Both of Rose's children told Ollie that Kevin was the kindest person that they had ever met. They were so thankful that Kevin was able to provide the best care for their mother.

Ollie called Paul Cannon that evening to tell him that he would be ready to leave the next day.

"After you drop off your car," Paul advised, "take a shuttle to the Executive Terminal. Be there about two pm. A Gulfstream private jet will be arriving about that time and a man named Tom Montgomery will be looking for you. Enjoy your reunion."

The next morning Ollie checked out of the hotel. He had one more place to visit.

He drove west through the town to what had been the coal company "patch" of his early childhood. The coal mine had been closed for many years and the houses had been sold. The homes were still there but most of them were now covered with aluminum siding and the rutted dirt roads had been covered with blacktop. He stopped in front of his old house and just looked at the house and yard for a few minutes while memories rolled over him like a warm fog. He had clear visions of his mother and father and all his aunts and uncles working in the garden by the side of the house.

`Time to move on, he said to himself, reluctantly leaving his childhood home behind.

He left the "patch" on its one main road and stopped and carefully made a right turn that would take him up the ramp to the by-pass and Route 30 west. At the top of the steep ramp, just before he merged with the by-pass, he pulled off the road and stopped and got out of the car. He walked around the car and looked down into the valley at his old home.

He forced himself to look to the left at the top of the hill. For a split second he saw his brother and his cousin helping him launch his first kite. He began to sob uncontrollably, burying his face in his hands. They were all gone.

It took him a several minutes to regain his composure.

He barely remembered the drive to the airport. His mind was filled with memories, both good and bad, and thoughts about the future. *What kind of a relationship could he hope for with his son? Would they be able to bond and make up for the lost years?*

Only one way to find out, he said to himself, Surely *it can only be better than the past.*

He returned his rental car and had lunch in the concourse and then took a shuttle to the Executive terminal. He had just finished a cup of coffee when a sleek, white Gulfstream jet taxied up to the gate. The pilot cut the engine on the door side of the plane and the cabin door swung open and the steps came down. A slender, casually dressed man bounded down the steps and strode quickly through the gate into the terminal. As soon as he saw Ollie he started toward him and extended his hand.

"You have to be Kevin's father," he said, smiling broadly. "The resemblance is uncanny. I am Tom Montgomery. Let's go I can't wait to see the look on Kevin's face when you show up at his front door."

Tom picked up Ollie's luggage and held the door and the two men walked toward the plane and started up the steps. As they entered the plane Tom stopped and said, "I forgot to tell you, we have somebody on board waiting for you."

Tom stepped inside the cabin and moved to the front of the plane. As Ollie entered the plane he stopped in disbelief. Standing there, with outstretched arms, was Tamara. She moved toward him and kissed him with such passion that he was barely able to breathe. It was several moments before they could bear to be separated by even an inch.

Finally they stepped back and Tamara said, "Why didn't you tell me your son had a Gulfstream. I would have been here months ago. This beautiful lady let me fly it in from Washington."

Ollie turned toward the cabin and looked at the tall, beautiful blonde woman, dressed in beige slacks and a white sweater, that Tamara was pointing to.

The woman flashed Ollie a radiant smile and said, "Hello, I am your daughter-in-law, Casey." She embraced him warmly and said, "I am so happy for you and Kevin."

Casey stepped back and said, "That's some woman," nodding toward the smiling Tamara. "I have never seen anybody just sit down at the controls of this bird and fly it like she did." Then she whispered in

Ollie's ear, "Why aren't you two married? I would love to have her as a mother-in-law and co-pilot."

"Lets get this show on the road," Tom said with exuberance. "I want to get to Hilton Head to complete the surprise."

Casey looked at Tamara and said, "Do you want to be my copilot into Hilton Head?"

"No thanks," she replied. "Ollie and I have a lot to talk about."

The trip to Hilton Head was smooth as silk. Ollie and Tamara barely noticed time slipping by. They were totally engrossed in each other.

When the wheels chirped on the runway, Tamara realized that they had arrived.

"So quick we got here," she beamed. "Did you notice how smooth the flight was? Your daughter-in-law is an excellent pilot."

Casey taxied to her assigned parking slot, cut the engines and started her post flight shutdown routine that took a few minutes and then she and Tom exited the cockpit to the passenger cabin. They exited the plane and walked to and through the small terminal to a waiting car.

The driver greeted them and stored their luggage in the trunk. As soon as his passengers were seated the driver pulled out on to the narrow exit road, drove the short distance to the four lane William Hilton Parkway and headed south through the subtropical tree and flower landscaped island.

Just past the Palmetto Dunes Plantation the driver slowed and made a left turn into a narrow road and stopped at a security gate. The gate opened and they drove through a lush golf course surrounded by expensive homes.

"How do we know Kevin will be at home?" Ollie asked nervously.

"That has all been taken care of," Tom replied.

After driving through the large plantation they approached another security gate that opened as they approached. The gate closed behind them as they crossed over a marsh on a stone bridge. The driver turned right as they exited the bridge and started south on the small island just off the main island. At the southern end of the island the driver pulled into a circular driveway in front of a large, modern house with huge, intricate metal double doors.

The passengers exited the car and Tom positioned them in front of the doors and rang the bell. A woman dressed in a maids uniform answered the door and smiled and then turned toward the inside of the house and said, "Mister Miller, there is someone here to see you."

Ollie waited nervously and in a few minutes a lean, younger replica of himself appeared at the door.

Kevin looked at Ollie and the people with him with total confusion, speechless.

Finally Ollie said, "Your nose looks a lot better now than the last time I saw you."

There was a slight flicker in Kevin's eyes as his brain raced to resolve his confusion.

"There is something vaguely familiar about you," Kevin said as he stared at Ollie. "Have we ever met?"

"I met you the first time shortly after you were born. You weren't quite a year old. That was in Japan in your mother's apartment. The last time I saw you, you were being carried down a jungle trail to a fishing boat in North Vietnam. Kevin, I am your father."

Casey started to cry, unable to control her emotions.

Tom was thumping Kevin on the back, shouting, "It's your fathers. He is back!"

Kevin just continued to look at his father, unable to speak. Finally he said, "Where have you been?"

As they embraced Ollie said, "That's a long story. I hope we have many years to catch up on our two lives."

Tears of joy streamed from Ollie's eyes. He was the last American hero to return alive from the Korean War.

EPILOGUE

Tamara and Ollie were married on Hilton Head Island in Harbortown, under the Liberty Oak Tree. Ollie and Tamara are now living in Hilton Head the majority of the time, just up the street from Kevin.

Ollie and Tamara bought a Cessna 172 Skyhawk that they fly for fun and "borrow" Kevin's Gulfstream for longer trips.

Tamara and Casey have become close friends and tennis partners and often go shopping and flying together. Most people think they are sisters. Tamara, who still has the body and reflexes of a twenty-year-old, is one of the areas top senior tennis players.

Colonel Shields kept his promise. In return for Tamara's lecturing on aerobatics, he arranges for her to fly supersonic jet trainers.

Kevin is teaching his father to play golf and tennis and Ollie works occasionally for Kevin as a consultant when Kevin's IIS intelligence organization has a project running in Europe.

Ollie remains in contact with Senator Mahoney and continues to help with the senator's project to determine the fate of the ferret program airmen and the last 2300 Vietnam War MIAs.

Ollie and Kevin have hired a private investigator that has been investigating the circumstances preceding Mary's death.

Ollie has spent many hours relating his life story to Kevin. After one particularly interesting session, while father and son were taking their evening walk on the beach, Kevin stopped and turned to his father and said, "You should really be writing this down. It's an interesting story that needs to be told."

The next day Kevin bought his father a computer and showed him how to use the word processor.

Ollie, using his de-briefing tapes for reference, is now deep into the third draft of his autobiography and Kevin is negotiating with a publisher.

About the Author

G. B. "Jerry" Mooney was born in Western Pennsylvania. After serving in the US military he graduated from the University of Pittsburgh School of Engineering. He married his high school sweetheart. They currently reside on the Gulf Coast of southwest Florida